MR. N

MR. NICHOLLS

Juliet Heslewood

Scratching Shed Fiction

Typeset in Iowan Old Style Bold and Times New Roman

Printed and bound in the United Kingdom by

Latimer Trend & Company Ltd,

Estover Road, Plymouth, PL6 7PY

For

Casper Jones

A Note on the Text

IN 1923, John Robinson was interviewed by a newspaper reporter from the *Keighley News* on the occasion of his sixtieth wedding anniversary. An article later appeared where John's reminiscences revealed more about the Brontë family than himself.

John had previously been interviewed ten years earlier for the *Yorkshire Evening Post*, but I have set his unique story from the later date.

His close association with the Brontës and, in particular, Mr. Nicholls, was unlike many that his young contemporaries knew. His memories encouraged me on an adventurous journey back into his unusual childhood in Yorkshire.

The Tower

*

THERE was a time when two suns appeared in the sky. People described them. Two suns, they said, were high up in the sky, together, at the same time.

'It is true,' they said.

From then on, generations believed it.

Slowly, the suns shifted from the sky and settled into memory. Here they were less dazzling, hazy perhaps, but they stayed there for ever.

I am sure of it. I am sure because I know that nature plays strange, teasing tricks upon souls that don't believe in such things, so it is better just to accept them as truth. Like the explosion of Crow Hill. Only a mile or two away from us that was, but the noise was heard wide and folk were fearful and the shape of the moor changed. The hillside was swallowed by itself.

That young man from the newspaper came round to visit me again and since he asked about events related to my past, I have become even less of a doubting soul. I've been given over to much reflection, but not to questioning. I remember much. I am not sure he believed me but I said he could take what I said or leave it behind him. My memory is occasionally faulty I know, but it is better to accept everything, even the blurred visions that at times will not sharpen. Because at other times things are as clear as the water in a cool, still stream.

He's coming back. He said he'd give me time to think, as if this is something I don't normally do. Still, he has set my mind on doing as he asked. The remembering. I now find I should like to go down those old paths again.

'If you don't mind, Mr. Robinson,' he said, moving around in our best chair as if its horsehair were coming through to scratch him. 'Since you were alive at the same time as them and you knew them, could you give us some descriptions of our famous local authoresses?'

I stared at him and I daresay I put him ill at ease.

'I know it was a very long time ago...' he went on, then he coughed as this implied my great age. 'Of course much has been written about them, but it would be so interesting to have some first-hand recollections.'

Did I have any first-hand recollections?

Did I half.

In my mind's eye I saw all three of them, the sisters. Each one different. Then there was only the one. I saw her so clear I could have drawn him the pattern of the cloth on her sleeves. I saw the glint of afternoon light upon her spectacles. Her reluctant smile.

I looked him in the face. It was full of eagerness and I guessed he was hoping for a revelation. No doubt he saw my words in print with his name at the foot of them.

'I was a lad,' I said.

He nodded and pushed the hair from his eyes. Sweat began to creep across his brow.

'I was very young and at the time did not quite understand things,' I said truthfully.

2

'Yet you knew them,' he said, encouraging me.

'I was taught a bit by the sisters, only...'

He was sat on the edge of the chair now. His fingers played with his notebook and his eyes widened. I should think his ears widened too, with waiting.

'What was it you didn't understand, Mr. Robinson? Was it their teaching?'

'Nay, not that. It was not them that taught me.'

'But you just said – I'm sorry, but I know they were teachers in the school at the time you were there. When you were a lad...'

'It were not them.'

The young man slumped upon his chest, bending forward so I saw the top of his head of hair. Then he looked up and pointed his pencil straight at me, as if he were holding a firearm and I were a nervous ferret.

'Mr. Robinson,' he said forcefully. 'I know my being here is because of your sixtieth wedding anniversary, for which – many congratulations. But I'd also like you to tell me anything that you remember about the Brontë family.'

I looked past him, out the window. I wanted him to go. Soon he did go. In minutes he was stood outside shaking my hand, saying he would be back. I saw him off. He walked over to our side gate and into the road, where he buckled up his briefcase and touched his hat to say goodbye. I nodded and turned round.

I saw the lifeless flowerbeds surrounding our small lawn where the earth lies dull in the cold winter months. Beyond our fence stand the sharp, upright lines of new buildings and warehouses, factory walls, greenhouses and all the like of this urban land. The sky was colourless, grey from gathered cloud and chimney smoke.

I could not get out of my head the idea that once two suns had appeared in that very same sky. Not here.

There.

Mr. Nicholls

*

WHERE I lived as a boy, it felt like the top end of the world.

Our house stood on the lower side of a single road that marked the top of a wind-blown ridge. It was let to us by the Taylors. They were the nearest you could get to being gentry, I suppose, though they did not have airs. We shared the house with Willie Forton who made bread at one end of it where there was a large oven. At the other end, near the outbuildings, lived my friend's grandmother who was deaf as a duck and who therefore did not speak much, not that she had many visitors. The Taylors moved out so as to live in the bigger more imposing house that had their initials and a date above the door. Between them and us was the road and their busy farmyard. Stanbury is the name of the village. If you stood in front of any barn or dwelling there, you could see right out of it. In both directions, right and left, the road became a mountain track again. I say mountain – because we do.

Years ago there was much traffic through the village. Pack-horses with lime on their backs used to come this way from Lothersdale. Nearly every house had hand-loom weaving or hand-combing being worked away inside them, which is why some homes have tall windows upstairs – to capture the light. Donkeys and mules were used in the wool trade and at the far end, going away west, was a toll house.

It is a mountainous land though there are no sharp peaks to mark it. There's rolling horizons. Wherever you are out there, there's wide open stretches and a few villages that have formed as if to make some kind of sense of it all. There are mostly the farms – scattered distant, far apart, clinging to empty hillsides as though their dark stone walls had unwillingly grown up out of the very rock that lies below them. Miles from anywhere.

You could call those wide fields and the moors our back gardens and it felt like we did live at some forgotten end of the earth.

The hills sometimes dropped steeply into cloughs like livid scars.

4

Yet on the northern side of our ridge the valley of the river Worth fell away gently with slopes all patterned by walls. Those fields still reach down to the river like a patchwork blanket of varied greens. That's where a few smaller mills used to lie, and them that remain are not as active as before. Griffe Mill, Lumb Foot. Though down in the valley beneath us, you could always see their chimneys sticking up.

Turn round upon the ridge and view the aspect to the south and you'd find a different land. Gaping sandstone rock in quarries high up on Haworth Moor. Falling away beneath your feet was Smith Bank that swept along and below that side of the village that our house looked down upon. It was always such a fine view, then. Farmsteads were dotted about, placed like sentries, all the length of Sladen Beck. Over to the west were much bleaker hills. Very wild, less green unless the heather was out to tame the wildness into something less than menacing. More foreboding. That way were few landmarks but for single trees like grasping black hands. Only a brooding mass of moorland. Wide stretches of shadow and light moved across those hills to shape them like giant shoulders of earth and rock.

Some have said it is a terrifying land. Not me. I liked to be out there and learned how to keep sensible in it. If I saw danger in the sky, hovering in dark clouds, I kept my feet to the tracks where the pack mules used to ride with their loads of wool. I'd not go down to the becks but stay high up with open views all about me. Or I'd keep an eye out for the low stone walls that move about the place like snakes.

As long as there was no mist, you could not go wrong. Always some distance away you could see one landmark that set you right. Haworth church. Watching out for it, you'd find your way about. You'd see the tower at the top of that village from where a mass of buildings spilled down the hillside.

Haworth lay just over a mile from us. Our village, high up on that ridge, was on its own like all the others in the neighbourhood.

But Haworth is where people went. They went to pray there and to have meetings and to learn things. Which is what I did too. Later.

*

I WAS not ten years old when I first found my way inside Haworth church tower. The new bells had been put in place only a short while earlier. Six of them. Great heavy things, they were. I'd seen them on the ground before they'd gone up. Solid iron. They hung from massive beams to which they were bolted hard. I knew the top of the tower outside was surrounded by battlements, which made me feel safe. If ever I ventured out there, in the open, I'd find the four corners and those fancy pinnacles that I could hold on to. But I stayed inside mostly and hid myself. So they didn't see me. So I could safely see them.

At first I went up only during the summer months while it was good and light. Early evenings. I looked down on the front of the parsonage. It was like a rectangular face, with four windows arranged up and down on each side and an extra one above the central door. A few steps led up to the door. The house stood stiff and upright and alone. Isolated. Hid from the village. Over on the right, Church Lane went up beside it but disappeared as a lonely track leading behind the house where a wide sweep of moorland went on forever.

I saw their movements, what they did in the parsonage and what he did, Mr. Brontë, their father, our vicar. I thought how peculiar it was that he'd once had me in his hands and baptized me, beneath where I stood in the tower, at the other end of the church. Many squealing babes he'd have held who were welcomed into heavenly places and not come in by the back door, the way I crept inside. If he'd've known I was up there, watching him!

They say that if a church is high up on a place, like in Haworth, it is named after Saint Michael. It's because Michael's an archangel and needs to be able to get to heaven quick. Up on that tower I was nearer the heavens than anyone else in the village. And with no wings to help.

I watched the daughters in the dining room and Mr. Brontë on the other side of the hallway, in his study where he had his meals. They seemed to lead different lives from each other, which I felt was ever so strange. Compared to us.

Often, as I set off home again, I met up with Martha. She liked to know what's what. She'd stop me in Church Lane by just standing there, barring my way. With her arms folded. And her tight little mouth turned into a piece of wire. Did she know what I'd been up to? Probably not. And she was probably wanting to know. But she didn't wait with questions. She told answers. All sorts of other people's business.

Martha Brown knew all there was to know about the Brontës. Well, more than most. Ever since she was a child she'd run errands for the family. She'd go only a few paces from her home down the lane where her father the sexton lived. On the dwindling health of the Brontës' old servant Tabby, she took over many of the household chores. Eventually she moved in with them.

I never let on a thing. Nor did I let her know what they looked like from above, from my private point of view. As if I were Saint Michael himself, staring down into the house, keeping my eyes upon them and their quiet ways.

*

BY the time I'd got back to Stanbury, dinner was usually on the table getting chill and my sisters already on their pudding. Willie Forton frequently came over with a newly baked loaf and sat with us when he wanted family company. Otherwise he was the owner of a fiddle which he was supposed to practise only at his end of the house, so's not to annoy. But he sometimes played outside which did annoy.

'He's been up that tower,' Betty'd say about me, not scolding. Smiling.

No-one really bothered their heads over me.

For us, evening time was sacred as that's when we talked. When

Willie wasn't with us (not often) there was me, my father and my two older sisters so we each had a side to the table. Father told us of all the people who'd come by in the day to have new shoes or boots. He was known to everyone. His were the interesting stories to tell and we liked to hear who had the longest toes, who complained, whose bunions were grown and if his new leather supplies had been delivered and would last the season. He described things well.

'If that young scoundrel Jim Pickles comes back to upscuttle my tools I shall bray him,' he said, recalling the antics of his favourite customer, a lad whose feet did not match. 'He's for ever fidgeting about.'

'He's playful, that's all,' said our Nancy, who only ever said things if she'd thought about them. 'He's growing too fast. He's bigger than other boys his age.'

Since my last brother had died I'd taken to keeping company with young Joseph Craven, also from Stanbury along the way. It was his grandmother also lived in the house. Dutifully he'd go and see her, but not for long since she didn't talk much. We went to school together, at the other end of the village. My sisters, being older, liked to tell on me and him.

'Our John's been acting daft with his young friend,' Betty declared, warmly. Father loved the tales.

'So he's not a good scholar then?' he asked, shaking his head. 'There's a pity.'

'I am that,' I'd say, defending myself. 'You can ask me what you like, I'll tell you good and right.'

'Well what's the moon made of?' asked Nancy, rising to the challenge.

'Nobody knows,' I replied.

'They do that. It's made of cheese and you don't know all, John.'

Of my sisters, it was usually Nancy tackled me on what they'd seen us do, we younger ones that were sat at the front of the class-room away from them. And I'd prove how I paid attention despite Joseph who once brought a mouse into school that he kept in his left

8

coat pocket. When I stood to declaim a rhyme, Joseph put the mouse in my pocket and I'd feel it wriggling, trying to get out, so I'd spread my hand over the pocket and continued to speak and sound more sure of myself. Joseph then got nervous his mouse would smother.

Chatter like this took up our evenings until we tired, though, if he were there, Willie Forton kept us up with old tales. More times than not it was Father carried me up to my bed in his room as the girls cleared the table of our scraped clean bowls.

*

THE sisters in the parsonage also took to talking, but not like us. Last thing of an evening they walked round and round the table in their dining room. There was something of a pace in the way they walked and, I guessed, in how they spoke to each other. As if they had things they urgently needed to say, after their silence. They'd been writing. They had a lamp at the table's centre and as dusk gathered, they sat themselves so its light fell on their many papers and books. Even at my young age I could tell they were bound close together ending their day in a way that was familiar to them, unusual to others. As time moved on, it was not by chance that I got to know them better.

Our school in Stanbury was given to the village like a gift from subscriptions only it came with all the trimmings of a schoolmaster who was led a merry dance. Mr. Abraham Sunderland was stern enough. He scowled when he punished us. He had a three-legged table in front of him on which there were a dozen or so sticks that he'd got out of the woods. When any scholar was inattentive he would throw one of the sticks at him and hardly ever missed. He was a good aim, I'll say that for him. The children came to school not only from along our road but by traipsing about the hills so its few rooms were crowded.

Since I had become the only young man in the family, it was decided I might do better for myself if I walked the mile or so to Haworth and go to school there. The teachers were the best that could be found in the neighbourhood, who knew more than most. Was I pleased! Though there'd be a fair bit of walking to do, I'd be rid of Mr. Sunderland for ever!

So I found myself spending many hours in direct view of the tower, on the ground. The school was in Church Lane, right opposite the home of Mr. Brontë. And it was him who'd built it – that is, not him with his own hands, but he found the money for masons to build it. On the outer wall was a stone carved with so many shapes of words it was a puzzle to try and make sense of it:

THIS NATIONAL
CHURCH SUNDAY SCHOOL is under the *Man
agement of TRUSTEES* of whom the *INCUMBENT*
for the time being is one: (*AND*) *was* ERECTED
A.D.1832 by *Voluntary Subscription*
and by a GRANT from the NATIONAL
SOCIETY IN LONDON
"Train up a Child in the way he should go
and when he is old he will not depart from it."
Prov. XXII.0

I always had the feeling that the gist of this noble plaque was something to do with me personally and that I should obey what it's fancy lettering said. It was named a Sunday school, yet we children went there on weekdays as well, for which thanks were again due to Mr. Brontë and his family.

The daughters taught there, but not regular hours. Miss Emily came the least and only if there was the need. She was taller than the others, very thin, dark haired and fearful frightening. I daresay had she been a better teacher, doing work she liked, she may have got more out of us. Her voice was strong and musical, as if it were not meant for words at all. She struck us dumb with the few words she did say so we stared and did not speak to her. But when I watched her from the tower and saw her walk round that table with her arms through her sisters' arms, I knew she was not so much the fierce person I'd thought her to be. She hardly spoke to a soul though she was hailed by folk in the street. It's not that she was haughty, nor had airs. She was alone, even when surrounded. Outside of school she could be seen with a terrifying dog that went with her everywhere.

Miss Anne we all liked. She smiled. The girls thought her the prettier of the three, though I'd not thought of beauty at that age. Her eyes were almost the colour of violets, big and kind. As were Miss Charlotte's eyes, only hers were hid behind that bothersome pair of spectacles.

Miss Charlotte spoke so soft you had to shut off breathing to hear her right. It was not a voice from round here, the way most of us talk. The way she said her '*r*'s was more like her father's, which I was told was the lilt of the Irish. She spoke English, though. As English as it comes, except for the '*r*'s. It was a hard task trying to pay attention to her, because of her quietness. Miss Anne's voice was quite soft too. Miss Emily's – well, as I say, there were no long sentences from her.

We had other teachers. There was Mr. Purnell and there were curates who'd come to help in Haworth and the outer parish villages. They went about the place visiting with Mr. Brontë. They mostly taught us the Bible. Rather, they gave us stories and we might have liked these better had each tale been told at once. Instead the curates broke off to see to the older children at the back who were having instruction for Holy Communion. I liked to listen in on what was said. There were words I heard that filled my head with wonder. 'Transubstantiation', 'Eucharist'. Never did I dream of spelling such words, not then.

Miss Sugden loved to gabble. At moments when she paused she had us turn our slates on their sides to make them wide so's the chalk letters fitted in. Then she'd say words more slowly for us to write: 'Harvest', 'Carpet', 'Farmer'.

When the lessons were finished Miss Sugden stayed behind in the school room, chattering on to us, tidying up our shirt collars so we went off looking neat. But Miss Anne and Miss Charlotte scuttled back to the parsonage, which was only a few yards away across the lane, as if they were in a hurry to be gone.

*

A TALL stone gateway stood in the wall of the parsonage and led direct on a path to the front door. There was no other entrance from the lane though a low doorway led from the end of their small garden directly into the graveyard. I saw it all very clear, laid out before me. And it was from the tower that one of the earliest recollections I have, and most vivid, told me this was no ordinary family living there.

It was when I saw Miss Emily outside on her own, just come back from the moors. A bedraggled, wandering dog was pacing fast up Church Lane. She saw it and quickly sent her own beast inside behind the gate before she paused to watch the stranger dog. It hung about the place, not leaving. I saw her run inside the parsonage, then come back with a bowl of water in her hands. She was stooped to give it to the dog when it leaped up and bit her savagely.

She did not cry. She lifted the hem of her skirt and wrapped it round her arm. She then walked back to the parsonage front door where she went inside, lost from my view. By now the dog had run off.

I wanted to know what happened but who could I ask? I'd give myself away, saying I'd been up there, watching. The chance came some days later when I met up with old Tabby, who was known to everyone in Haworth for being lame and specially deaf as well as servant to the Brontë family. In church she sang too loud, leaning on her stick and wobbling, fit to fall. Miss Charlotte always helped her to sit down, but once inside their boxed pew, she refused support and held on to its panelled sides.

She'd come into the churchyard from the small garden door and I'd seen her from the tower where I'd placed myself for a short half hour before school. As luck would have it, there was no-one about, so I raced down to meet her on the ground.

'Morning, Miss Tabitha,' I said loudly. 'How are you?'

'What's that? Who are you?'

'I'm from St. Michael's, usually of a Sunday. You may not know me, but I know you.'

'The divil you do…'

'Nice day to be out. You're looking well.'

'Am I heck with this pair of legs. What is it?'

'Only asking of you,' I said.

'Ask away then.'

I had every intention of engaging her in friendly conversation. She blinked and smiled and seemed to like me well enough. In order to find out what had happened to Miss Emily, I asked her about the whole family.

'Miss Anne, well she occupies herself well enough, they all do. Miss Emily likes to make bread and I've taught her many of my kitchen ways. Mr. Brontë, he's preparing words to speak, but are you from round here? Do I know you?'

'I'm from over Stanbury way but I come to school here as well as church. So how is Miss Emily – was she not bit by a dog?'

'Hey lad, and how do you know that?' she asked, stopping herself steady.

'I saw. I was – here. I would have helped only…'

'No she's not one for help. Sees to things on her own. Mind, if there were a choice, she'd save an animal before herself. She was that concerned for the dog.'

'Was it not a bite then, only a nip?'

'You what?'

'A nip. She was not bit too hard was she?'

'Oh, she was bit all right. Very hard. She burned it out. She came into the kitchen, walked over to the stove and took up my red hot tongs. Told me to tell no-one, but there I go, telling you.'

'She burned her own flesh?'

'That she did and all because the poor cr'ater needed water. The family was not to know, but she knew if the dog were crazed, it would do the same for her. Still, she cured herself, with no help from anyone. You'll not tell? You won't let on, will you? She's right as rain now and the wound is nicely healed though it's left a mark she keeps hid. But, there you are asking me and I don't even know who you are...'

*

DAWDLING over in Haworth, fetching up at the school across the lane from them, in time I got to know the Brontës very well. Especially from my high lookout post.

Now the brother, Mr. Branwell, he was a right card. His temper was not long. He was thin and red-headed and his moods matched the flames in his hair. In school he was little disposed towards us if we didn't read fast. Once when a boy was struggling over his words, Mr. Branwell shouted at him, saying he'd turn him out of the class if he did not get a move on. Well he got his reply all right. The lad turned on him, called him an old Irish and walked out. Sometimes after our school room hours, we went into the church where the curates gave us a short service. Mr. Branwell didn't join in. He'd sit hidden in the Brontës' box pew reading to himself. At times he'd fly into that short temper, even took our hair and coiled it round his fingers as he threatened to wrap us round the ears. You would not think this right in the son of a reverend man. Right or wrong, he made us laugh.

My friend Joseph would come over to Haworth to meet up with me and share the walk back home again. I told him all I'd learned in school and he told me the little he had. He'd wait inside the church porch where I joined him and often we'd see Mr. Branwell come down the lane in a storm. He'd arrive with a sharp halt at Sexton House. Joseph and I stood about, right loiterers, whistling, pretending to be minding our own business. We heard Mr. Branwell rant about the class to his friend, Mr. Brown, the sexton himself who'd built the house and named it accordingly.

'There he goes,' I'd tell Joseph. 'There he is, telling Mr. Brown he hates us and is fit for better work.'

"Do you think so? Do you think he'll join the mills?"

'Not that. He wants to be an artist but he'll not succeed.'

'How do you know that, John Robinson?'

'Because Martha has told me.'

'And who's Martha when she's at home?'

'Exactly that. Martha Brown is maidservant to the Brontës and daughter of the sexton who lives here. This is her family's home.'

Joseph went a little silent and kneaded one boot-toe between the lane's cobbled stones.

'Well why should she tell you?' he said, looking up at the door of the house as if it were the entrance to a cave of eastern mysteries.

'Because I asked. Did you not know that, Joseph? "Ask and ye shall receive." It's writ in the Bible. So that's why, when she's about, I ask Martha all sorts of things and because she's ever so ready to tell, she is.'

'Don't see why. Don't see what's so special.'

'Well it is. Mr. Brontë is a holy man. So his children are holy and all.'

'Then shall they be angels when they grow up?' asked Joseph, turning his head towards the graveyard behind him where a few stone replicas of the throng of heaven appeared to have just landed. Countless tomb slabs smothered the churchyard ground.

'Give over, Joseph. They're educated folk. Not like the rest of us.'

Joseph, at seven years old, did not take such an interest in teachers as myself. He preferred to imagine our world whereas I grew keen to discover it. So I hoped the teachers would help me in my quest. I did not like repeating what they said, just like a parrot. Nor did I care to chant long lists of names of unknown cities the teachers had likely never visited. In Mr. Brontë's son we had an entertainment. But he owned a mind that spun about and a tongue that proved its spinning. The daughters did not speak loud and I often thought that

15

Miss Charlotte, though not as impatient as her brother, considered us all to be dolts. If only there were some brighter spark among them I might have caught its glow.

*

HE came unexpected.

It was when Joseph and I were taking our time headed back for Stanbury that we saw him to talk to. I already talked a deal to my young friend who always was one to listen hard. I believe that if I'd told him Crow Hill had exploded from the fiery breath of a dragon that lived beneath the peat he'd have gone in search of it. As it was, living near the scene of the phenomenon we were familiar with the land where no trace of dragons had yet been seen.

We scrambled off after school, looking about us not only for his monsters but any living thing that caught our interest. Up away we went, through the churchyard, out onto the path that led towards the moor. We'd go down from the hills to Sladen Bridge where a row of houses stood by the beck. People from the nearby mill, Hollings, when they came home in summer daylight across the fields, they nodded their heads our way. Used to the sight of us. Joseph got ever so excited about things and it was not my job to put a stop to his fancying. He said the mill was haunted, which got his own spirit up. It was the beck that we loved most. To him it was a river that led to far off seas. I'd not tell him if things weren't as he dreamed, but tried to find some truth in them. I knew that water flowed its way somewhere. Becks, rivers, lakes, estuaries – they led to the great oceans of the world. These I had learned by heart, every one. So I told Joseph such seas might have started off here, out in the wild, not one mile from our home.

Muddying ourselves, throwing up great drops of beckwater, tumbling on the moss-slimed stones, we passed whole hours at play. We turned boulders into harbour walls and shouted at deaf minnows to swim towards them. We caught them in our hands then sent them back at once in sprays of noisy showers. We invented our own seas which we sailed with bravery, landing in foreign parts like the Duke of Wellington. Tired out, we climbed Smith Bank and the track back to Stanbury. Which is where, one cloud-lit evening, we found Mr. Nicholls.

As we raced through the village, round the road's gentle bend and came to a dead halt, we saw him.

'You two look as if you've been in a shipwreck,' he said.

'We have,' said Joseph at once.

We stayed still. A bit speechless.

He was a very serious man. On many occasions we'd seen him in church, taking over when Mr. Brontë was indisposed. Dark. Tall. Wide nostrils. Unlike the other curates. And unlike them he was to stay in Haworth and lodged at Sexton House along with the Brown family. The good thing about him was his dog, a brown retriever who was a friendly soul, obedient, neither shy nor overbearing. The dog was with him, panting gently, sitting at his side.

'Have you now,' continued Mr. Nicholls, not as a question. 'And where was your ship when it went down?' he asked.

Joseph looked to me for help.

'You say, Joseph,' I said.

'In the Specific,' Joseph replied.

Mr. Nicholls stroked one side of his face where dense, black whiskers framed his cheeks and chin. He stopped walking. He frowned.

'Could you spell that?' he asked Joseph.

'I could,' Joseph replied. 'Only I don't really want to.'

'I see,' said Mr. Nicholls.

He turned round and began to walk down the road from where we'd just come. He continued to stroke his chin as if it helped him think.

'What about you,' he said, facing me. 'Can you tell me about this sea? Can you spell its name?'

My throat went a little dry. Though I hoped to assist Joseph I did not care to seem ignorant.

'Most seas are a long way off here, Mr. Nicholls,' I said with caution. 'Only the sea Joseph and I are talking about isn't reached by carriages and sailing. You can only get there by thinking.'

'Indeed...' he said.

He paused in the road and tilted his great chin when he gazed up at the scudding clouds as if he'd forgotten us. His dark looks might have got the better of me had I not seen he was smiling.

'There is of course the Pacific, which is near China,' I said firmly, my confidence growing. 'I can spell that for you if you like. But the sea where Joseph and I have been is not the same one,' I went on, seeing he listened. 'It's rather secret.'

He set off walking downhill and we went back with him, as if returning to our homes was not the right thing to do. As if the day had not yet ended. The three of us and the dog. As if he'd more to say and we should trail along with him until we heard it. We were about to reach Sladen Bridge once more, before the ascent back up to Haworth. He paused and stared at the waters of the beck and seemed to find there those very same seas where we had wandered in our dreams. Joseph's eyes were wide, his mouth twisted in dumb silence.

'I should think the Specific is a very fine place,' said Mr. Nicholls as he watched the beck's lively flow. 'Perhaps you'll tell me more about it one day.'

He left us there. He walked away briskly, almost in a march but for the movement of his long arms that he waved about like a windmill. The dog, keeping apace, bounded round his legs. We watched until they disappeared from our sight.

*

AFTER that we saw more of him. There was him and others and they came over to stare about the place, so Joseph and I thought. In fact, they were considering a plot of land mid-way along Stanbury's main street. People got to talk and we heard what was said. They said another school was to be built. But funds were none too forthcoming, so a plan was made to have it as a church as well. A church for the Anglicans of our village. So's they didn't have to traipse over to Haworth every Sunday.

There were squabbles across our hills that I could never understand. They were not to do with sheep nor keeping the tracks nor oats nor turnips that were grown on the land. They weren't about the mills either which was surprising. No, the wrangles had something to do with a Mr. Wesley whom the Methodists were keen on and the Anglicans were not. So the two sides did not like to pray in the same kind of building. That's when I first started to look over the buildings, giving them some considerable thought.

To add to my confusion, there were the quaking souls. They did not have a chapel but met in Tommy Rushworth's house. Tommy had a grocer's shop and did a very nice business in it. Over his shop was the Quakers' meeting room which they reached by a short flight of steps on one side.

I knew there were churches that were sturdy and black and long. Over in Oxenhope a new one was built when Mr. Grant, the curate there, came to take over that parish. He'd teach us at times. He was always talking about 'his' church since he was the first one there and had raised the funds for it. With a voice like he'd been eating syrup he'd blabber on about his church being 'rather archaic in style, Norman don't you know' which made me laugh as I did not know. If it was high and hefty like other churches being built, I thought it should be known as Jack or Bill, but not Norman.

There were other churches, many of them. Chapels being raised all over. Square-faced with no coloured glass nor fancy shapes, they were more like the mills themselves, only not so big. Some were stranded out on open land. One great edifice was built for the Ranters, who'd previously gathered in a small dwelling and needed their songs to be heard. Of a Sunday they sang as loud as they ranted so's everyone knew they were worshipping.

No I never could make head nor tail of it all, not when we were supposed to be praying to the same God.

Joseph once told me he was a Dissenter.

'And what's that exactly,' I asked him.

'It means I dissent.'

'You never do!' I said, unable to hold back a tease.

'I do that,' he replied sharply.

'Then how come you spare the time of day with me?' I asked.

He chewed upon his mouth in search of a reply.

'You shall have to mind what you say to me, John. That's what.'

Some Sundays we often saw Joseph and his family go into the chapel that was only a few paces from our home. Crowds went. Most of Stanbury liked to worship there so it had to be made bigger, with a great gallery added and the roof raised so that all the singing they did could fill the space and God would hear them.

'You can't go in, John,' said Joseph once on a cold day as we blew our hands to bring them warmth. 'You have to walk across the way to Haworth...' he went on, looking out over the leaden grey moors. I knew his cheeky talk was learned from his folk and I saw them chivvy him inside as if he should not talk to strangers.

I did not care to tell him I did not care. By the time the new little church was going up, Joseph was that interested in it. Over the months we watched it rise, a building not one quarter as big as St. Michael's but snug and tight, fit for those of us in Stanbury who preferred not to make such a great song of things as the Wesleyans. We saw Mr. Nicholls arrive and pace with his dog up and down the straight path that led to its front porch where windows rose on either side. At one end of the ridge a bell was raised while at the other was a stone cross. For school and church.

'So can God come here weekdays too?' asked Joseph. 'Shall he come to the school and sit invisible at the classes?'

'He shall indeed,' said Mr. Nicholls.

'And shall you be teaching here?'

'Yes, I'll try my best to fly between Haworth and here, Joseph, as both teacher and priest.'

Joseph was silent for a while, leaning his weight from one foot to another, staring up at Mr. Nicholls with half closed eyes of keen inquiry.

'Is it because you are learning to fly that you wave your arms about when you walk?'

*

AFTER our first meeting and his words at the beck, I'd thought different about Mr. Nicholls. There was more to him, more kindly than his dark appearance made him out to be. My ears grew when I heard him talked about. Betty, Nancy and Father wanted to remain worshippers in Haworth so we continued to go there each Sunday where it was not difficult to hear folk at their gossiping. They came out to chatter. Many from the mills came as well as those who'd been working their looms at home. They all joined in the talk. They'd put on their better clothes and walked slow, not hurrying. Before heading for the church of their choice they gathered in Haworth centre to greet each other, below St. Michael's steps. These I reached from the churchyard where I took time to check the base of the tower, just to see that no lock had been fixed at its door.

When Mr. Brontë's eyesight was bad, Mr. Nicholls took his place performing marriages and baptisms as well as funerals. His great form and deep voice and outstretched arms swathed in white vestments were as familiar a sight as any in that church. He took to the golden eagle to read the Bible words or walked up the steep pulpit as if St. Michael had at one time dropped him there personally as his favourite. People appeared to listen to him. As they sat in their box pew, mostly hidden but for their bonnet tops, the Misses Brontë were silent and motionless except when they stood to sing hymns. Only Miss Emily sang loud. I noticed Mr. Branwell was often not there.

Martha Brown also attended St. Michael's and she lingered after the services and joined the busy gathering in Church Lane, which gave her a fine stage for an audience. I'd ask her things, like how Mr. Branwell fared since he'd not been teaching at my school of late.

'What do you expect from a man who spends more time in the inns than at home?' she said, her mouth, usually so tight, now twitching as she spoke. She smoothed her gloved hands down the sides of her skirts. 'With Mr. Brontë in a delicate state it's a wonder any of them can sleep at night and I'm sure I can't. Mr. Branwell nearly set his bed on fire last week and he sleeps in the same room as his father. If it weren't for Miss Anne, who happened to pass by their door and smelled smoke, we'd all be dead. Then who'd look after the parish...'

'Mr. Nicholls would,' I said cheerfully.

'Huh!' she exclaimed. 'As if he's a help.'

'Well the church is full now, every week. Isn't that thanks to him?'

'Church can fill as much as it likes. You should see what he's made of his lodgings...' she said, nodding her head at the door of Sexton House.

'Well I cannot see. So are you going to tell us?'

'Oh I'll tell all right,' she said, glad to be encouraged. 'First week he was here he drilled holes in his door. It was so's he could breathe, he said. Fresh air, he said again and again. It's what he needed. Look up there now – he has his window like that all day long, whatever the weather.'

I looked up to see a window on the upper floor wide open.

'There's draughts everywhere. It's not good in a place full of family, as ours is. Selfish is what I'd say. And priests should be nice to their flocks, especially those that give them lodgings and meals. Not thinking of fresh air all the time.'

Despite her tell-tales, I was glad to listen to Martha. She liked to describe her daily round of hazards, mostly complaining. When Mr. Brontë's eyesight improved following an operation, she found the benefit was mostly her own. It was because Mr. Nicholls, relieved of extra duties, could leave Sexton House for a holiday in Ireland.

'We must be glad he's gone in November,' said Martha. 'My family will have some warmth in the house without all his blessed fresh air.'

The Tower

*

DURING every month of the year, on days when there was no rainfall, the washerwomen of Haworth spread their laundry over the church tombstones. This was a particularly good place for them to put their sheets. Draped over a sea of flat slabs, the sheets did not fly up over hedges nor catch on thorns. In addition, the women had no need to traipse out up onto the moor but found this wide space right in the centre of the village.

When Mr. Nicholls returned from his spell away his name was on the tips of everyone's tongues. Not because of his absence. Because of the churchyard laundry. From his open window at Sexton House he had a fine view over the tombs and graves. The whiteness of the linen lay like snow over the yard. As the women chattered and laughed and threw up their drapes into the chill blowing winds, his temperament warmed. Martha told me it all.

'He flew out at them. He was racing about the place, calling them to respect the house of the Lord and Lord knows what else. They told him it was not his house, but the place where their own folk were laid. Some said they had more right to be there, sheets and all, than himself who was from across the Irish sea. They talked of the dead. And as their dead had always liked clean sheets when alive, it was a mark of respect from themselves who were left behind. Which made him rant even more. He said he would not listen to such – what was it now – 'distortion and blasphemy'. He ran about, he did, and was about to seize the laundry with his own hands. He was as mad as can be.'

'Did you see him, Martha?' I asked

'No, I didn't.'

'Then how do you know he did all this?'

'I heard it from Mr. Brontë.'

'So what were his thoughts?'

'Well, you'd not believe it. He thought it a fine jape. He was laughing. I found him in his study where he'd wrote a poem about it. That's when he told me. He even read it to me.'

Mr. Nicholls, with Mr. Brontë's blessing, went sky high in my esteem. I asked Martha what the daughters of the parsonage thought of their curate's exhibition.

'I can't say they were amused.'

'Really? So they don't always agree with their father.'

'Well, they're not so keen on curates, you know. Some people say that curates only become curates in order to find themselves wives, since they stand in front of folk in churches and are on display, you see, for all the ladies and their fathers to consider. And curates meet whole villages of folk, not like the weavers stuck in their homes nor at the mill. A curate has some clout too in that he'll have a regular salary.'

'And you, Martha. Weren't you amused?'

'To me, Mr. Nicholls is a strange one. Never one stranger than him. He sticks his neck out and he goes his own way. But then he works close to a whole family that's not like any other.'

*

WHY were they unusual? What made them different? Was it their quietness and their keeping themselves to themselves the way they did, their return to the parsonage as if it were a magnet or a compass point they had to follow in order to find home again? The house was alone, poised on the edge of moorland. But they only needed to pass through their garden gate, into the churchyard and down St.Michael's steps to be in the centre of the village. Where a whole throng of people passed by.

Our land was filled with folk of all sorts. There were them who worked in the fields mostly, or else in the mills. There were Haworth's shop-workers – drapers, grocers, ironmongers. Then there were those who made the iron into shapes – the forgers – and the same for wood, the carpenters. But there were also many of us who made a bit of merry of the wide, dark land, who made music – the choirs and the brass bands. There were the wealthier folk too, like the Taylors up our way and Mr. George Taylor who was ever so kind to let us have his old house. There were the Heatons over at Ponden who did not keep their gains to themselves, but put money into the music and the festivites, even if they were not Dissenters, like we weren't. Despite all this, the Brontës were not much in the public eye.

Not that they were cut off from the likes of us. Their servants were all in touch with villagers. Old Tabby, she'd lived with them for years though her own folk were a few streets away. I sometimes saw Tabby and Martha together on fine weather days, the younger helping the older to walk. They stopped and talked to the whole world. Before returning to the parsonage.

The parsonage. It was not the building made the family so separate. It was themselves, inside it.

As a lad I simply felt the difference. All I saw of them with my own eyes or learned from my own thoughts (less of other people's) informed me. I was over in Haworth once, mingling as I did, when a terrible stir took place outside Greenwood's, the stationer's shop. The noise was troubling, a mix of people's cries and something else – dogs' roaring. Miss Emily, being tall, was easily visible in the crowd. Spying her I thought it was her dog, that great bull-mastiff by the name of Keeper, who'd caused the scene. But for once, Keeper was not with her. Paper was all over the place – she'd come out and bought a sheaf but thrown it to the ground so the leaves flew about like snowfall. Mr. Greenwood stood at his shop door. Others also stood, startled.

Two dogs clawed at each other, raised on their hind limbs, snarling. Their strong, taut legs gripped each other's bodies so they seemed fixed together, yet moving, fighting hard. People stood back to form a crowd in a circle. Into the centre of this chance arena strode Miss Emily. Silent but with an expression of black purpose, she gripped both dogs at their collars, one in either hand. As the beasts continued to leap and twist and grimace, she held them apart, her thin arms like two iron rods. Until they stopped and quietened. Their owners nervously approached, nodded thanks to her and took the dogs away. That's when the crowd gradually dispersed, shocked. Not so much by the dogs. By her silence as she picked up her papers and returned up Church Lane to the parsonage.

*

MISS Emily hardly came to the school. It's not her I remember so much in that room. Miss Charlotte, she was often there and she set us tasks I thought were most difficult, at the time. Sometimes she gave us what she called the *Dictée* and not seeing how this was spelled we thought it was someone's name. When a lad asked her where Dick Tey lived and was he a Leeds man, she almost laughed. She lowered her head and put her hand to her mouth.

'No, this is not a person,' she said. 'I once lived in a town where I was a pupil like you and a passage of work was read to us which we had to write down, carefully, as we heard it. In English it is called 'Dictation', which means the act of speaking words that are to be written down.'

I quite liked Dick Tey. What was more difficult, but which I liked even more, was when she set us a subject and we had to write what we liked about it. We had stiff, clean paper and pens and inkpots that we had to be careful over (some children were given pencils after they'd spilled it more than twice). She'd give us a good twenty minutes at it. During this time she'd walk round the room like a shadow, noiseless and hardly there.

That time she gave us 'The Nest' to write about... I had a little think before I set my pen to paper. I thought for about five of the twenty minutes and she came round to me and saw my sheet was blank. She said nothing.

I watched the others scribbling away, some touching at their nostrils with their pens and others chewing the ends. Then, when I had my idea right, I set to.

26

The Tower

I wrote about how my friend's grandmother lived at one end of our house though we never saw her. I described our kitchen. We liked to have Willie Forton in at times, when he was not fiddling. I said how this was still a nest, a home, though without my brothers and one sister gone. The nest had got smaller only the missing ones were not turfed out into the world, but flown from it. Goodness knows where. I said our front door was not like others in Stanbury, but had great slabs over and on either side of it, which sheltered the door from the weather and made a grand kind of entrance. Which showed it to be a fine house, once, before the Taylors moved out. The entrance to the nest. Willie had a nice face, a bit like the bread he baked. So he was welcome. He made the nest feel less empty for Father and he made us laugh even if he often went to the Cross Inn and we were left waiting for him and Betty's cooking got cold.

For some time during the minutes we wrote, Miss Charlotte would stand up at the desk at the front and read silently from a book. She held it up to her nose and often raised her spectacles and rubbed her eyes. Then she'd start walking round the room again.

I felt her behind me, at my side. She stayed awhile. She read every word. I was a bit afraid of her, despite her being so small, almost smaller than me. So when she put a hand on my shoulder I was a bit perturbed.

'John – this is lovely,' she said so quietly I hoped no-one else heard. After that I was less scared of her.

*

OPINIONS were changeable, like the very winds. In our house, mostly thanks to me, our thoughts on Mr. Nicholls stayed fixed. Months went by with no need for us to alter those thoughts. The tale of the washerwomen only strengthened our liking. Joseph and myself, we began to accompany him on his way down from our ridge or up to it and he became a more familiar sight than any shepherd. A shepherd's flock kept him out on distant ground where one strayed sheep was bound to lead a soul astray. Mr. Nicholls walked steady.

People's general gossip turned upon each of the neighbourhood's curates and since Mr. Grant in Oxenhope went and got himself married, the subject of suitable ladies for the others was on the tongues of many. A popular subject it was in our house.

'If you were to ask me, John, I think Mr. Brontë should make Mr. Nicholls his son-in-law,' said Betty. 'He depends on him. There was never such a good curate. Think how fine their lives would be with Mr. Nicholls as a member of the family...'

Betty had grand notions of romance. As soon as she'd finished with school she made new friends who stood alongside her on a line of looms at Bridgehouse Mill. She met up with the girls at the village centre where I left her each day after we'd walked over from Stanbury. Though she began work very early, I liked to go with her and pass the time over there. I liked to see the throng of workers all making their way to arrive before the mill bell called a halt to latecomers. They clattered down the valley to make the morning's noise of working feet upon the streets. Father told her to keep a close eye on the clogs as he'd gladly provide any friend of hers with new ones, when needed. The sound of their steps matched their laughter and although the work was long and hard, she liked to feel herself grown and to be earning a wage.

On their traipse to work they met young men their own age. Some had not been at school with us, some were from Mytholme nearby and some were the sons of farmers. You'd think they were the sons of Adam for the interest they raised and our Betty seemed fond of one, Frank. At table, when she talked of him, her cheeks grew flushed and she ate too fast. She would tell of his many virtues and lay off the subject of his parents' Wesleyan ways unless Father or Nancy or myself thought to tease her. She would say we were all God's own (which of course we agreed upon), no matter the building where we prayed. So the subject would turn to our preachers and teachers and along the way the Brontës in their unmarried state.

'They're saying Miss Anne would do very nicely for Mr.

Nicholls,' said Betty. 'She's mild and he's not and that would make a fine balance.'

'Who's saying?' I asked, suspecting a new tale from Martha.

'Some of the women. Some who know.'

'How do they know?'

'Hearsay, I suppose. Heard what is said.'

Did it surprise me, what they said of Miss Anne? There was a time when she took a class and proved herself a very kind lady. Sarah Crabtree, a little one from Town End, she was poorly when she came to school. At least that's what we thought. Her face was reddened and great tears fell down her cheeks and she sucked her fingers enough for them to melt. Miss Anne took notice and when we were all at our slates, she drew Sarah from her bench, over to the door and bent down to speak to her. More than that, she put her arms round her and Sarah's face leaned upon her shoulder. Miss Anne let her cry. We were never to know what the matter was, but we saw she was soon well again.

I decided to find proof of a wooing between Mr. Nicholls and Miss Anne for myself. Up in the tower, at my secret post, I'd be sure to gain some useful clues. I'd learned by now that Mr. Nicholls had private meetings with Mr. Brontë on Monday evenings, so on one such night I stationed myself nicely to see how he was greeted at the door and by whom. Needless to say it was Martha let him in with no great signs of welcome. He went straight into the study on the right. I could make out Mr. Brontë's small round head and the white bands of his tight cravate. He sat away, out of sight. Mr. Nicholls, being big, filled out a chair at the small table there, his legs crossed, ready to talk parish business.

I might have slept and slipped with boredom, but was later woke by movement at the window-pane. Mr. Nicholls was stood as he shook Mr. Brontë's hand, about to leave. Which he did, letting himself out at once with not a single step towards the dining room where the sisters sat at the table. I heard his steps in the lane followed by the door of Sexton House which soon was closed behind him.

No courtship went on at the parsonage.

Mr. Nicholls

*

AT first, when he came into our school only once or twice a week, the children had not known what to think of Mr. Nicholls. In church he stood all robed and important, reading the holy words and making the sign of the cross. His crusade against the washerwomen had made some see him as a man to be feared, even despised. But I remembered him outside, pacing the hills to Stanbury with his dog and how he was always glad to talk to Joseph and me. I began to mistrust Martha's talk.

He brought us sweets to school. Some of the young ones at the front kept their eyes on his hands as he doled them out, one by one, to every child. When he took up his place at the front of the class we waited to hear why we'd been spoiled. But he made no mention of the sweets.

'Now I would like two of you, at the beginning of each class, to ask me a question. You can think of your questions during the week while you are not here, out at play perhaps. You see I need to know what you want to know,' he said. 'Two of you I will ask, and I'll decide which two when the time comes.'

'Please, Mr. Nicholls,' came a voice from the middle of the room. Lily Rawcliffe from along West Lane. 'Please, what kind of question? Can I ask my mam to give me one?'

'No, I want them to be your own. Perhaps something that puzzles you. Or perhaps some news that you have heard, like the troubles in France. Or to do with history or geography, if these interest you...'

Did he look at me? I cannot recall, but he went on making suggestions, all sorts of subjects, saying he felt sure that together we would find answers to the questions in the Bible.

'Are there any questions you can think of for today?' he asked.

'Mr. Nicholls, sir. Why do men have bigger feet than ladies?'

He did not reply at once but carefully chose a lengthy answer. He said men toiled in places like our nearby quarries. Or they built tall chimneys like down at the valley's mills. It was hard, physical work for which they needed great strength. Adam had been a gardener at Eden and perhaps he too had big feet...

He always had us listen.

In the corner of the schoolroom a basket was placed for Mr. Nicholls' dog, who ran to sit there whenever they arrived in the morning. The dog formed a part of our class and how often the younger ones asked questions about her. Why did she have a long nose? Why did we not have tails? When the children could not answer themselves, they waited for Mr. Nicholls' reply and believed his words were surely God's truth. He was a man of God, who spoke in our church. He raised his hand and blessed us all there. When he passed our parents the silver chalice, he turned its dark liquid into God's blood. He knew about mysterious things. He could even practise them.

We liked his lessons and I was glad to be no longer at Mr. Sunderland's in Stanbury. Joseph asked me what I'd learned when he turned up to meet me at the end of the day.

'Shall you ask why I breathe fast after I've been running?' he asked.

'No I shall not. I already know. It's to do with the air and lungs,' I replied, enjoying my older status with him as well as the privilege of being taught by our new curate. 'People at the looms are dying in their homes if their lungs can't get at air. That's why some houses here have tall windows and it's not only for the light. You've seen Mr. Nicholls' window, always open. Well air is good for you. It gets inside you when you've run, and your heart beats fast and your breathing does as well. We can answer that one between us, without asking him.'

'Shall we go and ask him to be sure?'

'No, Joseph. He's learning his books for tomorrow. We'll just head back on our way...'

Mr. Nicholls

*

UNDER snow the land goes quiet and hushed. And when there is no mist, it's a fine thing to stand about and watch. The snow lies for miles upon the outstretched heath. In the sun it goes bright white. The farmsteads and the mills are like stark, black marks on the white ground. Like insects. Usually when clouds are about, the horizon is hardly visible, being the same colour as the leaden sky. No sign of life. No sounds. A country caught between life and death. Everything frozen rigid and you wonder if a thaw will ever bring it alive again. Sheep stand still, their wool yellow-grey. Then sounds come – their bleating as if the cold has made them call for company. Their heads turn and stare, surprised to see a being other than themselves.

One winter saw the end of a year I'll not forget. So many things happened. Good things and bad. It was bitter cold.

All year my father had troubles that he tried not to show us, hiding them. But in the mornings I heard him groan as he woke. From my bed I watched over the blanket to see him stood with difficulty then lean first to one side then the other as he held his back, throwing his head up, closing his eyes tight.

Since in day-time we were mostly gone from the house, to school or the mill, we left him on his own already working at his bench. He seemed right enough with his lamp overhead and his tools hung up on the wall next to him. We did not know how he fared through the day. We hoped he'd go in to see Willie Forton who'd be at baking bread, the other end of the house. But by evening we saw things pained him. Heaping coal into the stove. Carrying a pail of ash into the yard. Whatever movement bent his back. Our Betty asked to send for the doctor which made him snap at her and walk out the room. We knew something was up but did not know how to help him. When at last Betty insisted he should see Dr. Wheelhouse, short work was made of the visit.

First thing Father was asked by the doctor was if combing was done in our home. A cramping of the lungs could be the cause of his aches. Betty tried to tell him that our house had not a single skein of wool in it unless it were wove into a shawl for herself or her sister.

'Nevertheless, all parts of the body do connect,' said the doctor. 'Lungs are life.'

'Surely if his back and legs hurt, it's not his lungs the cause?' asked Betty.

Dr. Wheelhouse told her not to bother her head with his profession. He gave her a bottle of brown drops for which Betty could offer no thanks. When she showed him the door, she felt his hand upon her skirt. She said so, later. And she said he was that ugly she did not care to look him in the face ever again.

Betty's young man, Frank, came to visit in the evenings. Sat round the table we made merry tales of the Wheelhouse visit. The doctor was generally not well thought of and there were more than Martha who'd seen to his ill repute. What surprised many was his marrying a young widow who became the talk of the hills. How did she deal with him? What was he like as a husband? A husband with a wandering pair of eyes? Marriage was always creeping in on our Betty's mind, but never voiced. When it came to herself and Frank, we kept silent and talked of others going down the matrimonial road. It was better than talking about illness. There were that so many weddings done, it was not an unusual event. Miss Anne became the subject of many an hour and probably in many a home, to be dangled like a puppet into each of our curates' arms.

'She's a pretty one,' said Betty. 'Of the three. I've seen her on my way to work, ever so early. She speaks out, says good morning. Neighbourly enough. But now that Mr. Grant is married she's no chance there. They say his wife is ever so nice and hated Oxenhope at first as she was from the south and missed southern ways. Miss Anne wouldn't have minded being married just a mile or so from her home. Well, there's another curate gone. She's missed her chance.'

'Yes, but think what Mr. Grant is like,' said Nancy. 'All rarified and with a silly voice. Miss Anne would do much better with Mr. Nicholls, though he's glum.'

'He's not,' I said at once.

'He is that,' Nancy went on. 'I've not seen many smiles come on his face.'

'He teaches us good things. He brings us sweets.'

'Well he's glum in church. But then church is glum.'

'Nancy, don't start,' said Betty who always seemed to calm things down.

Her young man Frank liked a pint or two. He'd stop off on his way over and arrive with a jar from one of the inns. He offered the brew to both Nancy and Betty, though Nancy had never tasted a drop and was inclined not to try. Betty offered up her glass cautiously. Through the evening the remainder of the jug was divided between Frank and Father. After a while, with Betty tending to the stove, I noticed how warmed up Father got. He talked loud and either laughed a deal or scowled. He sat over the table, his sleeves rolled up his thick arms that were placed squarely in front of him. He asked Frank about the mill, the family who ran it and what he thought of Mr. Wesley.

'He was here once or twice. Hundred years or so ago,' said Father. 'That's the reason for the great, square chapels you see about the place. It was then he got them all singing and praising the Lord and they've never stopped.'

Betty tried to change the subject, knowing Frank's parents attended the newly rebuilt Methodist chapel in Haworth's West Lane. Father also knew they did. He'd included the subject into his talk on purpose. Testing. Betty brought our dinner to the table and scolded Nancy for the slightest thing, making a noise of it. Nancy ignored her, Frank ignored the tone in Father's voice and I paid attention to everyone. Before the girls busied themselves over dishes, I suggested we searched for questions for Mr. Nicholls.

'Not to do with the Bible,' I said. 'Because it's him who finds the Bible in them,' I added, hoping the subject of the holy book, its teachings, preachings and its worshippers might now be put away for the night. Hoping I'd done Betty a favour. Hoping Mr. Wesley could be forgotten.

'What questions then?' said Father, his face glowing red. 'What's of interest to our young guest?'

I did not like the way Father spoke. He seemed to be putting Frank in a spot, asking too much as if he needed to know all. Of course if our Betty were to leave the house and marry, he'd want to be sure of any young man taking her off into the future and away from him. This was the likely thinking of a father. But Frank was giving the same back. So they became like two beasts meeting at a distance, watchful, cautious, sniffing at each other before one raised a paw.

Frank leaned back in his chair to put his arm round Betty's waist, drawing her near. Like the first move.

'The trains at Keighley. I like them,' he said. 'I like their sound, rumbling away. I like to think of where they've come from and where they will go.'

'Do you now,' said Father as he leaned further over the table. He looked Frank deeper in the eyes. 'You work among machines all day long. Are your ears not bursting with noise?'

'Used to it,' said Frank. 'So as I hardly notice. Railways is different.'

'Have you not thought to apply then? There must be some employment with the new line opened. Not one year's gone since Keighley had a station.'

'Do you think I've not tried, Mr. Robinson? Think I've not put my weight forward? Is that it? Not quite good enough?'

Betty drew herself away.

'I've not said that,' Father replied. 'Just asking. Look at myself. It's a fine thing to like your work. Makes more of a man of you, less of a slave.'

'Slave to the likes of the Merralls you mean? That I have work at all is a blessing, Mr. Robinson. Thanks to the Merrall brothers and their mills there are many in work. You must know that. There's people round here will fight and wreck to get employed...'

Frank stood his ground. So did Father. Which made our evening dinner less of a meal, more of a battlefield. As for myself I joined Nancy at one end of the table once it was cleared and the two men were sat by the stove. Betty came to sit with us. I looked at my trinkets and Nancy took up the needlework she'd been set to do. The jug of ale was emptied and rather than put an end to his visit, Father suggested Frank went out to fetch some more.

'I'll not be three minutes,' said Frank, as he left by our front door.

Father could have gone to bed then. It was his usual hour. A wide smile was spread across his face and if he didn't notice he was not aching, we did. By the time Frank returned, some half hour later, he was sat forward in his chair and on his haunches, waiting for more cross-fire. This was fought out as we played more peaceable games. I know Betty feared a quarrel. She busied herself all over, taking down pots and dusting them when there was no need. Their voices grew louder, but not in anger. They began to be quite daft. So Betty laughed and went up to Father and gave him a hug which he clung to and which made him suddenly cry. Then he talked about Mam, her passing away and how his girls were such gems, and that no man would take them from him unless he was truly worthy.

When Frank got up to leave we saw how Father also stood – straight – with not a groan nor a moan to be heard. Betty said later it was Frank's company had eased his pain. But I suspected it had more to do with the amount he'd drunk and I set my mind to thinking on the matter. Here was a question I could not ask my teacher, but I did ask myself. Could beer act as medicine for a man's aching limbs?

Frank did not always turn up at our house when he said he would and Father took to speaking less. That's when he held his back all the while. When he sat at the table he tapped his fingers upon his leg as if he could not wait long for his meal. My sisters noticed and we eyed each other without a word.

'It's men's company,' said Betty one time. 'That's what Father lacks.'

'He has me,' I said. 'I'll soon be grown.'

It was no great distance from our house to the Cross Inn, up on the main street. But of more amusement was the Black Bull in Haworth as long as you had time and a lamp in winter and you knew the way. Once he had it in his mind to go there after our dinner, Father could not be stopped. At home we could not get to bed, but waited, ears open, for his return. We knew that with Frank he'd end up with many of Haworth's drinking men.

Among them was Mr. Branwell who often caused a mighty stir. He would rant sometimes, loud and ever so miserable. I heard it at the door where I hung about some nights to fetch Father home. Once I carefully crept inside and saw Mr. Branwell in something of a blustering mood. He was sat in his usual armed chair in the corner from where he entertained the company. I looked about for Father who, like all the others, just stared and smiled, not really listening. But there was a stranger too, someone not from these parts and he must have taken a dislike to Mr. Branwell. There was almost a fight, with fists raised, then general laughter. I could not understand, then, the ways of drinking and drewling. I just wanted Father home.

Eventually, after some long weeks, Father stayed behind with us. He stood by the stove and warmed his back. He shook his head as if to clear it.

'I'm sorry,' he said, looking not at us, but at the floor. 'I'll not drink any more.'

He rocked away on his feet and held his sides.

'For I have seen young Mr. Branwell and there's a black cloud over him,' he said. 'He's half my age and with little time left...'

Word got round every corner and cobble of the village that Mr. Branwell was dying. On Sundays those who had never been to our church (nor any other perhaps) came to see him for themselves. The journey from the church to the parsonage was hardly a hundred paces, yet Mr. Branwell needed help to get himself home. Father offered his arm, but was advised to let him be.

'Demon!' shouted Mr. Branwell, as if he'd seen not Father, but the fiend himself.

The drinking was blamed. The drinking turned his mind.

Witnesses were many. Even I saw him, thin and in a sorry way, his tears enough to wash a tide through your heart.

Not long after as I stood outside the school I saw the windows of the parsonage all shut, with curtains closed. I knew it had happened. I was afraid to go inside the church in the afternoon's growing dark so turned away. I looked up into the sky as if to speak to whoever was God. The sky was not yet filled with stars, it being early dusk. I made my way to go home and found Martha in front of Sexton House.

'He's gone, hasn't he?' I asked her.

'He has,' she said briefly. 'He's at rest now.'

Her voice was sorrowful.

'He'd worn himself out, at the inn,' I stated, expecting her to agree with me.

'That what you think, John Robinson?' she said, the lilt of her words more like her usual snub.

'What everyone knows,' I replied flatly.

'Well you're wrong. You and everyone else,' she said, opening the front door. She turned to face me. 'Mr. Branwell has died of a broken heart.'

*

WITH passing months, something told me I should not lark about that old tower. Not while there was such sadness about. In daylight, if I was not at school, it was best to keep away from Haworth village, to stay on our side of the moors and go down into the river, fish there, get back up on the ridge safely before nightfall. The weather grew colder, but the crisp winds of autumn rode through a sun-streaked sky. Joseph Craven hoped to come with me, but I found I cared to be on my own.

'Try and understand,' I told him. He was surely grown enough for that.

'Well I'll try but I need to tell you about Mr. Sunderland and what we did to him today...'

Joseph was full of the Stanbury school antics that he felt sure I should know about and likely as not missed.

'No, Joseph. Another time.'

In the open air I liked to let my thoughts go. I let them move as they chose. Seeing the way Mr. Branwell went had shocked Father and I am only glad he had the strength to know what a sorry path our vicar's son had taken. We did not tell him how relieved we were to find him back with us of an evening, not in words, but he knew his children and what their pleased faces meant. We did not speak of Frank who, once he'd lost his drinking companion, found Betty's home less interesting. Not even Betty mentioned him.

Her face changed, for a while. It was brave and proud. We never saw her shed any tears. If she did, it was on her own, out of sight. Up at the crossroads I'd sometimes see Frank ahead of her, no longer seeking her out, his arms across the shoulders of other boys. They made a rattling noise of their steps, like a dance, and I almost wondered if he knew Betty was behind him. She'd look away.

The aches in Father's back did subside. Between us we'd no need of Dr. Wheelhouse and his useless cures. As Betty'd said, it was likely Father's work caused him the pain. At his bench, tapping and nailing, his back arched and stiff, he'd locked his bones into a rigid and painful state. So bad had it been, for so many months, he'd almost given in to the hands of a bone mender. He'd heard stories that some who were in agonies had gone to Rush Isles farm, way beyond Stanbury's ridge, and been pulled and turned while calling for salvation. Then they were set off right as rain and walked long miles back home.

'It's no bone mender you need,' said Betty. 'It's more common sense.'

'I've enough of that,' replied Father.

'Well give a thought to doing something else that will stretch you and keep you on your toes. Why don't you join the brass band at Lumb Foot?'

'Band? To join in with the singing of the Dissenters? I'll not make music with them.'

'Well we shall have to think of something.'

Father was not to sit hunched all the day, even if he had a thousand shoes to make. He should stand at times, stretch, avoid Dr. Wheelhouse and walk a deal more. He even accompanied me on my way to school, when I did not go early with Betty. But only so far. The short distance on his feet did him good and he knew he had his children to thank for it.

One of us, however, was less cheerful. This was Nancy, now grown enough to leave school and go to work. With little choice before her, she followed Betty to do the traipse down Smith Bank, uphill into Haworth, then down again to Bridgehouse. On her first day I could hardly wait to hear what she'd made of it. I hung about after school, before I raced home. When I saw Betty alone, I thought something must be up.

Before we even reached Stanbury, we found Nancy sitting by the road on her way up from the beck. Once she saw us she did not move, not even her eyes. Staring she was, at the ground.

'Nance – what's up?'

Her mouth folded up.

'Nancy, whatever has happened?'

That's when she hung her head, but still she did not speak.

I sat down next to her and as she didn't exactly help with her silence, I started to tug at the grass verge. I made a cleft of fresh mud where ants crawled about. They interested me, the fright and the speed of their flight. All over the place, in all directions. Disappearing into the crumbling mud. I went on and made a real furrow, finding more ants and then there were no more. All run off into hiding.

Betty sat next to her on the grass and put a long arm round her shoulders.

'I cannot do it,' said Nancy.

'What, up the hill? You that so tired?' I asked.

'No, John. I cannot do the work. I cannot.'

'But Nancy, you have to.'

'I cannot.'

'There now, love...' said Betty and laid her mouth to her sister's damp cheek.

'I cannot do it and I'm wondering what to tell Father.'

*

WHEN Mr. Nicholls came to see Father about a new pair of shoes, I asked to look at his feet.

'If they are of interest, of course you may John,' he said with as much seriousness as if I'd asked to see his mother's Bible.

'It's to do with what you said, before,' I explained.

'What I said? About my feet?'

'Not so much about your own, but about men's in general. A long while ago it was, but I never forgot.'

He sat down on the bench beneath Father's rows of model feet, each one a different shape and size. I explained to him the men's feet were on the top row, the ladies below though of course he could tell. I wanted to make him feel welcome.

'Don't mind him, Reverend,' said Father, who was stood with his measuring sticks and tapes. 'He has an eye and ear for everything. Feet and all.'

'Is that so, John,' Mr. Nicholls said as he rolled down his thick black socks to show his pale, unblemished flesh.

Straight away I saw what I'd expected to see.

'Well you said that men's feet were big for the labouring they do. Yours are also big, Mr. Nicholls. But you don't labour, not as quarrymen do.'

He looked up at me, blankly.

"Go on,' he said.

'You see I've been thinking,' I said truthfully. 'There's work like on the railways or the farms or in the mills. There's men moving about the place, using their hands more than their feet. You don't use yours in the same way. I mean, you turn pages and you pour water on babies' heads.'

He said nothing for a while and stretched his feet out ahead of him.

'Mr. Nicholls...' said Father, breaking the silence. 'Let's have your feet on this paper so's I can get their exact shape. John, boy, are you finished?'

'Don't send him off, Mr. Robinson. I should like to hear his argument,' Mr. Nicholls went on.

'I'm not arguing,' I said. 'I'm telling. From what you said it seemed that men who labour get the feet they deserve. Well, if you'll excuse me for saying, you mostly use your head don't you? Teaching, preaching and that. So why did God bother to build us in certain ways if those ways are not used? I mean, you've got the feet that might have served for labour. Instead you're more of a thinking man.'

'John!' cried Father. 'Leave off Mr. Nicholls with your talk.'

'No, no, Mr. Robinson. Your boy is a welcome challenge. When we're ready, shall we talk this through? I am a little fearful that what I have said lightly, only to demonstrate a point, has been taken too much to heart. Shall we do that, John. Discuss it together?'

I looked at Father for approval.

'Get on your way, lad,' he said. 'Mr. Nicholls, I shall send word round when your shoes are done. Can we offer you some tea?'

'That's kind. But only if John agrees to take some with me.'

*

THE trouble with looking back is certain moments keep returning, while the rest you have to think about with effort.

Sometimes a remembered incident passes to another with ease, especially if they happened at near times. Or else the more cloudy ones will arrive in your head slowly, with difficulty. Even unexpectedly.

The end of that year was marked by events connected in time, though they were apart in kind. Mr. Nicholls visited twice – to order his shoes and later, to fetch them. He sat with me and talked.

'Now then, John. What was all that about my feet? Or are you playing me up?'

'No. I wouldn't do that. It's just that I've been set thinking of late, as I said. I've wondered what I shall do with myself. I don't like to ask my Father as he'll say there'll be room for me to take his bench when I'm grown, and I fear to have pains in my back like his and fingers that are often nailed by accident. I should not like to be sitting in the same room all day. Our Nancy has feet that are not big neither, but her hands are doing work she hates. I know that Mr. Branwell wanted to be an artist, but never was. Then there's Mam, who died not long after our William was born. She said things about me, though she hardly knew me. She said that as I was the only boy left, she hoped I'd do well in life.'

Mr. Nicholls listened carefully I think. At least he hardly moved. And I had never talked so fast in my life.

'Father said Mam had a right hatred for the mills, saying they spoiled the look of the meadows and moors about here. I think so too,' I continued, pausing to take breath now and then. 'Only they serve the likes of our Betty and now Nancy's there and it seems a bit unfair. The work is not interesting, I know it, and is making Nancy ill. We had a friend, Betty's friend, who at the end of the day comforted himself with ale. The mills – I know they're ugly, great chimneys and the like, but they have to be don't they? It's what they're built for. Sometimes I count the windows on the warehouses and I multiply the ones across with the ones down, making a sort of mathematics game. It's the way my head goes. Only I should hate to be on the other side of the sheds, in with all the noise and steam. If you see what I mean, Mr. Nicholls, I don't want to disappoint our Mam, if she can see me. And I don't want to stand at the looms, indoors all the time. Not after all Nancy's said about them. But I – I suppose I am unsure and I – '

It surprised me, how many words came. Much of it I did not even know till it was spoke. All the while Mr. Nicholls had his head down and I saw his great whiskers against his cheeks, but not his eyes.

43

Then I did see them, when he looked up. They seemed clear and smiling like his mouth.

'It's a fine thing to be thinking of, John. But you need not worry your head with this, not now. We have to see how you do at school.'

'I like school mostly.'

'Yes, I know that. I can see that you try. If you do well, as your mother had hoped, you will not need to do something you dislike. There will be a choice ahead for you, a wide one. There are many professions.'

'I don't want to be a soldier, not with the wars.'

'Have no fear of that. No-one would push you that way. There are other things.'

'I sometimes think I should like to go to sea. I like the stories. But I may get seasick and I'm not so fond of salt neither.'

I grew agitated. The more he sat and listened, the more I found to say to him, that came from my mouth like a stream. As if the words had been there all the time and joined a current that took them away. So we went on, both him and me, him now doing more of the talk. He named different folk in Haworth, to let me see their lives – Mr. Greenwood the stationer, Mr. Ogden the draper, even Dr. Wheelhouse, which made me laugh out loud. I told him how Betty'd seen him off and that I should not like to meddle with people who were ill.

'There are many here, John. I visit the sick every day.'

'I'm sure that's very good of you, Mr.Nicholls, only I should like to live a long while.'

Then he said it. He said something I did not expect and it came as a terrible shock. It made me know he must have seen me, of an evening, as I dawdled about in Haworth before coming back home.

'John – have you ever thought of going into the church?'

*

IN an instant I recalled every time I'd crept into the tower.

Forgive us our trespasses.

Forgive me, Tabby, for befriending you and your talk. I was no better than Martha and her gossip. In climbing the tower, my eyes had trespassed. Into their garden, behind their windows, into their rooms. Into their servants' confidence.

Had Mr. Nicholls found the occasion to let me know I had trespassed? That I had spied on a family's privacy from God's own church? I wanted to say it, to ask his forgiveness in the hope that through him, the Lord's minister, I became blameless. The tower was not mine to go in, to climb up and to watch over Mr. Brontë's house the way I did. The steps were there so that the bells could be reached, not for a boy to scale. Sick at heart, I felt as if it thumped. I must have flushed terribly.

I wanted to run off and leave Mr. Nicholls, but he asked how I was. He'd seen me ill at ease. Being a kindly sort of man and not like the doctor, he urged me to explain my sudden look of faint. So I told him I needed fresh air, that was all. He'd probably agree, the way he kept his window wide. I said I just needed to breathe as the smell of Father's waxing sometimes got to my throat. He must have detected the fib. So, in my sudden thoughts, I became a liar as well as a trespasser.

He took a while leaving. Said he was concerned and should he call Betty. I said not. With another lie I told him these bouts of airlessness often happened. Going deeper into untruth.

*

'JOHN! John! We had ever such a caper today!' said Joseph, who I'd agreed to meet where the beck reached the lane at the bridge below Smith Bank. The great valleyside was wide and welcoming and made for a fine walk of an evening.

'What've you been up to now, Joseph...'

'Mr. Sunderland. We really had him we did.'

'Go on then. Tell.'

'Well, we were all in the schoolroom and he said he had to go inside his home – which he did – only he'd left the key inside the door, hadn't he? So we went ahead, we did, with the Plot.'

'The Plot...'

'Yes, John. What we'd plotted to do for months. While he was out we got the key didn't we, and we locked the school room from our side so when he came back he couldn't get in.'

'You locked your master out.'

'Yes. And he shouts out: "Open this door or I'll give you it" and so we asked him, we did, we said: "What will you give us, Mr. Sunderland? It will either have to be toffee or parkin or something for the fire".'

'You're daft you are.'

'Well, he just went on saying to open the door and we did not. So we stayed silent, all of us, all heaped near and listening and fit to burst.'

'So what happened? You got out I see.'

'Oh we did. But we made him promise and he said he would and when we let him back in he was that so angry. But he did as he'd promised. He went out again, warning us, but he came back with the parkin which he'd had all along at home. He had a knife too and he cut it in so many pieces there was not that much for each of us to have. Still, we had a deal of laughter over it even though he was that furious. He's not such a dridful one really. He sticks to his word...'

'You're a rum lot, you are Joseph. Larking about like that.'

'So shall I race you up the bank?' said Joseph, once his tale was over.

It was always a pleasure, at the end of the day, to hear Joseph's talk on my way home. And how glad I was to no longer be a scholar of Mr. Sunderland's school.

*

I MIGHT have laid off going to the tower for ever, but still the Brontës interested me. Because they were so different.

The Tower

Miss Emily was like a soldier – courageous, brave. In church she stood tall, upright and watched her father in the pulpit as if not listening to his words at all. After the service she never dawdled to talk with folk from the villages. Nor anyone else. We'd be on our way back to Stanbury and we'd see she'd already gone off on her own, changed from her Sunday clothes, accompanied by that brute of a dog, Keeper. As if dogs and the hills were better company than anyone else. She was a mystery to me. And to others.

Miss Charlotte was small, as sightless as a mole, but by no means meek. I never saw such tiny hands as hers with gloves made as if for dolls. I dared not displease her in case from her soft, smiling mouth she thought to scorn. But no, I was not afraid of her.

It was Miss Anne who you could talk to, more easily than the others. In the warmer months she'd come to school with flowers she'd picked just earlier, specially for us to draw. She liked drawing and she taught us how and it's thanks to her I found the lay of a pencil in my hand to be quite a pleasant occupation. Once she asked each of us what we would like to become.

Next to me was sat Ned Howker whose mam everyone knew was ill from the wool combing she did upstairs at their home. His father languished at church where he took Ned with him – both of them so sad. Miss Anne thought to kneel down and ask him, to cheer him up. 'Ned, what do you think you should like to do one day?' she said, looking into his tired, red eyes that he kneaded with his fists.

'Go to sea!' he blurted which made her laugh.

She picked up my pencil and asked if she could make a picture on my paper. Ned stood still, his tongue hung out as he watched her draw. Now and then she looked up to smile at him.

'I have seen the sea,' she said as she mused with her pencil. 'It's a wonderful sight.'

'Tell us,' said Ned. 'Are there whales and tall ships?'

'That depends where you go. In Scarborough, where I went, there are boats in the water and on the sands many things to entertain. Here, I'll draw them...'

With soft grey lines she fashioned the image of a bay and houses and people walking on the shore.

'Do us another!' said Ned as she finished shading the final details of the scene.

'I must tend to the other children,' she said. 'Another day, Ned, I'll draw a whale for you, if I can find out what they look like. You see, I've never really seen one...'

Ned watched her move across the room, his eyes gawping, his mouth open wide.

Yes, we all liked Miss Anne very much.

*

OUT of school, if not waiting for my sisters, I still had a mind to go with Joseph now and then and do a traipse. Once the cold got keen and bitter and the nights fell earlier, we had other escapades in mind.

We had thought to walk round the back lane of the village, the other side to ours, and wait for darkness to descend so that we could peer inside people's homes. But since I'd been aware of my trespassing, I was less sure this was a good idea. Christmas was near and Joseph had it in his mind that we might see the star in the east. I tried to tell him it came after the birth of Jesus, to summon the three wise men to get on their camels and find the child in the stable.

'Well the shepherds got there only just in time,' he said. 'If they'd had sheep out Stanbury way they'd have seen the whole sky.'

'They had angels tell them. The star was later.'

'Well them angels should be there now,' he said with his face all lit. 'Which way's east?'

'Over by Keighley. There's no star nor angels there, Joseph. Come on and let's turn back home. It's far too cold.'

As we returned we bent low against the wind and we blew our fingers and I could not help seeing the great, black shape of the church over beyond Haworth moor. It occurred to me there was only one way to set my thoughts to rest. I should have to make a confession of my trespasses right there. I'd do it the next day, on my own, just me and God, when the church had good daylight pouring inside, to remind me of salvation.

*

SHE was sat there alone, not in their family box pew, near the altar, shivering. Quiet as I could I stood still and thought not to move before deciding which way to go. She was knelt and she spoke, ever so low, in her soft voice. I felt like an intruder, a robber. I even thought to get on up the tower, but I had come to confess to God in His church.

She had her head bent low and her bonnet moved. Now and then it tilted backwards as she raised her eyes to the two grand windows behind the altar where grey skies filled their empty panes. From her sleeves she drew a handkerchief and wiped her eyes. Then she stood, tall as a child.

I could do nothing.

I went on and stayed stood where I was, quite still, sure I'd intruded on her. Any movement by me would be amiss. To run away from her would seem like I feared her. To speak to her would be like cheek. To do nothing seemed the best action.

She bowed her head towards the middle window above the altar, turned and at once saw me like the figure of a foolish statue, gaping. Still and dumb as stone.

'John,' she said.

'Miss Charlotte. I – I came here so's to, to – '

'I am leaving now.'

'Are you not well?'

She stood still in the aisle. Usually her wide eyes were soft and heavy-lidded. But they were glassy and they glared, fixedly, as if they did not belong to her, but to someone she'd thought herself into being. Her tiny frame then folded up as she was about to fall. She clutched the carved pew-end for support.

'Miss Charlotte,' I said again, going towards her. 'Whatever is up?'

She bent her head down onto her chest then raised a gloved hand to wipe her eyes. When she looked at me they were filled with water..

'My sister Emily has died,' she said.

*

FATHER was not a man to snore, but I heard his breathing and knew when he was sound asleep. Night time I was warmer. My knees reached my chin and I lay on one side and held myself close, eyes shut, trying to think what to do about my confession. When? Mr. Brontë would be very occupied now, with the sadness over at the parsonage. Would it be best just to confess to Mr. Nicholls since he seemed to have guessed my transgression? Or was it much better straight to God? And if it were to God did I really need to go into the church? As creator of the world and since he was all-seeing, why not out on the moorland where he'd get a better view of me?

I tossed about almost to a sweat. My sisters would chat and whisper late in their room next door.

Nancy had taken a fancy to a boy while Betty was trying to warn her off him without sounding harsh. Nancy scolded, almost to a shout. Betty tried to calm her. I did not hear the exact words, but I could tell what was said. Downstairs the clock in Father's workshop struck every hour and I lay there waiting for the sound. Still with no decision made.

At our window pale chinks of light crept around the curtain folds. I heard the sounds of carts and hoofs up on our road as the early merchants from Colne continued on their way towards Keighley beneath a lightening sky. By morning that sky was not bright which did not help once I got up. Father went down first, leaving me to look out the window in the hope that I might receive some heavenly blessing or at least some sign that would put my mind at rest. Nothing happened. Only the falling away green of Smith Bank in front of me and low-lying clouds that spread and hovered over the distant hills.

They noticed how I was speaking less, lost in thought. Something was bothering me.

'Now then, tell us –' said Betty. 'We're not so daft as not to notice.'

I could have told. They knew about the tower that I'd climbed for years. They saw it as a pastime, not a prank. They knew I was nimble on my feet and, with my liking for sums, calculating in my head. Betty wondered if I had fallen in love – a likely tale! I should have hated their teasing if that were so. I could have told the truth. I could have said it – 'Mr. Nicholls has asked if I have entered the church...' – but that would put them in mind of him as a scolding and fierce sort of man. I did not want that.

He had become a separate kind of person to me. I think it is because he took notice of the things I said. Father did not ask much and rightly hoped that the teaching at school would do me good. As long as he earned from the shoes and boots and clogs he made, he was doing as was expected of him. In the hands of people like Mr. Nicholls, Father felt I might achieve all that Mam had wanted.

Mr. Nicholls wanted more of me. I could tell it. So often in the classroom he'd turn to me when a question was asked. He knew I was likely to answer. Even if it did not have much to do with God. I was very unsure of God anyway. Since I never saw Him, I'd begun to find Him a strange one. I never told Mr. Nicholls this. I'd answer things like 'how do buildings stand up?' and tell the children about the girders made of iron instead of wood since no tree was long enough to spread the length of those great warehouses down at the mills. Their chimneys were circled with iron as well. I knew because Joseph and I used to straggle about there, on the sites where new ones were being built. We watched the men at work and Joseph, fearful, thought the bricks would fall even if the men didn't. Then when he saw the chimneys rising ever so high he felt sure they were going up to heaven. Angels would keep them up. He was always on about angels was Joseph.

Mr. Nicholls

As I still had not confessed to entering the church, I went off and tried to work things out, the way I did with my sums, over and over again. I wandered off in front of our house, down to the bank and to the beck which I watched. I liked to do that. I saw how the water went, over the stones and round boulders, always making the same patterns. Water flowed from upstream, from inside the moors. The look of the beck was the same. The flow was the same. It was alive and moving, but still the same.

If I admitted to Mr. Nicholls about going up the tower, before he questioned me, he might still treat me the same. The confession could be like a stone thrown into the beck. The water would find its way round it, moving all the while. Until it settled. The same level as it had always been.

I decided it was best to get the thing done before Christ's birthday. Then, when we were all sat at table, Willie Forton with us and of a mind to musically merry-make, I would no longer bear the weight of it. I made my way to Church Lane with every intention of knocking on the door of Sexton House and boldly asking to see him. But as soon as I'd turned the corner I saw them coming from the parsonage through the little gate in their garden wall that led straight into the churchyard. There was Mr. Brontë at the front and by his side was Miss Emily's great dog, Keeper. Behind these two came Miss Anne and Miss Charlotte, each holding a small book. Martha followed, together with old Tabby. Silent and solemn beneath a dull winter's sky they moved slowly forward behind Miss Emily' coffin, into the church.

After that, I hung away down the lane, still hoping to meet Mr. Nicholls. I had not sight or sound of him, but from inside the parsonage I heard Keeper, who howled all through that night and afterwards for day upon day.

*

EVERYONE feared the lung disease. Many in our village caught it, coughing and wasting away as they did. Plenty of folk, like Ned Howker's mam, coughed from the wool they combed in upstairs rooms. Though I'd been told by Martha that Mr. Branwell's death was due to his heart breaking, I did wonder about that. I believed hearts to be made of blood. I'd heard it said that the heart was a muscle and I'd seen muscles taut and strong inside Father's arms. Maybe hard enough to snap. The consumption was not something that happened quick. And by the time you called the doctor it was usually too late. That's what they said about Miss Emily. They said she'd refused to have Dr. Wheelhouse near. We thought that wise though it did not save her.

I had to stay well. I knew that if I did, I could get on in the world better than if I were shaky and coughing and fearful of work. By the time the morning sky lightened a little, though it was still cold, I hoped that spring would bring me the courage to begin a fight. My fight. I would battle with illness in whatever way I could. It would not be enough just to watch people walk by as they did every day on their ways here and there towards Haworth. I had to keep watch, to see how the healthy stayed living. This was surely how best to please Mam.

When our Nancy got ill we were that so worried we nearly did ask for the doctor. Luckily Mr. Nicholls visited. I was not sure whether it was on Nancy's account or to come and find me, but on hearing about the sick girl he went first to her. He stayed by her bedside for a good half hour then came down and sat with me in the kitchen.

'John, I've an idea for you,' he said.

Of late, since Christmas, I had not seen him out of school time. My doubts about confessing had set me a distance from him. Perhaps he had noticed this and was about to tick me off. Which is why I turned that so scared. Was he was waiting for me?

So when he came round to our house, I shook.

'How is she, our Nancy?' I said at once.

'She is well. She needs to rest and to drink and eat plenty that is hot. I am no doctor, John, as you know, but I believe she'll do best just staying at home in bed. That alone will do her good.'

'Well how is Miss Anne?' I asked, mostly on Betty's behalf since she still had it in mind that Miss Anne and Mr. Nicholls should marry. I'd say anything that would keep his talk away from me.

'Ah - how good of you to ask,' he said. 'She is very frail and we are most concerned. Miss Charlotte seems to have acquired an extraordinary strength that is timely and well needed. We must pray. We must pray that the same fate that took her sister – and her brother – will not take Miss Anne as well. But John, I would like to talk to you about other, more hopeful things.'

Here it was. Hope in salvation. After confession.

He told me of Keighley's libraries. He said that if I cared to go with him, I would find there a whole world of books that I could borrow and bring home. He said a subscription was necessary, but he'd be pleased to pay for that.

Which made me speechless. Why should he?

'Why should you?' I asked.

'Because I feel you would benefit from a little more reading than you have in school. Aesop is all very well for the likes of your friend Joseph. But the books you are given to read are not enough for a boy like you. Miss Charlotte feels the same. She has spoken to me about your work and we have thought of something that we feel you may enjoy. If you would agree to come with me, on a Saturday afternoon, we could look at many books. We would have the freedom of shelf upon shelf of books to choose from together...'

I was forgiven.

I had not needed to confess.

His godliness was bountiful.

*

The Tower

JOSEPH was grown bigger than he used to be and he liked to go further about. He never stopped his questioning ('if Crow Hill explodes again, will thousands of noisy birds come out?') but his child's ways were now very unlike my own.

We'd set off the far end from Stanbury and once the hard earth was thawed, the air warmed and the first green buds appeared on trees we took tracks well cleared of mud. Right past the houses we went along the old drovers' road, past the toll house then off over higher, wild land. Though the few farms there seemed far away, we did not take long to reach them. They stood isolated, stark and black on the sides of broad, sweeping hills. It was here Joseph made the acquaintance of Jim Clayton, more his own age than me and not a boy I cared to befriend.

Jim laid in wait for us. He must have seen us coming, like small spots on the back lane from Stanbury. Out on open ground we were exposed – Joseph calling, me whistling while crying curlews wheeled above us in an empty sky. Hardly anyone was about but for the cattle belonging to Withins farms. We went over stone walls, tracing the sandy paths where scratchy, colourless heather stood like splayed brush on either side. On and on towards the brown horizon.

We reached one of the farms. In a corner of the yard were tumbled walls where Jim had made a lookout post in the space between two great boulders. He was well hid there. Knelt down he'd seen our steady ascent up the moor while we knew nothing of his watchfulness. Stones came showering down on top of us. We looked up, startled as hares, and saw a bright and sun-filled sky.

'It's fairy folk,' said Joseph to which I said nothing, but walked on ahead.

I saw where the missiles came from and when more were thrown, I went forward through the gateway of the farm. Across the yard a goat was tethered in the open porch of a large barn. It bleated at the sight of me. I turned to see where Jim was crouched, trying to make himself smaller, inside the wall. His head of tufty hair gave him away and I paced towards him.

'What's all this?' I asked and was soon stood over him.

He remained bent low and stuck out his tongue at me.

'Back off our land,' he said with little threat, retreating further into his hide-hole.

'It's not your land and if you'd injured us, how could we have gone anywhere?' I asked.

'Don't know,' he said.

'Tell us why. Why do it?'

'Don't know,' he said again.

'Get out of there,' I told him which made him squeeze himself uncomfortably further beneath the hole's boulder roof.

A lone tree, bent to one side from buffeting winds, marked the edge of the farm. Standing by it was Joseph. When he saw Jim emerge from the wall he put his arm round the tree's trunk, for safety, as if it were the legs of a mother. Jim went over and stood a few yards in front of him, both hands on his hips.

'Your name – what is it?'

Joseph gladly told him his two Christian names, his surname, his age and his address. I stood by and waited to see how Joseph dealt with the stranger boy, hoping he'd see him off. But Jim was on home ground – that is, the land of the farms where he sometimes worked. Even though tracks and paths crossed the fields from this to other farms as guides across the moors, Jim claimed them all as his own. This was not the territory of valley mills, their masters and workers who met each day and knew each other's faces, their children and their cares. Jim felt the right to challenge any unknown figure who wandered on the lone and bleak hillside.

'Are we to go back now?' Joseph called to me, a trembling in his voice.

'No. I've a mind to stop,' I said firmly.

Jim was firm upright, his legs apart. He stood all threatening, right next to Joseph.

'What's his name?' he asked him, cocking his head towards me.

'He's called John.'

'Is he a friend of yours?'

Joseph said nothing but tightened up his mouth as if it were stuck with paste.

I might have been angry with Joseph not answering, but understood the poor lad was afraid. As I went over to them, Jim shouted loud towards the farmhouse and soon a mud-spattered dog came bounding towards us. It had been indoors and was let out by an old woman who stood at the gate watching, frowning. I kept the dog's eyes in my gaze and in an instant I thought of Miss Emily. What would she have done? When the dog was before me, barking and baying, I held firm, my toes curled inside the ends of my boots, still staring it in the eyes.

'Call your dog away,' I said to Jim.

He waved to the woman.

'Pestering me they are!' shouted Jim.

She shrugged her shoulders and briskly slapped her hands on her aproned thighs. The dog returned to her, wagging its tail.

'Come on, let's be going,' I said calmly, relieved there had not been a fight. As I made my way to the path we'd trod, I did not look back. I must have gone some twenty yards further up the hillside before I turned to see if I were followed. Joseph had stayed behind. He was still with Jim, both boys bent on their knees at the farm wall. They were making their way alongside it. I watched for a while, unable to guess what they were up to. Jim put one finger to his mouth, asking Joseph to be quiet. They were looking hard at something. I crept up myself. The rough, stony ground, not far from the tree, fell into a shallow ditch, one like many further down the hillside that gathered water underground to come out again as a spring or waterfall. Up here was all dry heath. The perfect open spot for curlews' nests.

I looked to see if any bird was about. The boys remained kneeling and very still. Until I coughed.

'John! John – there's four eggs here!' Joseph called to me excitedly.

I knew not to spoil their watch.

'I'll wait for you back down the hill,' I told Joseph. 'Down by the stones. Don't be long.'

Crops of gritstone rock jut out of those hills and stand as prominent landmarks. Some lie scattered about on high ground as great stones, as if they'd been flung from the sky. Standing on these you could look back over to Stanbury and see the whole village like a dark slug, creeping along that ridge. Otherwise there's nothing but open land everywhere.

My feet were not big, nor were my hands. The more I got to thinking, the more sure I was that to farm or to weave or to quarry were not for me. Since I'd been going into Keighley with Mr. Nicholls I'd discovered not only books, but other people there. Some of them lived out our way and walked the four miles to work leaving the country behind them. It was not as if Keighley was the other end of the earth. Nor even was Halifax, where our woven wool was sent.

As I waited for Joseph I thought how glad I'd been in the tower, to have that hidden place for myself when I wanted my own kind of secrecy.

In Keighley, where we entered the town, a new church had been built, St. Andrew's. It too had a tower with pinnacles and a clock on every side. I realised there were other churches beside archangel Michael's. Buildings were being worked upon that grew from week to week and I saw their shapely windows complete. As for the Mechanics Institute where Mr Nicholls found the books, it was a grand edifice with two flights of steps. The town, with its buildings, was a place of new discovery, allowing me to know there was more beyond our hills. Probably more adventures as fine as the hiding in my tower had been.

In the hills I liked to be alone. The hills were a fine place for dreaming. Joseph's dreams were of the fable or fairy type played out in his jaunts with Jim Clayton. I saw to it that whenever they went off to seek more nests or go knee-deep in the clear pools of the spring becks, I'd be somewhere near, usually on those stones, listening out for him. My play changed. I was no longer right for such scrambling. I still had dreams only they too changed – they became more earthbound.

*

'JOHN lad, I'll have a word with you.'

Father had combed his hair back and taken off the kerchief round his neck. He was sat by the empty grey grate with his feet not in his boots but in slippers he'd made from felt and wool bits. He usually put these on in winter, not on late spring nights like this. He was fitted for talk, spruced, ready for me.

'Mr. Nicholls came to see me,' he said.

He cleared his throat to talk well.

'He did?' I said.

'He would seem to have a high opinion of you, which of course makes me glad. He said Miss Charlotte feels the same.'

I said nothing. No words came to mind.

'He has it in his head that you're bound to do well since you've made a good start at the school. And those books you borrow, he says you treat them as you should and he is glad. He said he'd like you to do still better. That's exactly what your Mam wanted.'

His words did travel into my ears, on both sides, but they went no further. Not into understanding. Father was being all polite.

'He has asked me if I might agree to you having extra lessons,' said Father and he scratched the side of his neck then inspected his fingernails. I could tell he was uneasy, unused to talking this way. Still he went on. 'It may cost me some, not so much, but I've a mind to say yes to him. He wants to teach you the language of Latin and ancient literature he said. Other things besides. Such things he believes will go well with you.'

I sat still and watched him.

'I know he is going to come back, now that I've told you, to hear what you think on it,' he said and the more I looked at him, the more

I realised he was saying something that pleased him deeply. 'He thinks that with an hour or so, on Saturdays, he could get you prepared.'

'Prepared for what?' I asked.

'Only a suggestion, but he did wonder if, one day when you're fully grown, you might like to enter the church.'

Enter the church.

'Me? Enter the church?'

'Aye I know, it's not what any of us have thought, but he has. You're young and no decisions need be made, I told him. But the gist of it was that you were fit for learning more than other lads. Latin seems to be the way to rise a little. Church is something else. You don't have to be a bishop, nor a vicar. It's the learning he wants to do with you. The rest will get sorted later.'

*

MR. NICHOLLS did come back but with a look that was weary and worried. I was so heaped up with gratefulness and a spirit as light as a stray feather, I didn't see at first that he had not come to hear my reply. I was full of all we had talked about at home, round our table of an evening, with both my dear sisters saying they would help towards the lessons' costs. It was as if Mam had descended upon us all and her wishes were begun. I was full of telling him this.

But he was wretched.

'Mr. Nicholls, sir,' I said. 'Whatever is up with you?'

'I shall speak of what I'd suggested to your father another time, and you John – if you could wait. But I'm afraid I find it hard to withold the sad news I bear…'

'Come in –'

'No, I must get back. I am awaiting the return of Miss Charlotte from Scarborough,' he said and he shook his head. His face was all lined, crumpled up. 'She went to stay there with Ellen, her friend, and Miss Anne. But she has come back alone.'

'She has?'

The Tower

'Miss Anne died there. I'm afraid her return will be a sorry arrival to a home changed for ever.'

*

SHE came into school and we were all hushed as we stood about not knowing how to be. She told us to sit and gave us our readings, words and pages to decipher first in our heads then to speak out loud. When we were silent I saw her stare out the window, the spectacles like her thoughts perhaps, an obstacle to seeing clearly the bright day outside.

She was mild and quiet, taking the girls' needlework right up to her nose to inspect the stitches from close by. You'd never guess that things had gone so bad for her. She was still our teacher who came to the schoolroom door and stood before us like a trembling fern, as if she were hardly there. After the morning's lessons she went as silent as she'd come and we watched her go. Back into the parsonage across the lane.

That evening I was drawn to the tower. The weather had not been so warm for late May and the nights were blown through with a cooling wind. Unseen I entered the small door at the tower's base, closed it behind me and looked off into the wide church. Those two great pointed windows should have lit the spacious nave. They stood east where only a grey light found its way inside. This touched the brass eagle whose wings were spread to receive a heavy tome. It did not fly. It stayed still, tethered to its post, poised and unable to move. Globes made of glass hung either side of the high pulpit which stood solid, of wood, stern. I heard Mr. Brontë's strong words spoke from there as if in a distant echo. I saw Mr. Nicholls too, tall then stooped as he passed in front of the altar carrying bread and wine. Had I never noticed how damp the place smelled? How empty it was with no people inside. All that took place in the church I imagined, remembered. But no-one was really there. Everything was dull. It was no place for me to be, nor could I feel there any presence of God.

I climbed the stone steps until I reached where the heavy iron bells hung on beams. Carefully I made my way along the ridge that followed the walls round, but I did not go at once to my usual post. I took to the window opposite that looks out east. Through the slats I saw where hills were spread below me. In the valleys the chimneys of mills stood tall, rows of houses crept down beside them off the fields. I saw the outskirts of Keighley and thought how grand it was I knew the way into that town. I went back round to the window that looked down onto the graveyard and the parsonage. Once again.

Mr. Brontë, in his study on the right, was reading a newspaper. Miss Charlotte walked in and handed him a drink and I expected her to stay with him, the two of them together for the evening. She bent down and gave him a brief kiss upon the cheek. Then she left him as she'd found him only a few minutes earlier. I watched as she went into the dining room opposite his study. She lit the lamp on the table and sat at a small writing desk. This she looked at but she did little more. The light inside the glass flickered. She picked up her spectacles and carefully placed them across her nose. Her hands she then laid on the table. She remained seated, staring. Never had I seen such a sight so lone and sad.

Lessons

❊

HOMER was a writer and Mr. Nicholls told me much about him. He said that Homer lived ever so long ago, in ancient times, which made me think of him as ancient with a long beard and white hair and the way Mr. Nicholls talked about him, you'd think he was a close friend of God. Trouble was, Homer was born long before Jesus and that started me on many troublesome thoughts. Where did Bethlehem fit into the picture? When confusion began to set in I didn't dare stop and ask too much, especially once Mr. Nicholls got talking.

'The Greeks had many gods,' he explained and went on to name some of these.

My eyes wandered round his room. It was not a very big room, for a man who was tallish and well-built. The walls were a dull colour made dark by rows of books on shelves that I felt sure he had put up himself. Some were at floor level where single wood planks were supported by more books at either end. Larger volumes sat upon each other on the scratched wood surfaces where bare boards surrounded the room. The carpet's pattern had disappeared with time and tread, probably thanks to the many lively feet of the Brown family. I glanced at the door and saw four holes, each one the size of a penny. They made me smile as I remembered what Martha had said about him drilling them. The fireplace was filled with last season's ash and I thought to scold Martha about it, only she was well occupied at the parsonage. Other members of the large Brown family could have swept it for him. Many of them still lived at Sexton House while one sister visited with her husband. I got to know them by face, not much by words. I heard them clattering about in the back rooms, sometimes having a bawl. How did Mr. Nicholls work with their noise?

'...these gods gained great credence with the esteem paid to them all over the ancient world, so that by the time the Romans came to rule, they were adopted. Their names were changed. You have the Greek god Zeus becoming the Roman god Jupiter. The daughter of Zeus is Athena for the Greeks and Minerva for the Romans. Athena-Minerva was born, so the legend goes, when her father suffered a terrible headache and she simply came out of his skull.'

'She never!'

'That is according to the myth they all believed.'

'A bit like our Mary who suddenly found she was expecting.'

'No, not quite the same.'

'Why not?'

'Certainly those ancient gods were thought to be divine,' he went on. 'It took the birth of Christ to change people's beliefs in them...'

'Later on.'

'That's right. One inspired emperor, Constantine, allowed our Lord to be worshipped. Before him you were persecuted, imprisoned, even killed for your belief.'

'Go on then,' I said. 'Tell us more...'

'Thousands were killed for their faith. Many among them became our holy martyrs. You need only think of the names of our churches to identify them...'

Mr. Nicholls' voice was steady and serious, but this 'teaching' I found most enjoyable.

He had his thick hair brushed smooth, the way it was when he stood in church or came visiting to people's doors. He sat upright in a high-backed chair that suited him, gave him authority. Yet his talk was not high-sounding. And it helped that his voice was deep and rich. For a good half hour he told me about that ancient world, so far away in time and geography, and I listened hard. He even took down his globe from the mantelpiece and showed me the islands of Greece. Then off went my thoughts, how I should like to go there too. Such wonderful lands might please Joseph Craven, if ever we took up our old adventuring together.

Those early lessons contained many stories which I looked forward to hearing. When I returned home I'd repeat the intrigues of the pagan gods to Father and my sisters and also to Willie Forton when he visited. I feel sure he believed them. Everyone liked to listen. So on Saturdays we ate our meal with me put at the head of the table, in order to have some authority as a tale-teller, just as Mr. Nicholls had been only half a day earlier.

'Theseus sailed off to Athens with the maidens and youths. He had it in his mind to slay the Minotaur once and for all. When he got there he was helped by the daughter of King Minos. She knew a way into the place where the beast was kept...'

Willie's mouth was hung open as I talked. He told me not to stop though it was necessary for me to eat as well as talk and I had to pause from my story now and then, to give the others a chance to speak.

'Go on then, our John. What happened next...' said Nancy who particularly enjoyed the tales though she liked to point out she was no longer a child.

The girls served me royally and Father, despite being sat on the long side of the table, would ask for my plate to be piled upon first. My lessons with Mr. Nicholls gave me quite some clout. Not only at home.

I arrived each time at the same hour and knocked upon the door of Sexton House. If it were Martha opened up, down from the parsonage on an errand, she'd be as haughty as ever.

'So you've come,' she'd say.

'I have that.'

'He's been up and out in the parish and left his window open for us all to freeze.'

'And is he here now?' I asked, ignoring her usual complaints. 'Mr. Nicholls is expecting me, as you well know.'

'Oh hark at him now he's learning Latin. You'll not find a soul in Haworth will talk to you with those dead words.'

'As a matter of fact I shall,' I was able to reply truthfully. 'Mr. Brontë knows such languages. And so does Miss Charlotte. But not yourself, of course…'

*

MR. NICHOLLS spoke a good deal about Miss Charlotte. The whole village had wagged its many tongues for months since Miss Anne went away and died. Miss Charlotte, being the only child of the family left, was thrown into a new light, one that was not exactly bright. People felt sorry for her. Occasionally she left the neighbour-hood and nobody blamed her for not wanting to stay. Martha, who was the one in the know about most things to do with her, was at times proudly able to announce when there were visitors to the parsonage. There was the headmistress of the school Miss Charlotte had once attended. There was Ellen, the friend she had made there. Since Martha knew Miss Charlotte's every activity, she liked to present herself on intimate terms with these guests. She particularly liked to say when Miss Charlotte was in London, gone by train from Keighley, as if it were normal practice. Far from the likes of Haworth. She even suggested Miss Charlotte had important business there.

People expected Miss Charlotte to become unwell. In church they stared hard if ever she coughed. Everyone awaited the symptoms of threatened lungs that had killed off her siblings. Being on her own with only dogs for company, it was thought she'd fade away fast.

'She is what one might call stoical, John, rather like her sister

Emily,' said Mr. Nicholls when my lesson was over. I felt he'd been watching the clock, waiting to talk not of ancient Greece or Rome, but of where we lived in the here and now and of them, the two remaining members of the Brontë family. He did not send me off straight away. He liked to talk. 'She has seen much of death close by in her own home, but she has the great fortune to enjoy working.'

'Working?' I said, a little surprised. 'Martha and the servants do the work there, don't they?'

He hesitated. At that time he'd often smile. I suspected he knew many things that happened up the lane, that no-one else could know, despite Martha's bulletins. He spent those Monday evenings there. He was more and more involved with parish matters and often met with Mr. Brontë in his study. He'd be the one to know if Miss Charlotte was really fading away or not.

I felt she wasn't. In the schoolroom she continued as she ever had done, quiet and a little stern if ever a foolish answer was given. She scolded Jack Hey once, harshly, when he'd taken off his boots and laced them together, hoping to walk off home one foot in front of the other. He didn't even get to the door. Miss Charlotte's big eyes, normally so soft, turned into a stare as she asked if he'd come to school like that – or had he tied the boots together while she was talking?

'No, Miss Charlotte,' said Jack.

'No? No to which question?'

'No, I did not tie them while you was talking.'

'Then you're an astounding fellow. I believe you live in Butt Lane which is quite a walk away from school. Or should I say, quite a hop? I shall be most interested to see how you get yourself home.'

She was not to be fooled and I told Mr. Nicholls this very thing.

'No fooling Miss Charlotte, no,' he said warmly. 'As a matter of fact, John, she is a fine and clever person. Neither you nor anyone else in Haworth need fret too much that her being alone might mean she is bored. She has done much and has more to do. And one day you may know just what she has achieved.'

Mr. Nicholls

*

IT sounded to me as if he kept secrets. If so, that was his concern. Outside of the family and apart from Martha, he was the person closest to the life of the parsonage, a position we others needed to respect. Yet in order to maintain our esteem we had a right to know a bit about our vicar's life, did we not? When Mr. Nicholls showed me a veritable treasure he had come by through Mr. Brontë, I thought no more of Miss Charlotte, nor even her father but of her dead brother. Mr. Branwell, that poor wayward lad, now became a wonder in my eyes. The object of my fascination was a notebook filled with neat lines of writing. These were 'odes' or poems, written once by a famous man of ancient times called Horace and translated from Latin into English by Mr. Branwell himself. I held the book in my hands.

'So are all these words his work?' I asked, as I looked at the pages he had written.

'Yes, John. To translate from one language to another is no easy task. Firstly, you must find their exact meaning. Then you think in general what approaches that meaning, in the other language. To get the words to flow and to sound as natural as if they were the speech of you and me is not something anyone can do.'

'Do you have to be a poet?'

'It's best, if you're translating poetry.'

I turned the pages over and stared closely at every line. At times Mr. Branwell had drawn through some of the words and put a different one above them, as if he'd changed his mind.

'Did Mr. Brontë give it you?' I asked.

'No, no. I knew of it and asked if I might borrow it. He was very pleased to learn it would be used by you. He admires you, you know John. When you are ready we can try and work out our own translation of the odes. Then, if we get a bit stuck, we could see what Mr. Branwell has to say.'

'Do people know he did this?' I asked.

'You mean the people here, in Haworth?'

'Yes. Do they know he could write, that he was clever?'

'Some knew. He had friends here but they – they –'

Mr. Nicholls was not going to say what I already thought.

'They went off drinking together, didn't they?' I boldly asked.

'John...' he said, rising from his chair about to speak his mind. He walked over to the open window and put one hand upon the sill, the other at an upper pane. I could not tell how far his gaze led over towards Keighley, or what he saw there, if anything. From where he stood he'd have a fine view across the lane over the graveyard. It didn't occur to me that he might look in the direction of the parsonage that stood alone at the edge of the moor.

'People will say many things about others,' he went on. 'Often it is a guessing game, to try and find out what they do not know. We all know about Mr. Branwell, the young man who spent too much time at the inns. But he was no idiot. He was a fine person with much potential.'

'He didn't much like us at school. He hated teaching us,' I said.

'Possibly, yes. But that's because it did not suit him to do such work.'

'He could have taught us Latin if he knew so much about it.'

'Your hours in school are shared by many, of different ages and abilities. It wouldn't have suited all of you. That's why you are learning now, alone, with me. Mr. Branwell was simply... unfortunate.'

He returned to our table and held out his hand for the little book.

'You and I shall learn many things that no-one else will know. Here, already, in these pages, we've found a different Mr. Branwell to the one who is slandered in the lanes outside. I should like to be able to trust you, John, with all we learn together. Can I do that?'

'Oh but Mr. Nicholls, I have already told my sisters and Father the stories of the ancient myths and about Odysseus, that he sailed off and had all those adventures. And Willie Forton, he has bad eyes at times and he's afeared he'll end up with only one, like the Cyclops...'

'Those stories are for everyone to know. I'm glad you told them. And did they like them John?'

'Yes, but – am I not to say about Mr. Branwell's book?'

'You can, of course. But I should like us to be silent over certain things.'

For a moment a thought fled through my mind, from one ear to the other, as if it weren't meant to stay there. I remembered how I once thought we shared a secret – my stolen moments in the tower. Silence had served me well.

'I know how to keep quiet, Mr. Nicholls,' I replied.

'Well, let this book, the words of an enthusiastic scholar, be a kind of symbol for us, John. I would not ask you to swear on God's holy book. But I should love to share much with you. Much that no-one else must know.'

*

THE day of the shoes. There's a day I'll not forget. Ever.

Father's rolls of leather were delivered to a small warehouse in Keighley from where they came over on carriers that served the stores of both Haworth and Oxenhope. The leathers were usually black or brown coloured for the many hard-wearing boots he was asked to make. One lady required all the colours of the rainbow for her dainty feet. This was Mrs. Pollard from a house in Stanbury's back lane. Her face was soon to be one I took notice of. She wanted her shoes before time and preferred not to come to the workshop, but hoped Father would go to her. She presumed he'd do as she asked. Because of this he did not fancy the idea and made quite a creation of it in his own mind. He battled with himself and said she should come to his door like anyone else.

'You shall have to weigh up her worth in terms of the work, and maybe do as she asks,' Betty suggested one day.

Father's back had set him bent again, giving him pain right down his legs. Each day when she and Nancy returned home from Bridgehouse, Betty went straight in to see how he was. Not only did he ache everywhere, he began to have strange pains inside his chest.

'John, shall you go along to Mrs. Pollard's before you set off for your lesson?' she asked one Saturday. 'You can take your friend Joseph. Her leather has arrived and we need to see if it's the exact colour she likes.'

'And what colour's that?' I asked.

'It's green,' said Betty unable to hide a smile.

'Green as bad cheese?'

'Just green, John. But there's no knowing if it is the right green.'

'I'll go,' I said.

I went alone. The back lane ran along part of the northern side of the village and I could have cut down into it past the new school, but I had it in mind to practice speaking my Latin. So I took a long way round. I scrambled north, down the slope of the fields towards the river, then across and way up again with the present indicative of the verb portare in my mind's voice.

'Porto, portas, portat – I carry, you singular carry, he she and it carry, no carries. Portamus, portatis, portant – we carry, you plural carry, they carry. Porto, portas, portat...'

By the time I reached the Pollards' door I was sure that the whole world was fit to carry whatever it chose though I had to feel inside my coat to be sure I still carried Mrs. Pollard's green leather roll.

I knocked on the door and waited.

As bolts were noisily unlocked, I heard a voice complain.

'Oh pother and bother it...'

Two small hands gripped the door's sides to ease it open.

'Who are you?' asked a young girl who stood as still as a statue but for her blinking eyes. Her hair was a maze of light.

'I've come to see Mrs. Pollard.'

'Have you had breakfast?'

I said I'd eaten and wanted for nothing, but this did not make the girl move. I put my hand inside my pocket to feel the leather and kept it there.

'I've to show her the stuff for her new pair of shoes.'

'Can I see?' said the girl, coming forward.

She was not a servant, I could tell. She was herself. Across her brow a pair of dark eyebrows almost touched. Beneath these were two large brown eyes. The blinking stopped and she stared hard at me.

'You can see it only if you tell me your name,' I replied.

'Well why don't you guess. Why don't you?' she said and she hunched up her shoulders to her ears and grinned with pleasure.

'Let me think now. My sisters are Betty and Nancy. My mother was Mary. That's three guesses.'

'None of them are right!' she said laughing. 'One more guess and then I'll tell you if you're wrong.'

'Iphigenia,' I said in all seriousness.

'You're wrong! Wrong! My name is Hannah. Now you must guess my age!'

'Oh that would be too difficult,' I said and joined in her game. 'It's your turn and you have to guess what my name is.'

Her eyes stayed wide and she put a hand across her mouth and came right close to me as if she'd find her answer up my very nose. When a door opened behind her she turned at once. Into the hall came Mrs. Pollard.

'Ah, it's the young Robinson,' she said. 'Shall you like something to drink?'

'I've asked him, Mama. He doesn't want anything and good, good, good – I know his name is Robinson!'

'I'm sure he has another name. You do, don't you?' asked Mrs. Pollard who I never would have guessed, from her being so serious, was so closely related to the lively girl.

'John. My name is John.'

'Well, John. Show me what you have brought.'

We stayed standing, but not for long. I was almost afeared the lady would not like the leather's colour which would be a blow to Father, as if he had the time to sort through leather of every shade of grass, cabbage or leaf to please her. She was a little silent as she turned the leather round in her hands. Hannah stared at the roll.

'This is lovely,' said Mrs. Pollard at last. 'This is just what I want.'

'Is it, Mama? Are you quite sure? John may have other rolls...'

I left them to discuss the colourful shoes as I feared being late for Mr. Nicholls. Not long after I was back on our road I heard a call behind me.

'John! John Robinson wait!'

She limped her way towards me. So fast and so unwieldy was the way she ran, I felt sure she would fall over. Her arms waved and her legs would have done the same only she toppled into the road upon her knees and laughed when she drew herself up. As she reached me she brushed the dust off her clothes. Her cheeks were flushed.

'I have something to tell you. It's important,' she said.

I stopped where I was and waited to hear. She was almost breathless.

'If you would – talk to your father,' she began in almost a whisper as if fearful of folk listening. 'I wonder if there would be enough – enough for a pair of shoes for myself? Just – just like my mother's? I should so love such a pair.'

'I cannot tell, Miss Hannah. And besides, you'd need measuring. He can't make any old shoes in the hope they'll fit.'

Disappointment moved over her face like a cloud across the sun.

'Then – I may not.'

'I'll see what my father says. I'll give you his answer when I bring your mother her shoes.'

'You will come back, won't you?' she asked, almost pleading.

'I will.'

As I set off on my long walk, I knew she stood where we'd talked and continued to watch me. I turned and waved to her and saw how she stepped carefully over a puddle in the road. I heard her sing as she returned to her home.

Then I began a steady pace. A curlew cried as it circled the sky above me.

'...audio, I hear, audis, you singular hear, audit he she and it hears...'

*

USUALLY Mr. Nicholls and I sat opposite each other at his small table which he cleared. The letters, the writing desk and the pewter jug that had been on the table he placed on the floor, giving us room to work. In the corner his dog moved round and round until settled in a comfortable coil, nose to tail.

I was to recite the full present tense of the verbs he'd given me and I know I did them well, thanks to all the practise I'd done that made me remember. Then came our discussions of vocabulary, when he asked if I knew any words we used in everyday life that resembled their Latin forms. This was a fine game.

'Libro!' he said with some force.

'Liberty? Library? Liberal?' I replied, guessing hard.

'Library, yes. It means a book. Corpus!'

'Mmmm. Corpse. Corner. Corporal...'

'Yes, corpse first – but it's not what you think. It means a body and that often doesn't refer to human flesh and blood. Think of the word 'corporate' when a body of people is suggested...'

He divided up the lesson so that each task lasted only as long as I didn't yawn or falter. There were times when I was tired, when I'd gone to bed but not to sleep till late, usually when Father was up kneading his back as he stood in the dark. Mr. Nicholls could tell. He tried to change the subject or introduce what I liked best, which was the two of us reading together a piece of Latin text, just to get the sound of it right, even if I understood not a word. But some words spoke some sense to me, thanks to the guessing game.

The time passed quickly. But there were other times when something would halt our progress. This was usually due to sounds that came from outside. He'd stop whatever we were doing. He'd sit there, like a statue. Listening.

'Mr. Nicholls, is something up?'

'Sshh, John. Wait.'

Few horses nor wheels traipsed the cobbles. The lane went only to the parsonage and school, then led past the barn there into the footpath for the moors. Silent (I hardly dared breathe), you could almost hear the very words spoken by people who paused to talk right below his open window.

After a while he'd relax, to continue where we'd left off.

'Is it the washerwomen?' I asked.

'No, John. I don't think we'll be bothered by them again.'

'Did you scare them off?'

'I daresay I did but you'll be interested to know that not long after that time I received a splendid piece from Mr. Brontë. He wrote a poem about the whole washerwomen incident. As a matter of fact the poem – it's about me. He wrote about my victory!"

'He never!' I said.

'Oh he did, John. Should you like to hear it?'

'I should. Very much.'

I held him to it. I was that surprised to know not only Mr. Branwell, but Mr. Brontë himself was something of a writer. Mr. Nicholls went among the books that stood upright on the mantelpiece and between the pages of one of them he found a paper where the poem was set in fine, elegant words. He stood upright in front of the cold fireplace, big and serious, and his dog looked up to see what he was about to do.

He read to me.

> *'The females all routed have fled with their clothes*
> *To stackyards, and backyards, and where no-one knows,*
> *And loudly have sworn by the suds which they swim in,*
> *They'll wring off his head, for his warring with women.*
> *Whilst their husbands combine and roar out in their fury,*

> *They'll lynch him at once without trial by jury.*
> *But saddest of – of all the...'*

He faltered. In a matter of moments he'd lost his strong speech.

'Mr. Nicholls? Is that it?' I asked as I was sure it was not the end of the poem.

'No, John. There is a little more.'

'Well? What does he say?'

He cleared his throat and seemed not as sure of himself as he had been. Then he went on, his voice more hushed.

> *'But saddest of all, the fair maidens declare,*
> *Of marriage or love, he must ever despair.'*

*

IT was Betty did most of the making of Mrs. Pollard's shoes. They were to have no hammering of nails, she announced, only strong stitches and she would find the perfect match of cotton for the right green. The more she held them in her hands, the more she liked the idea of making such pairs as Father was less willing to make.

I asked Father, before he cut the leather, to keep to one end of the roll.

'Why? Are you thinking someone else might like such a colour?'

'I know it. Mrs. Pollard's daughter.'

'I see. And what size might she be when she's at home.'

'Well that's exactly what I was thinking of, Father. To visit her and to draw the shape of her feet for soles. Then if there's leather enough, we could surely make something of it.'

'Mrs. Pollard made no mention of it to me.'

'I'll make them if you like, if I have the time,' said Betty. 'It would be a change to make an infant's shoes.'

'She's no infant. She's nearer my age than a babe's.'

The green leather was duly cut with plenty left for a second pair of shoes. One Saturday, some weeks later, when I set off to Mrs. Pollard's I was pleased that Betty accompanied me. She insisted on seeing the mother and daughter who'd soon be the wearers of her handiwork.

The occasion was a rarity. Not often did I have the chance to speak at length with either of my sisters on their own. Though we sat and talked at the table, the rest of our daytime was all askew with doing things – making shoes, learning at school, pushing looms. Nancy had by now become used to the daily trudge to Bridgehouse and her continued dislike of the work turned her into a more difficult soul than Betty. On purpose I did not walk too fast. Betty, always conscious of the weather, flung her shawl about her shoulders.

'John, come on now. We should make way at some speed.'

Deliberately I did not heed her. Something about Mr. Nicholls had been lodged in my mind and I knew this was a time I could try and get it out. Since Betty was generally a wise one, perhaps since she had taken on Mam's place in the family, I knew she was the right person to hear my thoughts. As we turned into the back lane the wind blew up. She bent low and pulled her shawl about her head. But I stopped.

'John, whatever is it?'

'I – I should like to ask you things.'

She put her arms about me, warming us both.

'Now what's up?' she said.

'Nothing's up with me. It's about Mr. Nicholls,' I said.

'You mean with no lesson today? You'll have one next week and after. He's busy. He has the new Institute to manage and it will be a fine thing for us all, especially for you. Imagine all the books coming to Haworth and folk not having to go into Keighley for them now. He's much to do with all the arrangements.'

'Oh I know all that. No, it's not to do with it.'

'What then?'

'More to do with him.'

'With him?'

'Yes. Betty, you're a girl. Tell me, would you think him unlikely to wed?'

'You what? Is this a thought that troubles you?'

'No but I'm thinking it might trouble him. You see, it's to do with the washerwomen – you remember. He was at war on them. And Mr. Brontë, he was glad of it. Only he felt that such – such women pitied Mr. Nicholls and not in any kindly way. It's said he'll never marry because of it. Do you think that's true?'

'Bless me, John, are you now set on thinking if curates can be married or not? That's usually what we girls talk of. Mr. Grant, he's wed. And Mr. Sowden over at Hebden Bridge, he could if he wanted I'm sure. He's a nice, gentle sort. They do get married, you know, and as likely find a willing girl. Being married to a clergyman is a fine thing I'm sure.'

Betty urged me forward, still with an arm about my shoulders. When we were almost at the Pollards' house we stopped.

'You're fond of Mr. Nicholls aren't you?' she said.

'I suppose I am. I like the lessons.'

'That's what they say about good teachers. They set their pupils up for life. Well I'm sure there'll be ladies will come to be fond of him. I know he's not popular with everyone but I think he's a good man.'

'Do your friends say so? What do girls in the mill think of him?'

'Not much. That is, few of them go to church so they don't say. For them Sundays is a time to stay at home. Has he said anything to you? Is he sweet on anyone?'

'No. I just wondered if you thought him – peculiar say.'

'He's stern. And he's serious. But that's probably a good thing in his work.'

'Is serious not likeable then?'

'Well, he could loosen a bit, I'll say that.'

'Loosen?"

'Yes. You know, perhaps laugh some. Loosen...'

'Loosen...'

*

HANNAH jumped on the spot when she found us at the door. She chattered at speed as she led us through to their parlour. The ceiling was low and crossed with dark beams that gave the room a feeling of weight and age. A wide fireplace, so welcoming with flames in early autumn's chill, took up the space of almost an entire wall. The room's far side brought light through a row of windows that looked out across the green valley of the Worth.

'Do you like our view, John?' asked Mrs. Pollard when she saw how I stood there, looking out.

'I do,' I said.

'And do you see how finely carved the mullions are?' she asked as she came to stand next to me. She almost stroked the stone between the window panes. 'We are proud of the house. It is not big, but it is adequate and dear to us.'

Most people's homes had straight and plain upright windows, especially those built for people who worked at wool. I did not like to say we lived in the Taylors' old place and that it too had them – these 'mullions' she called, as if they were close friends. She wanted me to admire them, to take in what she said about the house. It seemed a bit strange to me and I was a little unsure of what to say. As if my tongue had clamped tight inside my mouth.

'That was how windows were built, well over a century ago. You'll have seen the date above the door where you came in.'

'I saw it,' said Betty who was standing by the fireplace. Beneath her arm she still held the parcel of shoes that Hannah eyed in silence. 'There were numbers and letters writ up on a stone, like where the Taylors live now.'

I had to get Betty off the subject. I felt it not a good thing to let Mrs. Pollard know that we were renters off the Taylors who were generous in the sum they asked. The way she talked gave her an authority that I did not like. Airs. To do with a lofty station. Luckily she was not for asking about us.

'Indeed, yes, the inscription. Not many homes up here have such. They are a reminder of old families – families who have done well for themselves. Do come and sit down. Hannah dear, go and ask for refreshment.'

'Shall you want oat-scones? Mrs. Parker could do them quickly if you like,' said Hannah and she moved as if she were the pendulum of a clock.

'Go on now and say we have company,' said Mrs. Pollard. 'But go easy. Slowly.'

Hannah would not move from the room but fixed her eyes upon the package that Betty still held close.

'Please consider yourselves my guests,' said Mrs. Pollard as she patted the cushions beside her on the sofa. 'I know your mother passed away some time ago. Are you able to manage?'

'We are,' said Betty who remained standing. 'Thank you.'

'So, to the shoes. The moment I think has come for me to see them. Give them to me, do.'

Hannah had stilled herself and stayed by the door. Her eyes widened as she watched Betty hold out in both hands the pair of shoes she'd so carefully stitched in the evening lamp-light over the last few weeks. Slowly, almost reluctantly, she gave them to Mrs. Pollard.

'I do hope they'll please,' she said a little nervously.

Mrs. Pollard took them from her and as she inspected each sole, each tongue and each lace threaded inside them, the silence of the room was not broken. She placed one shoe to her nose and breathed in its smell.

'Pure leather. Pure delight. And green... green...'

*

THE green fields that lay wide across the hills above the Worth had not entirely lost their summer's glow. Gleams of light were thrown across them and reached from a sun hanging low towards the west.

Down by the river's edge the tall chimney of Griffe Mill rose like a finger, pointing to the sky, though the growing darkness around it lessened its stark outline. I sat by the windows as the women talked and Hannah's feet, once captured, were measured and drawn by Betty.

With no eyes upon me, I touched the stone mullions. Each one was finely set into the sills of the wall's openings, each one solid, bearing weight but of a pleasing, tapered shape. I tried to imagine how they must have been put in place as the wall went up around them. And how the house had once looked as it slowly rose. Just like I'd watched the new school not fifty yards away. Such things were of interest to me. I liked to see the way things were built. Here at the Pollards' the broad fireplace had one great slab across it to form a lintel and beneath it, to one side, a nook, a corner, a space all of its own. Surely Hannah sometimes tucked herself away in here...

'We should be headed home now,' said Betty, as she stood to leave.

'Mrs. Pollard, if you please,' I said, interrupting her perambulation round the room in the new green shoes. You mentioned the stone above your front door. Are the marks to do with the name of the mason?'

'No, no!' said Hannah who seemed to project herself across the room in single bounds of enthusiasm. 'There are letters and numbers. The letters are 'P for Pollard and 'R' and 'E' and 17 and 27 and they are full of mystery and only a few people understand what they mean. And a sorcerer has passed along the lane, on his way to join the drovers' road, bound for Lancashire on winter's nights and he has tried to change the numbers and letters round but failed, stopping as he rearranged them. They remain as they are, fixed for ever, wonderful...'

During her short speech Hannah managed to come right up to me and take my hand that she kneaded with moving fingers, as if she should implore me to believe her. I did not have the heart to check her tale and was glad to find that neither did Mrs. Pollard. She watched her daughter and waited to give me some measure of truth once the girl was finished. That's when she said it, and she stared straight at me.

'I expect you know the tower of Haworth church?'

At which point I believed the sorcery to be true and Hannah its magician.

*

HANNAH did not go to the school in Stanbury nor any school as far as I could understand. I told them about Mr. Nicholls, how he'd been so busy at the work he'd done, even to the extent of building Stanbury's new school where occasionally he taught.

'Mr. Nicholls, yes. He is to be congratulated,' said Mrs. Pollard. 'I've heard about our own Mechanics Institute in Haworth, with himself presiding over that as well. Such energy in a man so sobre in his looks...'

'The schools are his main concern...' I said, and hoped to return to the subject. For some reason I wanted to let Mrs. Pollard know that I took extra lessons from Mr. Nicholls. I was educated.

'Hannah must learn here, in this house,' she said decisively.

Did Mrs. Pollard teach her herself?

I fell into silence in that window sill. Hannah tried to cajole me out of my thinking. She sat with me, took my hand again and sniffed as she rapidly talked. Her wild hair fell over her brow and she pressed it back away with the palm of a hand that soon returned to my own. Mrs. Pollard talked of her difficulty in finding people who were willing to come over as far as Stanbury in order to teach Hannah.

'The right type of people,' she said with some emphasis.

'And what type of lessons?' I asked.

'Music, drawing with graphite then water-colours,' replied Mrs. Pollard. 'She'll also have to take up deportment soon.'

Hannah, suddenly tired of sitting, stood upright then turned upon her toes and collapsed to the floor. At this Mrs. Pollard herself stood and we took this as a move for us to leave. She saw us to the door which she firmly closed behind on us, and so shut us out.

'Wait here,' I said to Betty outside before we left the low back lane.

'I must get on. We've stayed a long time and it's getting dark.'

'No wait,' I said.

Hurried footsteps approached us from behind, as I'd anticipated. 'John Robinson, do wait!' came Hannah's voice. 'You've not looked at the strange carved stone! Do look,' she said as she urged us back and pointed above the door. She clung to Betty's arm.

I read the initials and date as she had described them to us earlier.

'And when you're next in Haworth, go back to the tower and look at it a little closer...'

*

I DO not recall when I went there to do as she asked, but it was some time afterwards, late and just before nightfall. As I approached the small door at the tower's foot, I heard laughter – loud, generous laughter. The noise came from Sexton House where a window was wide open with no curtains drawn across it. Lamplight glowed throughout Mr. Nicholls' room and I saw the shadow of his form pass over the walls. He was walking about, laughing. At one point he stamped his foot and his dog barked. I heard them both.

Since I was unsure of what to look for at the tower, I was more inclined to discover what the noise was about. The front downstairs room was dark – the Brown family were in their back kitchen. All I needed to do was call.

'Mr. Nicholls! Mr. Nicholls!'

What with his laughter and his feet pounding that way, my voice was not heard. He clapped his hands and stamped a foot and again he laughed fit to burst.

'Mr. Nicholls!' I called much louder. 'Sir – Mr. Nicholls. Whatever is up?'

His great shape appeared at the window.

'Who's that?' he asked.

Once I'd told him who I was, he said he'd be at the door in a trice and that I should come up to his room. I could not see his face well when he came to meet me, but I sensed there was a smile across it because he chuckled all the way upstairs.

'Sit yourself down John,' he said as he drew out the chairs from the table that he usually claimed for our lessons. He remained stood up. Yes, smiling he was, broadly.

'You heard me.'

'Yes, Mr. Nicholls. Is anything up?'

'Is anything up...' he said and seemed entertained by the question. 'Is anything up...' he repeated as he paced about the room.

'Well, is there?' I asked.

'John,' he said, once he'd stopped still. He leaned on the table and his face stared down into mine. 'We have a genius in our midst.'

The smile made his nostrils broaden.

'A genius?'

'Yes, John. She is wonderful.'

'This genius is a lady?'

'A fine woman. She has written a book that is going to be the most significant volume in the new Institute library. It was published last year. But another book has also been published and I have just been reading it.'

'You have? And it's that one's made you laugh. The one written by the lady genius?'

He sighed deeply and stared into the growing dark of the window, his gaze towards the parsonage.

'Yes it is. Both books were written by Miss Charlotte.'

*

FOR a while I believed he'd caught some kind of brain fever. He visited so many sick it was not a daft thought. That was it. Gone a bit mad. Plenty of folk had been unwell. There'd even been a health inspection of Haworth – the drains, the middens and the like. Both he and Mr. Brontë were hoping to get cleaner water brought into the area. Maybe the dirty stuff had touched him strangely.

When he told me that about Miss Charlotte, and I'd seen how he laughed, at first I thought him crazed. He sat in front of me with a book in his hands that he passed over for me to look at. The name of the author written on its cover was a certain Currer Bell. The title of the book was *Shirley*. So I stared hard at him, almost sure of his upscuttled mental state.

'Whatever are you on about?' I asked.

He just shook his head and his unusually unkempt hair fell about his temples. 'I know you must be confused John, but – '

'Me confused?'

'Listen to me. Listen. You're in no hurry are you?'

'No. The dark won't mind.'

'Well then, let me explain...'

He told me Miss Charlotte was a famous writer. More than that, her sisters had written books before they'd gone and died. All three of them had published but under different names for fear they'd not be taken seriously.

'Are the books they wrote that serious then?' I asked, still not able to understand what he told me. He talked loud and with this smile over his face. As I'd never seen him before.

'That they are women and have written unusual, powerful stories could be held against them.'

'Why?'

'Well, John. You're someone who knows Miss Charlotte and you knew Miss Emily and Miss Anne. Did they seem like the kind of women who would scandalise society?'

I had to think hard about this. I was very unsure of what he said and still felt his head was touched.

'This is what has happened,' he went on. 'Their books have shocked the public.'

'Why? What did they write about?'

'Well, sometimes books are thought to be dangerous, if they offend. They were unafraid and wrote of truthfulness. The way people really feel.'

He leaned back in his chair and drove his fingers through the dark, limp hair. He sighed as he gazed at the window where night had settled as a black screen. He collected his thoughts before he spoke again and the minutes allowed his surprised dog to settle back nicely in her corner.

'All three sisters were well known to me, John, as you must be aware,' he began. 'And I work closely with Mr. Brontë every day. I believe it is thanks to him, their father, that they grew to be exceptional people. He gave them education, you see. There were other sisters before them you did not know. Maria and Elizabeth, these two died, as did their mother. There was also an aunt, Aunt Branwell...'

'That was the lad's name.'

'Yes, he was named after her side of their family, their mother's. She also died, most unfortunately. So you see, he was left to bring up his family alone. It was not Mr. Brontë's fault that he sent his children to a school that was both cruel as well as limited in what it offered its poor pupils. He was incapable of knowing that such a fine sounding institution, a school specifically 'for Clergymen's Daughters' was to be a harbour of disease. The elder two died from appalling conditions there, which prompted him to bring home his other daughters at once. He controlled their education at home until they went to school at Mirfield, some twenty miles away. The idea was they would become teachers themselves. You see, he made learning something that was inviting and enjoyable. This is how he in his turn had risen from – let's say a lowly start. With a love of learning he reached Cambridge university. From there he entered the church. He knew that learning in itself could be a home, a place where the mind is nurtured and can flourish.'

He began to explain things so I understood. Like a story. I listened close.

'His children grew up in this environment, not the place that most of us are familiar with, this cold clime of moors and farms, mills, warehouses, smoke. They grew up in conditions inside the parsonage that allowed them to develop fine-tutored minds. Later, Miss Emily and Miss Charlotte, they went abroad to learn even more.'

'Where'd they go?'

'To Brussels in Belgium.'

'Did they sail on the seas?'

'Well they sailed across the Channel on not a very big boat, but after some time Miss Emily came home. She suffered terrible homesickness.'

'And Miss Charlotte, she stayed in the foreign land?'

'Yes she did. She became a teacher in Brussels until she also came home. The sisters even thought of having their own school. They began teaching here in our school. That's how you have known them.'

'I never knew they'd been on boats...'

It's a strange thing to have your thoughts turned downside up. Not one person that I ever came across had ever been in a sailing ship apart from Mr. Nicholls who'd come over from the Island he told me about. I'd have thought myself hard pressed to find another such soul, living where we did. Miles from all oceans. The very idea that Miss Charlotte, who was so tiny and pale, had boarded a ship and gone off away on the tide was something I could not easily believe nor conjure up in my mind's eye. She was the shy lady whose presence in the school-room, in the lane or in her family box pew at church was so quiet you almost did not notice her. How was I to go thinking of her as a traveller, a genius? How make of her a famous writer?

'Was Miss Anne famous too? We liked her. And Miss Emily?'

'Miss Anne wrote much about her own experiences as a governess. I think you must have found her a gentle person.'

I did not like to say that Betty and half the neighbouring villages were once after him marrying her.

'She was especially nice to the little ones.'

'Her time spent as a governess was arduous. She could not work in the way she thought best. The children in her care were undisciplined and rude. The fact she was not allowed to punish or curb their bad behaviour caused her great concern.'

'Well, she was very kind. She'd not beat a soul.'

'The children's parents spoiled them and said they did no wrong. Those young things were believed and defended more than their educated teacher. But she was able to write about it. This helped her finally when she returned home. You see, John, when people have had unusual experiences, as all three of the sisters had, it is possible to turn the bad into good, into art. Writing is a form of art.'

Mr. Nicholls was telling me such things I tried hard to comprehend. The sailing off in ships was one thing, the writing another. As I sat with him and he talked, I began to feel his lamp-lit room with all its shadows cast about was separate from Haworth and everything in it. Ever so slowly it turned into a place of wonder, rather like young Joseph might have thought of it.

'Their home was one of books, the books they read and the books they wrote. They began with stories when they were very young. They wrote tales in tiny books. Eventually, their whole world was books and the world itself got to know them. I must ask you, John, do you follow what I am saying?'

I did not move much. My ears listened hard and since I liked the sound of his voice, like Mr. Brontë's, it was not difficult for me to listen to him. Understanding had to take its time.

'I am trying, Mr. Nicholls. Will you go on, I mean about the books and what Miss Charlotte has writ. That's not her name there,' I said, my head tilted to the book on the table.

'Ah – yes,' he said then moved over to look out onto the chill darkness before he pulled down the window's lower pane. I kept my silence and waited for him to talk as he pleased. It was not often, not usual that is. Not at such length. He drew the short curtains then turned up his lamp and the light grew and flooded the room wider with its warm glow. Outside the church bells struck the hour. The dog shifted her hind legs and moved a fraction into a changed position as if she had been disturbed by all the interesting news.

'The book that was published a year ago, along with two by her sisters, has become very popular. It is the story of the life of a young woman from her childhood to her marriage. In its early chapters she wrote about her own experiences at that terrible school I told you of.'

'Then it can't be a very nice tale,' I said.

'She overcomes the obstacles in her life. She has faith.'

'Does she have only a father, like Miss Charlotte?'

'No, she has neither parent, but she has her wits, John, and great integrity.'

'What's that?'

'She knows herself and is true to herself. In her actions her honesty leads her finally to fulfilment.'

'Well, if you don't mind me saying Mr. Nicholls, this *Shirley* does not sound very amusing to me. Why is it you were laughing so much?'

He sat down, reached for the book and that odd smile returned.

'Forgive me, John. I should explain. It is this second book that made me laugh though it is no frivolous work. The first, about a girl called Jane, is very unlike it. In *Shirley* she writes about the mills and people whom we can recognise, not unlike those we know round here. All the looms and the troubles and the things your sisters experience down at Bridgehouse, these can be found in *Shirley*. She has written about the place she knows and John – she also describes the village curates and it is those descriptions that have made me laugh. She has Mr. Grant from Oxenhope exactly! Not only him and Mr. Smith from Oakworth but – I do believe at the very end – she has studied and written about me!'

With his new outburst, I sat still and said nothing more for a while. I recalled how Mr. Brontë had written about him and the washerwomen. Now I tried to conjure up this new Miss Charlotte, also a writer, and it was not a grand leap for my dizzy head to remember what I'd seen from the tower. The sisters in the dining room of an evening, walking round that table where their papers lay. And her, when her sisters were gone. By herself. Still writing.

'Well go on then, read us it,' I said at last. 'Read us where she's written about you.'

He settled himself in the chair, his elbows resting on its arms. Several scraps were wedged inside the book as markers and one of these he took out. He leaned forward so the lamplight fell on the whitened page and read.

'"...*there came as his successor another Irish curate, Mr. Macarthey. I am happy to be able to inform you, with truth, that this gentleman did as much credit to his country as Malone had done it discredit...*" Now let me see... Yes, here she speaks well of me. Listen. "*He laboured faithfully in the parish: the schools, both Sunday and day schools, flourished under his sway like green bay-trees. Being human, of course he had his faults; these however were proper, steady-going, clerical faults; what many would call virtues.*" John, do you hear that? This is her own voice, these are her own thoughts. But listen to this...'

He was laughing now. Though I could not follow all that Miss Charlotte had written, I guessed it had gladdened his heart and brought to his nature something I had never discovered there before. He was loosened.

'"...*the circumstance of finding himself invited to tea with a Dissenter would unhinge him for a week,*"' he went on, '"*the spectacle of a Quaker wearing his hat in the church, the thought of an unbaptized fellow-creature being interred with Christian rites – these things could make a strange havoc on Mr Macarthey's physical and mental economy; otherwise, he was sane and rational, diligent and charitable...*" Oh John!' he laughed aloud and stamped his foot on the ground so's the dog looked up and her ears stiffened with surprise.

'She is an extraordinary woman!' he went on as he took my hands in his own. 'Yet I must say that although she is a famed writer,

I cannot approve of such fame. I know the whole nation must know her worth. I know she will be glad of the recognition, for herself and her sisters. But to me, she is – she is not a writer. She is the person that you and I both know. She can only be our Miss Charlotte!'

*

ONE thing that was not muddled but clear as daylight for me was that I should not tell Martha Brown what I'd been told. Likely as not she already knew most of it and would try to find me in the lane to let on some half-baked information just to annoy. Armed with all Mr. Nicholls' revelations, I held them close as a pearl that lodged inside my head where I let it shine in secret.

Miss Charlotte's fame was not to be learned from the mouths of neighbours. Soon it was printed in the *Bradford Observer* where she was named not only as the strange-sounding Currer Bell but as the daughter of Mr. Brontë, incumbent of Haworth. The village was no place for secrets now. She was known for her success and the newly opened Mechanics Institute kept her books for everyone to read.

I believe Mr. Nicholls' pride in her swelled. When I arrived for my Saturday lessons all the chanting and declamations of my walks across the moors seemed to reach his ears as music. Then I'd take my place at his table as if I were a welcome long-lost visitor and we'd read our texts and I'd write and speak and his high spirits raised mine. He almost sang. I thought it was because he was glad of her success.

But when he was glum, he was drear as granite. His moods drifted like breezes, blown by any news he learned from across the lane at the parsonage.

'Miss Charlotte has taken the train to London,' he said once when I arrived and before I'd hardly sat down.

'Well she would do, would she not?' I asked. 'If she's so well known, she's bound to go off visiting there.'

'London,' he said, mumbling fit to moan into the knuckles of his hands that he held tight to his mouth as if he'd nibble them. 'I'm told she is to be introduced to some very well known names. She'll go to dinners and the theatre. She is even to sit for her portrait...'

At moments like this his eyes were small and shadowy. He did not stand to go towards the window. I daresay this was because he knew there was no chance of seeing her in the lane below. Fresh air blew throughout the room and his dog raised her nose to sniff the sudden coolness. Everything was bleak, when his mood was.

He set me long translations that were a trouble to compose as he sat there silent, his eyes turning wandery and wet. How he dragged his hair about, shoving it over his head or round about his ears. He chewed up his mouth when there was nothing to be ate inside. All of a nervous trembling, he was. Still I tried to do my work but was hard pressed to make it good. When I asked him for help, he did not scold me – I had no fear of that. He answered me with a dull, flat voice. As if he took no interest in my efforts.

So afterwards I'd make my way home with a heavy heart. I could not help but feel I had failed him and determined to do better the next time we met. Then come another time and he'd be changed, his spirits winging their way across the leaves of our books, his voice lifted, his eyes alert and his attention fully upon my work.

'Miss Charlotte has returned home,' he'd say, which meant that all was well again.

*

AS the months passed, though I tried I could not look on her in a new way. Still Miss Charlotte did not seem like a genius to me, which is how I thought of Homer and Ovid and even Mr. Branwell when it came to Horace. William Tyndale, who'd first translated the Bible, was the bravest hero I knew since because of it he'd been strangled for heresy and his body was burned at the stake. Then there were other people in history who'd come to similar terrible ends and the very idea of a young girl like Jeanne d'Arc getting herself in that fire when she'd only been tending her sheep out on the hillsides - this was another fact that I found gravely unjust but thrilling to know. These were people of bravery and genius.

I did not see Miss Charlotte as one of their number.

Mr. Nicholls brought in literature as well as history into our Saturdays and long before I knew anything about Miss Charlotte and her writing, he'd led me to read all sorts. We did stories from the *Tales From Shakespeare* before I dared to touch the real plays which he had in one fat, worn volume on the shelf above his hearth. The last fifteen minutes of our literary hours were spent in reading loud in turn, and in making something of the dialogue in books. Best of all I liked it when he became Mesty, the ship's slave from Captain Marryat's seafaring tale.

When I asked if we could read Miss Charlotte's books he did not reply at once. I believe it was because her work was sacred to him. Yet the books were out in the lanes of Haworth, borrowed, read and talked about and as public as any daily newspaper. Did he not want to lend me his copies? I saw them above the fireplace, together with books by Ellis and Acton Bell that I guessed to be Miss Emily's and Miss Anne's. I fidgeted to get to read them but he would not listen and quickly changed the subject, suggesting that since I was so keen on seafaring and adventure, we should travel the pages of *Robinson Crusoe* or familiarise ourselves with the foreign lands of Gulliver.

There was only one thing left for me to do. I would not ask Martha Brown (would she have a copy?) nor join the list of subscribers for it at the Mechanics Institute. The next time I saw her, I would ask Miss Charlotte herself.

But it was not her, it was Mr. Brontë I asked. I met him as he walked away from the parsonage. The day was an early one in spring when the tips of trees begin to sprout green and a brightness in the air holds promise for future months of light. He was carrying a few books beneath his arm and he walked slowly, his eyes set firm upon the cobbled surface of Church Lane that had seen no rain for days. My own steps almost crossed his as I closed the door of Sexton

House behind me. 'John, how nice to see you,' he said, steadying his stick as he paused to talk.

'Mr. Brontë, sir,' I said in haste, knowing the opportunity might pass. As ever when I had something urgent to say, it came out tumbling quick. 'I should like to ask you for one of Miss Charlotte's books. You see, I do know about them and they say she is a famous lady now and I would like to see why since I can read well and I know much about books and the like since I've had ever so many lessons now these past many months.'

'I have heard, John. So I've heard. Both Miss Charlotte and Mr. Nicholls tell me you are a fine pupil and it is a pleasure to teach you. It won't be long before you're doing the teaching yourself, I should think. We could do with more of you.'

'Then have I to buy my copy of *Jane Eyre*? Mr. Nicholls will not part with his and I'm thinking that my sisters may like it, it being about a young girl and with Nancy now on the power looms it could take her mind off the work if I read it aloud. She loves stories and she listens well.'

'I'll see to it, John. I'll find you a copy and give it to Mr. Nicholls when he next comes to the parsonage.'

I was led to believe I should soon have a copy of the famous tale, only I never did. Not then. He must have forgotten as he went about his parish and attended to the business of Haworth's drains. Sewers were to be blocked, pipes to be installed and more importantly for him, the overloaded churchyard was to close.

*

WHEN Hannah Pollard had asked me to look closely at the church tower, for a passing moment I believed she owned some supernatural power that had detected the occasions I had trespassed there. At one time I'd almost feared the same of Mr. Nicholls.

The churchyard became a drear place for me. Laid out with a sea of stone slabs at the lower end of the parsonage garden it was too much a reminder of the end of people's lives. I was only at the beginning of mine. My lessons had introduced me to a world that lay beyond our homely hills and I was ever tempted to discover it.

I crept round the tower, unsure of what I would find. Then I saw it, a sundial with an inscription: 'Richard Pollard of Stanbury, buried the 25th day of August 1735...'. This was what Hannah had hoped I'd discover. He must have been her ancestor. Wealth and good fortune created this man's eternal memorial and yet his bones, like so many others, were feeding and fattening silent worms in the damp, cold earth. The suggested closure of the churchyard made me think on all that lay beneath it. People dead and gone. Mostly forgotten as time went by. The sisters from the parsonage might also be forgotten in the years to come. Such was the way of the world. Yet buildings like the tower stood up to time.

If I could only do something, one day, that would remain.

This, at that time, was the drift of my early wandering thoughts.

*

'SO this Island, where you lived, does it have sea all round it and funny trees with coconuts?'

'Ireland, John. It is an island called Ireland. I know the words sound a little similar, but just try and associate them, if you prefer. No, there are no palm trees and coconuts there, I can assure you. If you're thinking of Captain Cook's journeys, those were the other side of the world where it is hotter, where all vegetation grows according to the climate.'

'So what do thy grow in – Ireland,' I asked, trying to pronouce the '*r*' as he did and Mr. Brontë did and we didn't normally.

If we wandered off to other lands like that, he wouldn't bring us back sharp, but explained and described things. And he certainly seemed to know a deal of things which is why I so liked to be there, in his room.

As I moved forward – and Mr. Nicholls said I was doing just

that – the learning became no more of a chore than it had ever been, more something I enjoyed. Of an evening I was able to take myself up to the room I shared with Father and look over the work I'd done in preparation for each Saturday. It was a short, quiet hour or so which I looked forward to. In that time I went over the words, the verbs, the names and the scribbles I had made in a notebook bought for the purpose to be replaced by others and kept beneath my mattress. I did not find it difficult to concentrate, even when there were noises downstairs that told me dinner was on its way.

So when our Nancy got bad, I was not put out that she took up so much of our evenings with her tearfulness. Right from the start she'd been wretched during her daytime hours at the new power loom. Though Betty went with her and they were able to see each other at times during their daily routine, and though they walked there and back together, Nancy became ill from working at Bridge-house Mill.

"I cannot do this for much longer,' she said at the table when our voices had done enough of talk of other things. 'The machines make me feel like a machine. I have a head and I have thoughts and the noise bangs those thoughts right off over goodness knows where...'

She kept in the feelings she'd held in all day and was bursting to tell us them. No longer did she keep her wretched state from Father. Early on he saw how she'd changed, since she took up the work. As she talked, openly, her face went all pink and her cheeks all puffed and the water welled up in her eyes. It was a sorry sight that we did not know how to dispel. There seemed no solutions. We put together our puzzled heads to try and think what else she might do. She'd always liked the little ones at school and would have taught them well. Had she been able. Money was needed and could only be found by working for it. My heart was particularly sore when I came to think how some of the money she earned went towards my lessons. And how she would have liked those lessons! When I'd been doing them for a very long time, I gave the whole matter some thought. If I stopped, at least Nancy's money would be her own.

I became determined. I put on a rigid face of it and walked to Haworth one Saturday with a mind to put an end to my learning. I should not listen to whatever Mr. Nicholls had to say. I had to keep in my mind's eye a clear picture of Nancy bent at the looms and all their clattering noise. I had to hear in my ears the sounds of her sobs at night when Betty tried to comfort her and their sisters' talk went on late. I should not forget how, in the mornings, those two girls were both weary, but off they went, smiling that kind of smile that isn't a true one, but one that goes with a mask of bravery. Such masks were useful.

I knocked on the door of Sexton House, my own mask in place.

'Oh it's only you.'

'Yes, Martha. Only me. And don't suppose it'll be only me for much longer.'

'Well there's a fine bit of news. Moving away are you?'

'No I am not. Just the possibility of 'only me' moving onwards.'

'Don't talk riddles, John Robinson. He's not here.'

'Is he not?'

'No. He's at the parsonage. And don't expect him to be in a good mood either. He's like that all the time. It's probably to do with his father passing on, but I'm not so sure. Seems more like simple doldrums to me. The way ladies have them.'

'What's that supposed to mean?'

'Doldrums. Istericks. Every now and then at funny times they come, only he's a man and it can't be that. It's just plain moods.'

'Then I shall cheer him up,' I said and at once realised that what I was about to suggest – the end of our lessons – might do the opposite.

Martha let me into the house and I went up to his room and found his dog who was pleased to see me. I ruffled her curling ears and stroked her head and did not mind those great paws on my shins. I sent her to her basket and gently paced about. The table was not cleared but scattered with books and papers and a pen put aside by an ink-pot, as though left in a hurry. A large drip had fallen onto a single page making an insect-like shape – as if it were about to walk over the table. I glanced at the paper.

> *Returned from London, 15th July. Cheerful.*
> *Not one month home – departed for the Lakes with K-S's.*
> *Martha warns of visit to Ellen or worse, London again.*
> *George Smith?*

I heard Mr. Nicholls' steps on the stairs and stood aside and whispered to the dog that yes, Master was back. As soon as he walked in I saw that Martha was right. Doldrums.

He was near dumb silent. I could always tell when something was up as his hair was not in a neat clump, where he'd been drawing his great fingers through it. He did not scowl, but his fine, wide eyebrows turned wrinkly. Frowning, worried. And the cheerful greeting he gave me did not ring true.

'Ah John, you're here, good. And I'm a little late. I'm so sorry.'

'That's no bother.'

He quickly cleared the table. When it lay ready to receive our lesson's books, he paused and stood very upright and held his back as if it ached. He sighed.

'Is something up?' I asked, not expecting much in reply.

He remained stood up, his hands in the small of his back. He faced the window. I always felt that the window, wide open of course, was like the framed opening to his thinking and he'd look at it sometimes with longing, sometimes with dread. That day it was dread.

'I – I am a little afeared   '

'How, Mr. Nicholls? Of what?'

'Sorry John. You must not mind me...'

I pulled out a chair as I felt sure he was not well.

'You must sit down.'

'John, thank you.'

He sat there, but he was still twisted round, looking out the window.

'Have you to tell me what's up?' I asked again.

Which is when he turned his face to me and it seemed to belong to another man. Not the great square-set face of the master who liked to teach me, but a face all weak and crumpling in on itself.

'I – I have been speaking to Mr. Brontë. He has told me some news, that's all.'

'Bad news is it?'

'Is it John?'

'Well, I'm not to know.'

'No, you wouldn't. I'm sorry.'

Again he looked at the window. Outside was the sun and the blue sky of a day as bright as any in warm, late summer. But that did not cheer him.

'You would not mind, would you John, if I spoke to you as something of a friend,' he said. He then turned himself back to our table and I saw how he put his hands upon it, not gently, but gripping the edges as if to crush its very wood.

I hardly knew what to say, so said nothing.

'You see, I cannot speak easily about certain things and I feel I must,' he went on. 'I – I have considered Mr. Grant, but feel he is not the person to whom I should confide such thoughts that have begun to beset me. And Mr. Sowden at Hebden Bridge – he is certainly a friend, a good friend. My concern with both of them is their proximity to Mr. Brontë since we are all three curates in the neighbourhood and I cannot risk their knowledge of my – of my – unfortunate situation...'

The dog held up her head. She was sat as usual, round in a brown heap of fur inside the basket, but as he spoke and his voice changed, going high and all anxious, she woke from snoozing, at once alert.

'I shall be glad to do whatever you think best, Mr. Nicholls,' I said.

That's when he stared. Not out the window but at me. Again, he was like someone else, not him. His eyes were fixed at mine.

'Some time ago I was under the impression that the entertainment offered to Miss Charlotte by her publisher was of more than a professional nature. Do you remember when she went to Scotland earlier this month? She was not entirely alone on that visit. She went to meet him there, after she had stayed with him in London. Mr. Brontë told me how she had enjoyed seeing the home of Scott and the abbey at Melrose...'

The dog settled down, snout wedged beside her tail.

I was not entirely comfortable. What I'd planned to tell him was now certainly impossible. Nor would I be able to console our Nancy with the idea that the money she earned from the work she hated so much was entirely hers – not a penny to be spent on me. If he wanted me to talk to, I would need to come as usual for lessons every Saturday.

'I suppose, John, we have seen Miss Charlotte so confined to this village it does not enter our heads to suppose that her marvellous books might be the means of her leaving us. Look at us. Look at the company of mill-owners and merchants, of farming lads and us – curates! Just think of this, John...'

'But – you said you liked how she wrote about you. And that the book, the new one, is about the mills.'

'John, yes, she is a writer. She observes and she perceives and she will look on all that takes place here as one removed from it. This is the role of the writer. This is what she and her sisters have done, so brilliantly. They translated their own experiences into fiction. A writer can do that. A writer is a person set apart.'

'That doesn't mean she's better'n us does it?'

'No, not better. But yes. Her father will think so.'

'He's always very nice to me. He stops and talks and he knows who I am. That's something.'

He shook his head.

'As it should be in a lively village between the pastor and his sheep,' he went on. 'I am not questioning that, John. I am thinking of Miss Charlotte's success. She is the talk of London. Her books and those of her sisters are written about, discussed, loved and hated – across the nation. And she – she has become a great name in the literary world. She's part of that, now.'

'Well she still lives here. She may go away now and then but she comes back.'

'She has moved beyond us, by her own efforts, her own needs,' he went on, as if not listening to me. As if he was sorting his own thoughts. 'All of them did. They – they transcended Haworth. Miss Emily, Miss Anne and Miss Charlotte. It was not enough for them to be daughters of the vicar, to socialise with the music-lovers or take tea with the wives of the Merralls and the rest of them. They were educated beyond this. Their vibrant brains required channelling and release. They could not go away, nor wanted to, being so home-loving. But they needed to feed and nurture what they had become. And they did this – in writing books. Do you understand this, John?'

'A bit. Only I don't see as how that's bothered you. Or has it bothered Mr. Brontë?'

'Oh John, how can I say. Her success is a source of great pride to him.'

'Well then, what has bothered you?'

He put his elbows upon the table and cupped his head in his hands, as if to help him think straight which I hoped it would. I saw no reason why Miss Charlotte's writing, that he liked, should put him into moods such as this one. He lifted his head and ran the fingers through the front locks of his thick hair. Again towards the window he gazed.

'The publisher. No, both the publishers. I have only just today learned of the second one.'

'What's wrong with them?'

'Nothing. They are learned men, one of a brilliant social sphere. The other, it seems, is in attendance...'

He was at last beginning to give me an explanation. It was best to let him reveal the picture, even if it appeared in fragments. What I did know was something did bother him, sparked off by seeing Mr. Brontë and to do with Miss Charlotte and her books. And London.

'Go on then, I'll not speak,' I said which seemed to give him the courage to talk much more, at length.

'John, I can honestly say that I was a little alarmed to hear of her trip to Edinburgh to meet Mr. Smith. His mother, who has given her much hospitality in London, was also there. Naturally Miss Charlotte, though travelling alone, would look forward to being with them. She is stimulated not only by such travel, but by their company – his company. I am unsure of what he is like, in appearance, and can hardly ask Mr. Brontë this, but I gather he is a young man and his admiration for Miss Charlotte is proved by his recognising her achievement. Apparently he did not sleep the night he read *Jane Eyre* but would not put it down until he had finished it. Then came the decision to publish, despite the probability that it might offend public taste. He knew what he held that night. He read her writing. He knows her. He knows her great worth.'

Still I could not see where was the harm in this. He went on.

'There was a visitor to the parsonage this week. I met him. He was as unknown to me as any person coming from a foreign land. He arrived by train to Keighley and took the time to reach these hills. He came with a purpose. He is not exactly a publisher like Mr. Smith, but the firm's managing agent. He it was who suggested to Mr. Smith that he should read *Jane Eyre* and it was he who came to Haworth another time, to collect her written manuscript of *Shirley*. You see, John, they come a long way for her written words, in person. They take the pages back with them from across the road there, from the parsonage front door and all the way to London to be turned into print. And from there, for the whole world to read...'

Beads of sweat were creeping over his brow. He stood up to take water from his pitcher on the mantelpiece and without looking at me, he sat in his place again, next to me at the table. By this time I believed I was getting something of a drift of his words. Would he have preferred Miss Charlotte to stay here, to teach in our school, and not to become famous?

'This other, he is going away to India. He talked to Mr. Brontë.

And Mr. Brontë has talked to me about him. He spoke as a man pleased, even relieved. He invited me into his study and told me that this man, this Mr. Taylor, is likely to make an offer of marriage to Miss Charlotte. He said that if it were deferred for five years, until the time when he returned from his travels, then he would not be averse to such a prospective union. There now, John. I have said it!'

'Mr. Nicholls, should you not like Miss Charlotte to marry?'

That's when another look came into his eyes. Like drizzle. As if I'd shocked him and a cloud had opened with the fright of it.

'John, you don't see. I am beside myself. It's the thought of these others, these publishing people she knows, who have now made her acquaintance. You know Miss Charlotte – I know her. In the six years that I have lived here I have become so admiring of her, so fond. But they – they are now her - suitors. John, can you not see the difference? How can they know her as I do? They know her through her books, yes, but I am one who can truly say that I know her well and I love her. Yes, I do. I love Miss Charlotte, deeply, with all my heart.'

*

WELL, what was I to make of that?

I could find no way to make him happier. It was not for me to walk up to the parsonage and knock at the door and invite myself into Mr. Brontë's study and beg him to send Mr. Taylor to India for eternity. Mr. Taylor was not one of his curates who had to do as he said, mostly about church services, Haworth's sewerage or visits to the sick. Mr. Taylor and the other, Mr. Smith (George with the question mark I guessed but never asked), were from London and literature. And Mr. Brontë was bound to like them well, seeing as he liked books so much.

If only I could talk to Miss Charlotte herself. To tell her...

...go up to the parsonage steps and ask to see her. Go into the dining room and sit at that familiar table and explain that Mr. Nicholls loved her. The more I thought of it, the more the daft idea became not daft at all but a solution. Anything to put his mind at rest and to keep him cheerful...

...and if she was pleased to know this, she could consider all it meant. Mr. Nicholls could be the one to marry her. Her fame and fortune would be enough to see them settle where she could continue to write and he could teach boys like me of a Saturday and through the week. More than likely they'd want to live in Ireland, where he was from, where his family lived. Then he would be happy. And she'd no longer be alone.

But Mr. Brontë would.

*

'YOU'D best find out more on Mr. Taylor,' I said, which was a shorter thought that came to mind. 'At least he is going away.'

'Ah but John...' he said with a huge sigh like a chimney blast. 'There are likely to be others!'

'Then you must go to her quickly, must you not?' I asked.

This made him move to the window again, as if he searched there for guidance. That window was no ancient oracle. No light nor voice came through it to give him the answer he searched for. And who was I to presume I'd be of help? I said what I thought only because he'd told me so much, most of which was a muddle. Did this allow me to speak out? Did he want this of me?

'Mr. Nicholls, if you ponder your thoughts like this, you'll make yourself sick.'

'I am already, John. Can you not see? I am becoming quite ill.'

'Well you should do something about it, like most folks do when they're out of sorts. I don't know if there's a medicine, but there must be a way.'

I left him soon afterwards and walked from Sexton House in a mood of my own. I went off fast and as the bright light in the sky was so welcoming, I decided to go the long way back to Stanbury. At the end of West Lane I did not go down to the beck and return that way. Instead I took to higher open land. My feet went steady, pacing the turf. My mind raced. I was ill-at-ease.

Mr. Nicholls had given me so much, for so long, a time now moved into years. Together we had ridden down channels of learning, sailed oceans of knowledge and been glad of each other's company on those travels. I'd seen no end to our discoveries. Friends we were already without a need to name the way of friendship, nor chart its journey. Was this about to change? He was now steering me on a different course and I was unsure how to embark upon it.

I looked over to our ridge, its line of homes clinging fast to the hillside. My folk were there and those I'd known since infancy. We grew and we thrived or failed as time marched on.

Was it time that changed us? That's what I asked myself that day when Mr. Nicholls seemed no longer to be my teacher. He'd shown he was a troubled man. With the passing of time I was no longer his cadet. Was I now to be his helmsman?

I went far. As I walked up and over towards the horizon's moor, I saw in the distance the highest of Withins farms. Stark and black it hardly changed its threatening look, no matter what the promise of a day's blue sky. I knew that Joseph often went there. I'd seen him skip through Stanbury's street, down to the turnpike to meet the back lane on his way to those heights. Where I was now headed from the valley's other side. For all I knew he might have been there, seeking out birds' nests with Jim, building up forts from the great scattered stones.

I was between all of them, the people I cared for – behind, in front and to the sides of me, each one on familiar land. No matter which single direction I chose, I could find some one of them waiting for me.

But I'd never had to take another's hand, to take the lead on an unknown track. I'd always been the one to be cared for. I didn't know how to be other than this and I did not like it – or rather, I felt the ground, once solid, was giving way beneath me.

*

SHE did not wave. Maybe at first she was not sure who I was. Once I was nearer, she raised both arms. Her light hair was up on the wind.

'John. John Robinson!'

'Hey...I never did! What are you up to young Miss?'

'My mother has gone into town and Mrs. Parker suggested I took a walk and I am to walk you know and cannot stay indoors on days like this. And what do I find but you, after so long not seeing you! How are you John?'

If she'd had an older sister I'd have thought this was her. I had not seen Hannah for months, a year maybe, when, without announcement, she and her mother left Stanbury and the old house was kept by Mrs. Parker alone. There had not been much talk about their whereabouts, since they did not take a public place in the village and were hardly missed. Living on the back lane, behind most people's homes, meant they did not join in the throng of everyday meetings in the street. It was only after some months I knew they were gone when, as I passed on my way to the river, I looked up and felt no life was in that house.

Now here she was. Hannah Pollard herself. It was not just that she seemed taller and fuller in her frame, the expression of her eyes had also changed. Lidded, subdued. Most different was how she came towards me, with careful steps. When she took my arm with both her hands, in order to steady herself, I felt bound to make myself stand upright, secure and strong.

'Betty wondered where you were. She missed making you more shoes,' I said.

'Oh those shoes...they will last me for ever. I hardly wear such pretty ones now. They even talk of giving me heavy black things. Don't you know, John, there was something wrong and it hasn't really come right. It was to do with the way I was born.'

As she spoke, I found I was that pleased to see her, I hardly listened to a word she said.

'They are still unsure of what the trouble was – is – the doctors. I saw so many of them. You cannot imagine how completely shameful it was to undergo their objectionable examinations and worse, their deliberations on my state. None of them could come to any agreement and so each one made his own theory. John, I was measured and weighed and pulled and given hot poultices and strange things to eat and it was when I was about to be placed inside a wooden frame, with straps and weights, I told them no. No thank you very much. No.'

'Were you not at school then?' I asked.

'I was abroad you know. I learned a great deal of French from listening and –'

'Betty thought you'd gone to school.'

'She was probably told that by Mrs. Parker. Why we left was not something my mother wanted to be known in Stanbury, which is why there were no announcements. She hoped that by the time we returned, no-one need have had the slightest idea.'

'That you were gone away to get better?'

'Yes. That I'd needed to learn to walk properly. She hoped it would appear as if nothing was ever wrong. Well I can walk properly, John, can't I? Just look...'

No puddles lay in the road for her to jump across. No grass verge for her to fall upon. Only the dusty track of the old drovers' road that ran beyond the village. She shook her arms to send me away so that I could see how well she stood balanced on her own. One foot before the other she moved forward, her head held high and her eyes fixed to the first house on this side of the ridge. With full concentration, her mouth chewing about her teeth, she faced the length of the road and did not look my way. After fifty paces or so, when I thought she might have forgotten me, she turned round and waved and called to me and laughed. That sight of her conjured up a new feeling in my heart. I felt as if the curlews that reeled in the clear, bright air had lifted me with them to join in their flight.

BETTY was tending to the mud behind the house, in the yard. After weeks of rain that seeped into the earth and found its way between every sturdy stone, a mossy layer had thrived near the paving cracks there. Without putting a stop to her work she nodded and said she was the only one at home.

'Shall you and I have some lunch outside?' she asked. 'Father has taken Nancy into Haworth. Did you not see them?'

'I came the long way. I saw Hannah. She's returned.'

'Has she now?' said Betty and she stopped and stood to lean on her broom. 'Is she here to stay then? Has she finished school?'

'I didn't ask.'

'Well, that's a fine piece of news. We should try and see more of her.'

'How?'

'I don't know. You'll have to work that out, John. You're the clever one.'

'I'm not you know. I mean, I think I must let up a bit. I was going to ask you something...'

We brought out chairs to sit and watch southwards to Haworth moor ahead and the sweep of the bank in front of our house. The sun was out of sight but we felt its welcome warmth in the air.

'So, what is it John you were going to ask?' said Betty as she brushed the crumbs from her skirts. She sat back in her chair, arms folded, settled, ready to listen.

'For some time now I've had a mind to stop my lessons with Mr.Nicholls. It's mostly because of Nancy and you – your pennies going to pay for them.'

'He doesn't ask much.'

'Well then, it's the idea of it. There's Nancy who hates her work and you never one to complain and there's me learning about the wonders of this world while the two of you are at Bridgehouse which is no wonder at all, more like hell itself.'

'There's nothing wrong with earning, John. We all must do it.'

'Well I'll never do something I hate and I don't like to see Nancy that way.'

'Is it really to do with us?' Betty asked. 'Or is it him?'

'Who?'

'Mr. Nicholls.'

Trust her. Betty had a way of knowing things before you knew them yourself.

'It's mostly to do with you,' I said. 'And a bit to do with him now.'

'What's happened?'

'He – he's not himself. That's all.'

She didn't move but her face stayed smiling, all spread with a beam of light that crept its way round our end of the village. So long was she silent I thought she might have dozed off, but every now and then she twitched her nose and sent a fly from her cheek.

'I think it would be best,' I said.

'It would not, John. You've to go on.'

'But I've surely learned enough?'

'No. There's never enough. And the more you find to learn, the more there'll be. Think of our Mam, what she wanted for you. If you don't want to be in the mills, you'll need every bit of the things Mr. Nicholls teaches you and more besides. So what's up with him?'

I could not tell her his secret, but perhaps make more of his recent moods. These she could take as reason enough for me to stop the lessons. If he had been a widely disliked man, she might have encouraged me to stay away from him. But she and many more had seen the deal of good he'd brought to his work alongside Mr. Brontë. More than those other curates. They may have been 'loosened' in their manner, not given to stern ways or blackish looks, but Mr. Nicholls had raised one school and brought more children to another.

By the time Betty and I had finished our talk, my mind was beginning to waver. Should I not, after all, give up my Saturday place in his room? It was not really him, nor was it me, but Miss Charlotte's invisible presence in that room that had to be changed. And since he was so chary in speaking his heart to her, so meek in advancing his cause, then once more I decided I was to do things for him.

The task was going to be difficult. With caution, I plotted it.

First, there was the matter of the publishers. I needed to find out what Miss Charlotte felt about Messrs. Smith and Taylor. An easy path to take would be to hint their names to Martha in the hope she could tell me any word Miss Charlotte said that smacked of feelings. But from the start I knew Martha should be kept at a safe from trouble distance.

Mr. Brontë was familiar with me. Apart from after church, he'd greet me if ever he saw me in Haworth and asked about my studies. I wanted to tell him about the book I'd once seen of Mr. Branwell's work, but to mention his dead children seemed not a good idea. Instead of Horace or even Homer he'd tell me news from the paper beneath his arm, as if politics not publishers was a subject I should know more about.

To speak to Miss Charlotte herself was the only way. But how was I to do it? She had not taught in school for months. She was too busy on her travels here and there (with or without publishers and literature people I was not to know). Only after church did I feel I might see her and even then, out in the street in view of everyone, not to speak at length.

People from far away had begun to come to Haworth just to have a glimpse of her, to seek out the vicar's daughter who'd written those books. I knew well enough she did not take to being approached in public. So I let things be. Unexpectedly, one day the opportunity turned up. I found her out on the moor alone, but for the one remaining parsonage dog, Flossy.

Normally I would have gone in another direction, so as not to disturb her. Since she had become famous, although her small, shy looks seemed the same, I wondered if she talked different. Would she speak to me the way she once did? With a mission in mind I knew that I should try my best. Being nervous I'd talk anyway.

Lessons

Flossy was a friendly sort of spaniel, the type called after King Charles and very unlike Miss Emily's great brute. Poor Keeper had died, never quite the same since he'd followed his mistress through their garden gate for the last time. Flossy was nice and silky, black and white, and he bounded about in the heather. He came to heel when she called him – just like she'd dealt with pupils in her class. She patted him, bent low and kissed his ears then threw a stick ahead of her and watched him chase after it. She walked quite fast, lifting her skirts, her feet dainty and agile as a goat's in the purple brush. She seemed less a silent figure of mourning now, more akin with the wide outside.

The moorland was unlike the lanes and alleys of Haworth over which her father's name was spoke with awe. The sunlight shone not on her name that lived in print – and that a name of disguise. Here she was free to be herself. As I was. The place at times so wild or like that day, so mild and lit with gold, belonged equally to both of us. So I approached her.

She held one hand to her brow to shield off the sun.

'John? Is that you, John Robinson?'

'Yes it is, Miss Charlotte.'

'I don't bring my spectacles with me when I'm out walking. I wasn't sure. Now I see perfectly, of course it's you.'

'How are you Miss Charlotte? We don't see so much of you now. I was even saying to my sisters the other day, what with her writing books and travelling and seeing her words on pages, hundreds at a time, whole chapters and more, it's no surprise that Haworth sees much less of her. And are you off again?'

'Perhaps. I should like to see my friend Ellen. She lives not far away.'

'Is that so? Where's that?'

'Birstall. Her family have been there for years.'

'And then there's of course London which Martha says you have visited often, for long days at a time. There's the people who make the books there, aren't they? I wonder how that's done. And are you writing another? Such a time it must take.'

I was asking too much at once and needed to draw in the questions, to make them go in one direction. My nerves raced about in my stomach.

'Are you able to see them, the publishers, away from London? It is ever such a long way,' I said.

'We write to each other of course, but they do come here when they need.'

'I have never met a publisher, Miss Charlotte. What are they like?'

'Well, each one is himself I suppose. As any person is.'

'But they must be different, knowing what to print and what not.'

'That is what makes a good publisher. The ability to reach through the darkness of the wood and find some sapling that may be helped to flourish.'

Flossy begged for his stick to be thrown.

'May I?' I asked, hoping my arm might send it further than hers, keeping Flossy away from us.

She handed me his stick and the dog crouched and barked then bounded off once I'd thrown it as far as I could.

'Mr. Nicholls tells me you have achieved much,' she said. 'He is very pleased with you.'

'He talks to you then?' I asked.

'Of course, John. He is my father's curate. We see him often.'

'And the others from the villages. Mr. Grant, from Oxenhope...'

'Ah dear yes. I am very glad you don't have him as a teacher. But forgive me, I shouldn't speak ill of him. Mr. Grant is a true university man. I doubt he has ever left Cambridge in his heart. I fear he prefers to talk to graduates, not lively minds like yours. I believe he feels he has been planted on these hills as if in the Sahara...'

'Mr. Sowden? We don't see him much.'

'A dear man,' she sighed. 'He is well-loved in his own parish. Unlike Mr. Grant, he has a thriving town about him, not so many empty hills.'

I was making no progress. Possibly I'd annoy her, talking like that while she wanted to walk alone. Her big eyes looked over to the moorland heights where the farmhouses were almost invisible, lost in day's sunlight.

'Then we're lucky with Mr. Nicholls here,' I said, I hoped not too pointedly.

'Very,' she said. 'He's a solid man.'

'Well, if you don't mind my saying Miss Charlotte – I mean, I have sisters fully grown and our Betty almost made a terrible match at one time. Her young man was not what she'd hoped after all. Certainly not solid. I was wondering what it is that allows a girl to know if someone, some gentleman, is solid or not? I mean, is solid the right thing for a girl to admire?'

'John,' she said, her eyes down, watching where her feet went. 'There is no recipe for the perfect match. There must be respect and mutual interests. It is often possible to admire where others despise. Your Betty's gentleman was not right for her...'

She stooped to pick a piece of heather that she placed in the buttonhole of her jacket. If only she'd go on, I thought. I'd got her talking much. I had to keep it up.

'Well, he'd not be right for anyone. He was a monstrous type,' I said though I hadn't wanted to talk of Frank at all. I wanted to jolt her. To tell me of her publishers.

'Ah, but he may be right for someone else. Even monsters deserve affection. Did you never hear the tale of the beauty and the beast when you were young? It is always good to let time do its work.'

'Yes, but – let's take the people who make your books, Miss Charlotte. Would you mind telling me about them?'

'Tell you about my publishers?' she said, surprised.

Got her. Now to find out.

'Yes please. If you don't mind.'

'My publishers... well, they are educated people, trained in their work through a love of books and yet much more. Their discernment is often quite alarming...'

There she went, trailing off with her words again. If only she didn't. Just as I hoped for information. Without her glasses maybe she couldn't see the land as I did. Maybe it was blurred like her thoughts.

'Yes, Miss Charlotte. How come they're alarming?' I said

'For myself, I am glad of their critical minds. I enjoy the stimulation of their judgement rather than being left too much on my own to question the fitness of my work.'

'You don't like it on your own...' I said and she stopped and glared her wide eyes at me. I had perhaps gone too far and needed to bring her back. 'I mean, I know you are on your own now, without your sisters, as we all know Miss Charlotte. It must be ever so difficult to write books all on your own. I've not read them, I'm sorry, nor the ones Miss Emily and Miss Anne wrote as I've been led along such ancient tales and more adventurous ones as well, more suitable for me as Mr. Nicholls thinks. Only I know he likes yours because he told me.'

'Yes,' she said, a smile appearing briefly on her face. 'He has also told me.'

Then she must like him. At least.

'So – if you're writing still, on your own which is hard I know, shall your publishers make another book? Shall you be seeing them again?'

'They wanted three in all. I am finding this third one difficult. It is perhaps to do with being alone, I admit. You're not wrong there, John. It is very hard.'

Nothing was a help. I knew of no ways to have her give me the answers I needed. Was she being courted by a publisher – or two? Was she likely to marry one of them? I could not ask her straight. Yet the rare opportunity of being out there, with empty moors around us as we walked, was too good to lose.

'I've not known London people,' I said. 'Mr. Nicholls kindly – ever so kindly – used to take me into Keighley to the libraries there. But I've never seen grand folk more than Mr. George who owns our house, and Mr. Merrall and others at church who were more smart and learned than us. Will you tell me, Miss Charlotte, will you tell me what your publishers are like?'

'Do you really want to know, John?' she said, perhaps by now puzzled by my insistence.

'Oh yes. Everything. How they speak, how they look – even their names. Everything!'

'Well, there's Mr. Taylor, to whom I must be thankful for reading my first book. He is intelligent, quick, searching.'

'Is he now? Would you call him a fine man? Do tell us!'

'I should love to be able to, John! But I am afraid he has a determined and dreadful nose in the middle of his face which cuts my soul like iron!'

There now, a small triumph. I tried to ask her more and I hoped she wouldn't tire and we might stay on the narrow path that led down towards the beck.

Mr. Taylor could now walk out of the picture, all the way to India, and was no cause for alarm. Though she felt gratitude and respect for him, she was able to describe his short stature, his red hair and beard with a humour I'd never seen in her before. Maybe it was something to do with her fame or even that part of her that came from the island, Ireland, I thought. Maybe because she had travelled far. She was perfectly loosened and not like a teacher at all. So I expected the same when she came to describe Mr. Smith. But I was wrong.

The brief gleams of mirth she'd shown me were soon lost when she described this gentleman and she almost became quiet. 'Shrewd' he was, 'kind' 'handsome' and a formidable partner of his firm.

So I was left unsure of things. Did those words mean she had feelings for him?

On our way back before I left to return to Stanbury she pointed to the hills and came up with a subject that was her very own, possibly nearer to her heart than the publishers and their world that were so far from ours. She asked how it was for me to live here, as she had done, knowing that a wider world existed, of men and women whose lives were filled with incident that we'd never know. Was it enough to stay here and not discover more?

'I cannot say, Miss Charlotte,' I said. 'I suspect we shall always be wanting to wander abroad. But there's much at home enough to cherish. There's people who are good, solid and who've already proved their worth...'

*

TWO things had to be done. On a Saturday. Soon.

First, Mr. Nicholls had to ask for Miss Charlotte's hand.

Mr. Brontë, if he gave himself even a minute to think about this possible son-in-law, in his right mind would discover what a fine idea it was. He'd known him for years. Mr. Nicholls had taken over the ministering of the parish whenever sorry times had fallen on the parsonage like the time of Mr. Brontë's operation when his eyes were bad, the terrible deaths, even the repairs to the roof when there was noise and dirt everywhere. Mr. Nicholls was always near. There were some folk in the village who had not taken to him at first but who turned grateful once he was in their homes and by their sick beds. He was a man of books as well. And even though Mr. Grant over the hill in Oxenhope was also a learned man, he'd not let you forget it. I'd heard he'd sulked for weeks after he'd read Miss Charlotte's book, knowing he was pictured there as one of the curates. Then he'd started to visit the parsonage more often, once he knew how famous she'd become. She'd not have liked that.

Considering the other curates who, unlike Mr. Grant, were unmarried, they'd maybe not thought of Miss Charlotte in the way Mr. Nicholls did. She had no fancy ways about her and she did not flap her lashes about the way some girls did. I knew those ways. I'd seen girls at it. One such scamp from Butt Lane had even done the same to me while I once waited for deliveries from Keighley, minding my own business and the time of day. Some girls asked for trouble.

Miss Charlotte was that so serious she'd rather scowl than flirt. And Mr. Nicholls loved her. He'd grown to know her slowly, the way she thought and acted, without a care for her pale, plain looks. This was bound to stand in his favour. This and all he was to the parish. There could be no obstacle on his suitor's path. I had to encourage him.

The second thing was for me to end our lessons. Definitely. I was not to waver nor doubt that this was best. My sisters could keep their pennies and my conscience would be clear of them. Besides, once Miss Charlotte had accepted him, Mr. Nicholls would need the time to prepare for his joyful nuptials.

*

ON my way over to Haworth with my resolutions in mind I met up with Joseph Craven. He was sitting on the bridge and he kicked his feet against its side with a force that told me he was out of sorts.

'Joseph? What's up with you?'

'Nothing.'

'Well something is. Are you to tell me?'

'No, I am not.'

'Very well, I'll be on my way. If you waited a while till I was finished in Haworth, we could go off rambling.'

He folded his arms and kicked the bridge more fiercely, both legs swinging in time.

'Have you not been up Withens way? Not seen Jim?'

'I'm never going there again.'

'Ah. He's bothered you has he?'

Joseph stopped his banging limbs and looked up at me.

'He made me watch him. He said I should learn how to do it. I didn't want to. He made me.'

'Come on with me or I'll be late. Tell me what he made you watch.'

'No, no – I have to stay here. I must.'

'All right Joseph. I'll stop a while, but I'm not to be late. Now what was it Jim did?'

Joseph jumped from the bridge into the road and looked down into the water then up where the beck flowed from the hills.

'Tell us, Joseph.'

'He said I was to see how it's done, killing puppies. His dog had some only that was a week or so ago. He said it was good to wait so that the dog got fond of them first and they were a bit bigger, better to drown. He made me follow him into their barn where the dog was lain and the puppies scrambling up to get at her teets. He was that so nasty, he took them one by one, slowly, and she snarled when the last one had left her and would have scratched him fierce as a lion only he kicked her hard. Before she had time to leap at him he'd put them in a sack and ran. I wanted to stay but he was running so and told me to follow. I heard the puppies squeal, I did.'

Joseph's mouth and voice were all quivery. He blurted Jim's misdeed, his head full of it as he kept his tearful eyes staring down on the swirling surface of the beck.

'He said I was to carry them down to the small waterfall where there's that pool. Only I wouldn't. He said he'd wrap me one if I did not. Well he forced the sack on me. I went a short way and opened it then I dropped it and ran. I came all the way down here. And if he got them and has drownded them, they'll come along in the water to the bridge and I might be able to save them.'

I was about to put my hand on his arm but knew he'd shrug it off. He could be prickly like that, rather than take comfort. He stood and stared up at the heath where the sun, coming overhead behind us, had made of the hills a brilliant purple land. He blinked as tears fell down his damp cheeks.

'All right, our Joseph. I'll leave you, but I shall be finished in an hour or so. You could meet me up in Haworth or shall you still be here?'

'I'm staying.'

Lessons

*

MR. NICHOLLS was not there when I came to his room. For a long time now whichever member of the Brown family greeted me, they knew to let me in and upstairs. With the dog not there I guessed he was out for a walk and had missed watching the time. For a brief moment I hoped he was kept in Mr. Brontë's study while he asked him for his daughter's hand. Fine hope of that. I heard the front door close and the flurry of the dog on the stairs. I heard her master's tread approach, slowly.

He had been out. Over to Oxenhope and back. Mr. Grant was unwell and his wife, Sarah-Ann, afeared it might be the lungs.

'Were they not to call the doctor?' I asked, knowing how Mr. Nicholls' skills were preferred to any doctor's medical knowledge.

'No need. You know, John, sometimes there are illnesses which are not physical at all. They are brought upon us by ourselves.'

I knew what he meant. I already saw in his face that look of dullness that had little to do with his skin or its blood supply, more to do with the workings that went on inside his brain.

'Well he's not sickening for a sweetheart is he?' I said rather pointedly which Mr. Nicholls missed. He searched hard for our books and laid them on the table and had he sighed I'd have not been surprised. The prospect of teaching me had never been a chore, but I could tell his heart wasn't in it that day. So I had to change his present mood. Pull him up short.

'I'm thinking this may be my last lesson with you, Mr. Nicholls,' I said straight.

Some life did come into his face.

'Whatever do you mean?'

"As I say. I think it's not fair on my sisters and I must surely know a very great deal by now. More than most.'

'But John, I was going to talk to you about this. In fact this comes as rather an opportune moment. You do indeed know much...'

He was shook into a speech. At least he was less dull.

'As for the payment of my lessons, it is hardly worth discussing and your sisters shall not continue to pay for them. I like to teach you, it is a great pleasure to me. But in return – well, Mr. Brontë and I have been discussing this, only last Monday evening. You were the subject of a whole hour.'

What was he on about? Surely not the old business of the tower. Was I not doing so well in my lessons, despite what he said?

'We have both thought you would do well in the classroom as a teacher, John.'

His announcement shut out everything I wanted to say.

'There has been a system in our schools for a while now,' he went on. 'Boys like you were then called monitors. That has changed only in name. Now they're known as pupil-teachers and they are perfectly capable of taking a small class. What would happen is that you, as teacher, could attend the younger children as your own pupils. You would have to have some instruction and then, at the end of each year, you'd be examined. Eventually you would receive payment.'

No I said nothing. I hardly knew what he was on about. As if my ears were blinded.

'Officially, you should be given seven hours a week of instruction. What we'll do here is simply continue our lessons on Saturdays but make them longer, or add extra hours before or after school. I believe you might find this most stimulating and of course, should you want to become a professional teacher in a year or two, your training for a college would already be set in place...'

*

JOSEPH was not at the bridge. I admit I was glad of it. My head was that filled with thoughts going this way and that, I could not have helped him out much.

I knew I should find him back in Stanbury, his tale of puppies hung off his tongue. Our paths always crossed. I stopped and watched the water and the old stones, the ones that had hardly budged since we were younger lads. Now we moved about while they stayed still.

Gladness filled my heart. Glad and joyful I was and my pace was fast and the sun shone down on me and I felt the world was a kindly place to be in. I could hardly wait to get home and tell them all that Mr. Nicholls had spoken of.

But as I went I did not put aside that other thought I'd earlier had in mind. A ruse occurred to me, born of hope, wily as a dare. Yes, I'd be a teacher at the school – as long as Mr. Nicholls asked Miss Charlotte to marry him.

*

'NOW don't you go bribing me John,' he said when I told him. 'These are matters entirely unrelated, one of which is known to you through an exchange of confidence.'

'Yes but I could say no. I could refuse to teach and only you would know why. You could tell Mr. Brontë anything you liked and I'll bet it would not be the truth. We both know we should not lie in this world. He'd ask you why I'd refused, he'd want to know. I don't believe you'd say "as long as I may ask for your daughter's hand, then John'll teach the little ones." No, you would not say it.'

'You're right. I certainly would not.'

'Then go on and do it.'

'Lie?'

'No. Ask him. Ask Mr. Brontë for her hand.'

'I – I am so fearful.'

'What of, Mr. Nicholls? Whatever holds you back?'

'The possibility of his refusal.'

'He'll not do that. Not when you think how you stand with him and the parish.'

'I cannot be so sure... He is her father and she his only child.'

'Do it, Mr. Nicholls. Before someone else does.'

*

IT took him until the winter.

I stuck to my bribe as well. As each month went by I said that I would not think to become a teacher in my class until at least the new year. I told him what Miss Charlotte thought of one publisher and he wondered how I knew. So I went and told him the truth which was always best. I said I'd asked her and she described that nose of his. This made him laugh and indeed, it gave him a speck of hope. But in time he became fretful and nervous and hardly ever the kind of man who would please a girl and make her heart burst with happiness at being his wife.

At my home they came to believe I was in a strange state of hesitation, lacking the confidence to move forward as a teacher. I was quite good at it really, pretending, but then I too was fearful. How should I have the kind of authority that would make the likes of the schoolchildren listen to me and follow my words, the way Mr. Nicholls had done?

So the two of us, him and me, we went in line, holding back, unsure of ourselves in certain ways while the Saturday lessons took on a greater value. There, in the books, in the foreign vocabularies, in the maps and through our steel nibs we were secure, our roles defined, unchanging and bringing familiar rewards. I almost hoped those hours would never end.

They did end, abruptly. Because of his proposal.

He told me he was going to do it and since he was in such a sweating state of fear I was inclined to come over and stray about Church Lane until the deed was done. I even thought to go up that tower again, to see him in Mr. Brontë's study or else in the dining room, where Miss Charlotte wrote alone. I wanted to see him in front of her, on bended knee.

He said he'd wait until she'd finished her third book. It seemed to me that everyone concerned was waiting, putting off the moment, knowing it would come yet fearing its arrival. The more he hesitated, the worse he became. He worked himself up into a right stew. He waited for one of those occasions when he had a formal meeting of a Monday night with Mr. Brontë. They sometimes lasted until nine o'clock. He said he'd tell me how it went.

And he did, he told me. How it was frightful. Terrible.

He said he was in that study with Mr. Brontë talking over parish and school matters until dark was well set in. But instead of asking for his daughter's hand in marriage he said goodnight and stood to leave. He did not leave. He went over across the hallway and knocked at the door where Miss Charlotte was quietly at work.

He said he explained to her – how he'd felt, not just recently, but for months and months. He knew from the start he was making a fool of himself but he was conscious it had to be done. And although he might have appeared nervous – shaking, unsure of his words – he was glad of it, the doing. He told her of his suffering that he could no longer endure.

When he said all of this to me, I could not help but wonder how she'd felt. She'd known Mr. Nicholls as her father's curate, doing her father's work and stepping in when he was unfit. Her meetings with him had mostly been held in her father's study or during the hours of church services. Was this the way to be woo-ed?

And if he'd been such a spectacle of nerves, would this encourage an acceptance? Would it lead to love?

I tried to make out what Betty or Nancy would have made of such a man. Younger lads were more to their favour. A man all-a-quiver who'd made himself ill was not their idea of a sweetheart.

Miss Charlotte did not reply but asked if he'd had words with Mr. Brontë. When she learned that he had not, she sent him from the parsonage, saying she'd give him her reply the next day, once she had seen her father.

Her reply was grateful in tone, but a firm refusal.

*

IT was Martha who told me much more.

'Never, not in all my years at the parsonage, have I heard nor seen such a wild commotion,' she said. 'The words that came from his mouth are not the usual ones you'd expect to hear from a vicar.'

She was describing Mr. Brontë. She'd been startled from her quiet chores in the kitchen to come out at once and see what was wrong. Miss Charlotte had hardly said a word and gone up to her room. Whatever the trouble was, it had caused the terrible stir in him. He shouted more loud and full of threats than ever he had from the pulpit of a Sunday. He banged things. He strode about the room and banged more, thudding his fists on the furniture she'd polished only that morning. She hardly dared go in, but when he came out, like a thunderbolt, she saw his face was changed.

'Red with spleen and anger it was. His eyes flashed and his temples were grown lumpy, as if they'd explode.'

'Are you not exaggerating Martha?' I asked.

We were stood on the front steps of the church where they led down into Haworth's small square. The space was exposed to the wind and it was cold. She wrapped her shawl about her, she blew on her fingers. No-one was about.

'No I am not zaggerating, John Robinson. I saw him with my own eyes. And what I have thought since I've seen such a sight has turned my stomach tight. To think of it! To think that Mr. Nicholls should so dare to presume! That's what is thought. That's where the trouble lies.'

'Why, Martha? What's so wrong with him?'

'He's not fit for someone like her! He's no-one. We all know it. We do.'

'Who's "we", Martha?'

'Me as has known them all, and my family as has given him lodgings. My father says he should like to shoot him. And what's more, my Mam has tried to stir him. But since he came back from the meeting that Monday night, he's not moved from his room. He's not eaten nor come into the fresh winter air he likes so much. We've walked his dog, but he won't come out hisself. I always said he was a strange one, well he's more than strange. He's impossible.'

Word soon got round Haworth as Martha's vocal complaints encouraged widespread news. The story went that Mr. Nicholls had asked for Miss Charlotte's hand in marriage and as she'd refused him he'd become so ill he was likely to perish. People waited for his appearance much as they had waited to see who would be next with the lung disease. The neighbouring curates were called to replace him and his duties were reduced, thanks to the 'illness'.

My lessons also stopped and how odd it was to think of the reason why. I knew I needed to get to him and that the Brown family were almost holding him as their captive, walled up in his room. Imprisoned by his wretchedness. I did not find it hard to think up some excuse to visit him.

John Brown the sexton answered the door.

'He's seeing no-one,' he said firmly.

'But I am to be a teacher at the school, and I've to take on some of his work. We need to discuss it. I've not come to gape.'

I found Mr. Nicholls with his arms cradled round his head where he leaned on the table. In the corner his dog leaped from her basket to greet me. I ruffled her ears and patted her sides and sent her back to the corner.

'It's me, Mr. Nicholls. John. I should like to know how you are.'

He did not reply at first. Trying to stir him was not easy, though I knew he was conscious. Great sniffs accompanied his breathing. At last he raised his head and his hair was everywhere. His eyes had gone small.

'Read that,' he said, pushing towards me a piece of paper, a letter from the parsonage.

It was from Mr. Brontë. The words were cruel, very nasty and I was shocked to think of them being from the old man who had always acted so kindly towards me.

'This is unfair, Mr. Nicholls. What are you to do?'

'He and I have not met to speak, we have only communicated in letters. Extraordinary, is it not, that having worked together all these years, so closely, he now sends these missives over the road, delivered by the Browns who must be very entertained.'

'Well, have you heard from her? From Miss Charlotte? Whatever does she think?'

'Look at the end of the letter. See – she has added to it. At the bottom she has written a few lines. She knows he has been harsh.'

'Am I to read them too?'

'Please do, John. It is a little bit of comfort to know she does not share his vehemance towards me.'

I read her words – the only time I ever saw her handwriting:

> *I have no wish to be in any way associated with the senti-*
> *ments my father here expresses that seem calculated to*
> *give you pain. I ask you, Mr. Nicholls, to keep up some*
> *good spirits. Courage!*

'Well then, she's not averse to you. That's something.'

'Not enough, John. Not when you think what I hoped for. There is only one way for the whole matter to be finalised. I gave Mr. Brontë my resignation –'

'You never!'

'I did John, and then I thought how my work, built up over these years, would be diminished if I left. The schools...'

'I shall keep them going. We both can.'

'John, I have no doubt you will do well and I have given thought to you, believe me. I would not leave you without direction after all the years we have known each other.'

'Well you're not going are you?'

'I offered to take my resignation back, hoping the disturbance it would cause in the parish would strike him as unwise. He is bound to know this. But he gave me one condition that I cannot obey.'

126

'What? What can be so bad as to send you away?'

'He wrote again having considered my return in a new light. He said that yes, I should stay. But – but – I was to give him a written promise that never again would I bring up what he called 'this obnoxious subject' either to himself or to Miss Charlotte. In other words, I was to stamp out my love for her and pretend it did not exist. John, I cannot do that.'

'Then are you to go?'

'Yes, John I am. I have already made a decision. People will no doubt talk since they've seen Mr. Grant and Mr. Sowden take my place on Sundays. But I trust you will put their minds at rest. I am not going to die of a broken heart...'

'Like Mr. Branwell?'

That he should laugh, with his face so pale and grim, was some relief.

'No I'm not like poor Mr. Branwell. I've too much to do with my life.'

'What then? Where?'

'I have applied to take up missionary work, overseas.'

'Over the seas?'

'Yes, John. I am hoping to go to Australia.'

Exile

✳

HE did not go suddenly. His departure was a long time happening what with so much to be done and a delay that was difficult for everyone. For us all. The absence of Mr. Nicholls was noticed by those that lived near to him and throughout the whole parish – even to the outlying villages. All due to his captivity in misery. Much was talked of and understood in that time, above all Mr. Brontë's refusal to forgive him for his presumption. His anger endured as did Mr. Nicholls' suffering.

Yet there was a hesitancy in everything, as if uncertainty lingered in the air like thinning clouds. No-one had anticipated such a great reversal of routine and orderliness. The question was, how to adapt?

Miss Charlotte went away. The parsonage was not a comfortable place for her. Her sisters and brother were gone and her father believed he had done right in sending off her most ardent suitor. He alone stayed. It was his home, his parish, his will. Her duty was to obey that will.

A replacement curate was sought immediately. Mr. Grant and

Mr. Sowden were often too entrenched in the demands of their own neighbours to take on Haworth in the wake of Mr. Nicholls' long and fruitful occupation there. Tongues wagged and Martha took on the status of an oracle, approached by many for news of the turbulent times that were being acted out in the parsonage. She upturned her nose, deigning to speak only where she knew her words would fall on eager ears, occasionally remaining dumb, to annoy.

I was allowed access to Mr. Nicholls' room in the hope that our lessons would continue as before. But little was said between us of my studies. He talked as a broken man and during this time if he taught me anything, it was the true meaning of love-sickness. He was indeed sick from it. Never had I witnessed such a state of mind. It touched me deep.

I took him oat-scones and haverbread that Betty baked specially and delivered with them the good wishes of my own family. To amuse him I thought to give him news of Willie Forton who, on hearing of a newly widowed lady in the neighbourhood had decided to become her suitor and was greatly enjoying himself demonstrating to her his skill at the fiddle. Then I thought best not to talk of other men's successes in that line.

Over in Stanbury, people were lost to know what had gone on in Haworth and I was eager to let them believe only real things, not the tales that were said at the inns and over walls in our small street. My family had witnessed and understood the years I'd spent so close with Mr. Nicholls. And since I was not banished from his room they knew my news was likely to be nearer the truthfulness of facts than other folk's fond chat.

The worst of it was when Mr. Nicholls was obliged to come out into the world with Mr. Brontë as they performed in church together. Yes, they were like two dogs, just as men are at times when they bear a grudge. When dogs suspect each other they stand at a distance, still, frozen, waiting. These two had to move from altar to pulpit to rail, but their flesh was up. If by chance they touched each other, just in passing through that narrow holy space, I felt sure the slight brush of a white robe would make one of them turn and snarl. Mr. Brontë showing his teeth. Mr. Nicholls cowering.

Like a tired, exhausted hound he was. I could not bear to see it.

*

STILL I knew there was ways to enjoy myself well enough, back at my home. As Christmas approached I thought to join in the antics of Joseph and the children from Mr. Sunderland's class. Years had gone since I'd attended there. Out in the chill streets we'd had many a lark in the past and I hoped I might still feel the pleasure of a child's carefree play.

What we'd always liked best was to serenade some of the over-trusting of our small village - with carols and hymns which, sounded from our mouths, were not as sweet as they should've been. The tunes were the same as ever, familiar enough by those of us who were not Wesleyans. But then, for the likes of Joseph, church-going did not come into it. There was him, Nathaniel Spencer and Rob Hey, all of whose families were regulars at the chapel and never seen in Mr. Nicholls' small church of a Sunday. As I say, being such young ones, devotional thoughts did not enter the matter. To have some fun and to make the festive season the cause of it all was every child's delight.

It was decided we should divide into two groups. I found myself beneath Harry Whitaker's window, not far off our main street. He was a quiet, harmless man and I was a little worried he'd find us bothersome. The other gang went off down Pepper Lane, towards our house, where they did the same kind of warbling at old Abe o' Sam's.

We shouted and larked and made something of an uproar and when I saw the old men's heads come out of their windows, as if these had been separated from their bodies, I felt oddly sorry for them. Beyond childish play.

'Come on, let's be away!' I called and we were soon on our feet as both men came out of their homes and took up the chase. They went round after us and met up face to face, surprised as hares. It's said they were out of sorts until well into Christmas morning.

The lads were for setting off down the length of the village, to see where more mischief could be made.

'Come on John,' called Joseph whose lantern-lit face was a-glow with excitement.

I had thought to return home.

'We're off to Joe Bills now,' said Joseph, his boots hopping on the black night's ground. Into the empty street he raced not to lose sight of the others. In my heart I felt I should still like to be with him, if not his friends.

Joe Bills was a man of many occupations – grocer, draper, carrier to Keighley and all about. At one time he had been the village constable. He lived in a farmhouse at the other end of the village, a little too near to gaping darkness for my taste, though the daring of Joseph's companions helped them think nothing of it. So I went along. We stood there at Joe's door and angelled and three kinged his household with a raucous, screeching voice of one unholy accord. Then came a fumbling of locks behind the door.

'Any red-heads or white-heads among you?'

'Nay, Joe! Not one!' called the carollers.

'Are you sure?'

'Yeay, Joe, it's Christmas tide!'

'Then come on inside!'

He took us all in and gave us ale and cakes and he and his family were that so welcoming, it warmed my heart.

Arm in arm with Joseph I returned to where the winds from the moors did not reach to whip around our sheltered east end homes. As I patted him goodnight I thought how glad I was not to be quite grown.

*

AFTER those early weeks of uproar, once Christmas festivities and the new year were past, the villagers of Haworth began to wonder what lay ahead for the reduced family and servants in the parsonage. The damp, cold air sent people indoors where, huddled near their stoves or by flickering flames of fire, they had the subjects of the vicar and his daughter and the continued presence of the curate to stir their hearthside talks.

'Miss Charlotte has come home, and she's brought her friend Ellen with her,' Martha reported to me. 'Having company is better for her really though of course Ellen cannot stay. When she goes I dare not think what will happen. It's all very well Mr. Brontë having us around him. Nothing much has changed for him. He gets his food nicely cooked and his study cleaned where he sits and reads endless papers and is always writing letters. He stops me at times and talks about troubles brewing abroad, that he's read of. Well I'd like to say to him "Yes, Mr. Brontë and what about the troubles on our doorstep?" only I know he'd scoff at that, saying nothing was amiss.'

'Everything is amiss, Martha,' I said.

'Well you would think so, wouldn't you.'

'From what you say, Martha, your young mistress has a bit of a dreary life, does she not?'

'Her new book is a success. She's famous.'

'She doesn't care for being famous.'

For once Martha's tongue did not leap ahead of her thoughts. She sighed a long, weary sigh. She didn't fold her arms nor twist her mouth into the kind of shape that said 'I know best'. She looked down at her feet.

'I suppose it wasn't that bad,' she said quietly.

'What wasn't? People not speaking to each other?'

'No. What he did. Mr. Nicholls.'

'What he did was wonderful! He loves her,' I blurted to Martha as I detected the beginning of a slight change of heart in her. 'All he wanted was for everyone to be happy which they would've been if she'd been kind and said yes,' I went on. 'She might have said yes, but for her father. Or she might have asked for time which would have been more like her. Cautious, not to go racing ahead. We all know she's thoughtful. That's how she got those books done. But now look where've they got themselves to. Just the two of them in that cold parsonage on the edge of the moor. Reading and writing and being ever so quiet. All very well, such fine activities, but they could've been a family again.'

'How?' asked Martha. 'The family's dead.'

'Children, Martha! New little ones. Such happens when folk get married. Did you not know?'

'I never thought. No-one ever thought. It's because he's - he's so stern. He's always got a frown on his face.'

'That's how all you at Sexton House have come to see him. You've begun to believe each other without looking closer, without a kinder thought. Not all Haworth feels like you. And yes, I do think everything's amiss because I know he's a fine man, even if he doesn't smile so much. He's given me the world. He'd have given her the world too. Only now she's got much less than she had before. And look who she's got to share it with. One bad-tempered old father. She could have had a husband.'

Martha, in something of a novel way about her, mumbled rather than spoke. If it had been summer, perhaps she'd have been more sparked, more talkative. I guessed that for her, working in the parsonage had also become very drear, especially when Mr. Brontë was there alone, mostly hid in his study.

My teacher's role was now upon me and I had to meet with Mr. Brontë to have this new position explained. One of the most difficult situations I ever was to face loomed on the cloudy grey horizon.

I could not go straight into the work. I could not bound upon a group of little ones as if they were the very images of Joseph and myself, the way we had once been. I may have gained much knowledge and with it, an understanding of how to keep knowledge inside me, alive and ever-searching. But I was still to have instruction and guidance.

As far as I could see our schools were run by the church. Churchmen made the rules. Our most senior churchman was Mr. Brontë himself and I now had to answer to him. This meant I was required to go to him where he spent most of his time – that same room I had seen from way up in my tower – at the front, right hand side of the parsonage. I called on Mr. Nicholls first.

'John – just be yourself. He likes you so well.'

'Yes but – how can I be easy with him, after all he's done?'

'You must not think like that. He has done nothing to you personally that should affect your exciting new role.'

'He has! He's cruel and –'

'John, stop. Go peacefully. Think of all we have done and all there is for you to do because of it. There are young children in our neighbourhood who see no further than their homes and streets, the mills where their parents go each morning, where their siblings will also go, too early in their lives. They know the farms, the bleating of sheep, the changing colours of the moors and the movement of the skies overhead. This is all they know. They don't know there is the possibility of much, much more. You do. This is the great value of being educated. So remember this when you talk with Mr. Brontë who is there to help you make the lives of our children better. John – this is the achievement of all our Saturday lessons. It is what we have done together. Remember that.'

*

FIRST thing I did inside that study was check the window to see how the tower looked from inside the parsonage.

What an adventure it had been, to go there, to climb up even at dusk and to peer into the depths of the very room where I was now sat. The tower stood this end of the church, a great bulk in the grey winter's air, the only feature of the village I could see. Behind it were the familiar hills above the Worth, cloudy, indistinct, patterned grey.

Fortunately Martha had given me a wink when I'd arrived. If she'd been haughty I might have felt small. She knew this was a rare occasion for the likes of a lad like me. Not many people entered Mr. Brontë's study unless from invitation. For once I was not a trespasser but someone who'd been called upon to visit. Yet I was not at ease and with little courage. So when I was in there and I turned my attention to him, I knew I had to muster some kind of strength. I even tried to pretend I was Mr. Nicholls, since I was sat in the same chair where he used to sit. From this chair, when all was well between them, he had faced Mr. Brontë.

He really was a thin and rather dry old man. His mouth was not firm, but his smile was set, as if pushed up into position by the bands of cloth about his neck and chin. Their whiteness matched his cropped hair and whiskers. His eyebrows had not whitened so much. His fingers were long and his nails too. Though tall and upright, he seemed not very supple and shuffled awkwardly. His slippers were worn right through. He fussed with clothes that were none too new, until he got himself comfortable in his chair. Then he hardly moved, as if moving might make him snap. I felt sure his neck, all wrapped the way it was, would fall limp if the swaddling bands were removed.

He seemed calm, what with that smile, though I had heard from Martha that lately he was a bundle of nerves and these were hard for him to keep in check.

He nodded to the open newspaper on his small, upright table.

'A ship's gone down, near the Baily lighthouse. Did you know?'

'No, your Reverend.'

'There's all about it in the paper, here. The ship was called the *Queen Victoria*. A hundred aboard, eighty or so have lost their lives. Set sail from Liverpool only the day before and hit a snowstorm off the Irish coast. They say she went down in only fifteen minutes. A terrible, terrible thing.'

I wanted to ask more, interested as I was, but my throat had become tight.

'I myself sailed over from Ireland,' he said which reminded me his particular speech was Irish, if a bit croaking. Like Mr. Nicholls'. And Miss Charlotte's was nearly like it, though it did not croak and was still very quiet despite her being famous.

I had to remember not to mention her.

The room was unlike Mr. Nicholls' room. Very unlike. Here Mr. Brontë was secure inside his own home surrounded by his own choice of furnishings. A small fire burned in the hearth on the other side of the room. The walls were scrubbed and gave the room a pleasant kind of pale light. Pictures hung on the walls. A tall piece of furniture stood against the wall opposite me. The top half was covered by a large expanse of cloth pleated into folds that met in the centre like rays of the sun. This was framed by polished wood, all part of an upright whole with piano keys on the bottom half. It seemed a waste of space to me, too tall and very fancy.

I looked at the pictures. One was big, the width of the fireplace where it hung. It had no colour and though only black and white was something of a confusion. It showed a strange kind of city, with buildings that were mostly huge columns and distant arches. The scene was struck with harsh light that streamed in from one side onto a huge mass of terrified people. Hundreds and hundreds of them there were, mostly women with their clothes falling about and their arms waving, fleeing, flowing like waves away from the light. A flash of white fire spiked through foaming clouds. Over the walls of the city, in the far distance, was another building like a tower but not like my tower. It was as big as a city itself, pyramid shaped with floor upon floor of more columns and arches rising up into the stormy sky. Not in any way peaceful. And I'd have thought not the right kind of thing to set your mind at rest.

'...but there has been great progress in our steam-powered ships that now go all over the world. Did you know, John, it takes only two weeks to reach America though of course, going East would be a much longer journey with great land masses in the way. John?'

'Oh I'm sure of it, Mr. Brontë. I have imagined it might be so.'

'Yes, well let's get down to some business. You know why you're here.'

'Oh I do.'

'I believe you'll do well in our schools. You're quite ready for it. Away from here there are boys younger than you who have been teaching for a number of years. How old are you now John?'

'Fifteen next birthday.'

'Mmm. We should have thought of it earlier. I should have thought.'

'But I might not have wanted to.'

'Is that so?' he said, and he raised the dark tufts of his brow above his small circular glasses. 'Does the thought not appeal to you John?'

'It's not that, sir. I don't think I would have been ready before. I should not have been one of the older pupils and as far as I can see I'll have more clout now that I am. I know the children. I see how they learn, or not, and how they choose to behave. I need to have authority with them. That's not a thing that comes easy you see Mr. Brontë...'

I was talking fast, the way my voice always ran away with me. I hardly knew what I said, but though I was nervous I knew the words I spoke were all true. I had so much to say. 'There's only one or two good teachers around here, Mr. Brontë,' I said.

'That's certainly true, John,' he said, clearing his throat. 'My daughter does not have as much time as you probably guess. And I myself am not as young as I used to be.'

Best not to say his name. The name of Mr. Nicholls. Nor even hint at it.

'So, let me explain a few things,' he went on. 'You probably are unaware that not far from here, over the border in Lancashire, there is a fine old hall, Gawthorpe Hall, which is owned by a new acquaintance of my daughter. His name is Sir James Kay-Shuttleworth and he was made a baronet only some years ago. It has been most fortunate for her, getting to know him, as he has the potential to introduce her to many good and influential people in London, as well as in the country, and I am keen for her to do just that. Now, to come to the point. Sir James, who was originally a doctor...'

I was feeling chilled. I wanted to go over to the fire and place more fuel on it, but he was that far in his talking I dared not interrupt. I tried to pretend the cold was a piece of clothing that prickled, like some coarse wool. If I could only see the fire's flames, that might have warmed me. I guessed Mr. Brontë wore sturdy underclothes beneath his shabby coat.

'...and he has been profoundly moved by the condition of children working in poor circumstances, such as he witnessed in Manchester. His philanthropic ideals have stretched into education and that's where you and I and our schools come into the picture. He has been instrumental in setting up the system in schools whereby pupils like yourself may become teachers and it seems only natural, since we have this social contact between himself and us, that we should go ahead and show our profound appreciation, our awareness of its need – and use it too. Do you understand this, John?'

'You speak very clear. Is he a churchman?' I said

'No, he is not. He is concerned that all children, no matter what their social background, have the right to be educated.'

'I see. Good of him.'

'But to come back to his system. A pupil is selected to be apprenticed to a master or mistress of a school and examined by an Inspector at the end of each year. If all has gone well, the master or mistress is given a grant to keep the pupil in a paid situation. As I have said, normally the apprenticeship should begin in children of a younger age, but we have not had anyone quite as suitable as yourself, John.'

The way he looked at me then was yes – kindly – smiling as he was. But I could not return the pleasure, despite all he told me. I was to be grateful, glad, honoured at being so chosen. The idea that I should be taught and to teach and then to be paid for doing it was something beyond my usual trail of thought. Yet since the news came from him, and since I had been turned against him, because of his treatment of Mr. Nicholls, I almost wanted to refuse the privilege despite my knowledge that it was more than a stroke of good fortune.

He talked on, explaining things.

'...as you said about few teachers here. Our problem is how you will be instructed and examined. I am going to look into it but it seems you must be taught by someone who has graduated from university...'

I had to remember how I got there, into his study – thanks to the lessons. Lessons from a man from university.

'Well now John, you must know how dear to my heart is the subject of education. I had the school across the lane built for the children of Haworth.'

'I know. I've read the stone.'

'All my children taught there. I know you experienced each one of them in that classroom. That makes me rather partial to the idea of you – you being one to inherit what we began. So, to come back to you, I must tell you that I believe you would do better to start off in your own village, Stanbury, before we put you here. There's the small school there, more recently built and used as a chapel-of-ease for the Anglicans. I'm sure you know this. I know you follow my thought...'

Oh I followed it all right. The school built by your curate. All thanks to him.

'Since you and your family live over that way it seems not a bad idea to place you there. Between us university men, we will hopefully find you an instructor. Mr. Grant is nearby and has created his own domain in Oxenhope. Mr. Sowden over at Hebden Bridge – well, he is really very taken up with a larger parish. Then there is of course myself here, but I am unsure of making a commitment to teach. You may be interested to know that my daughter will give occasional help to the schools despite her changed position.'

He mentioned, almost in passing, that there was to be a new curate who might also prove fit to instruct. As if I needed anyone else. As if I could bear to even set eyes on the new man. An intruder.

'For us to be relieved of the often treacherous walk, in winter that is, over to Stanbury would be a great relief. Of course you would still have Miss Atkins who I believe teaches the girls at times and possibly Miss Sugden. And we have yet to see the ability of this new curate, once a suitable person has been found and established in Haworth. Meanwhile, until we have everything set in place, I'm going to suggest you make full use of the Mechanics Institute library here, another blessing in our village. You could also go into Keighley for books...'

He heaved a sort of sigh, a breath to end his words when they were all said. He looked over towards me. 'So, tell me, John, how does all this sound to you?'

'You have explained everything, Mr. Brontë,' I said.

'At home, the conditions in your house – would you be able to study?'

'Not like in here,' I said and glanced round the room.

I knew I should soon have to leave, once I had found a voice that gratefully accepted all he told me. He could never have guessed how my collar was hot and the palms of my hands had gone into a sweat. It was not to do with my nervousness nor the thought of the task ahead of me.

He'd made no reference to him at all. Though I had kept my silence over him, the name of Mr Nicholls had not been mentioned. After all he'd done.

*

THE Cross Inn is not far from where you come into our village from Haworth. It's named after the old cross that stood nearby on the wayside that's remembered by some though I never saw such a stone. Drinking men may have dreamed it up. Not far from the inn is the beer shop that had got itself a licence late, so making the east end of our street a fine watering place for the thirsty traveller. Or for the thirsty trouble-monger. There were plenty of them. They were that noisy and they spilled out of the Cross like sheep falling from a hill. Tumbling and bleating. Half the night long.

The damp air made me out of breath at times, or else it was the cold that went with it that caused me to hunch my shoulders and ache with a longing to be indoors. When I saw Joseph on the bench outside the Cross, my first thought was that he had joined the drinkers who had thrown him out. No-one sat there in winter. There was nothing to see but thick, grey fog that made formless ghosts of passers by. But he was mumbling to himself, kicking his legs.

'Now then,' I said. 'What's up with you?'

'Nothing.'

'Got no news for me? If you haven't, well I have for you. Very interesting it is too. Only maybe you're not for being interested today.'

'I am that,' he said and he stopped his legs still.

'It's about the new school.'

'What of it?'

'It's to have a new teacher.'

'It is? Mr. Nicholls coming back then?'

When he said that my speech stopped short. I wanted to tell him the surprise of my new role and instead his chance remark had robbed me of my words. That he should hope to see Mr. Nicholls again wrenched my heart. How was I ever to take his place, if lads like Joseph hoped he might come back?

'Nay not that,' I said and I sat myself next to him. I thought to tell him all that had passed. Although I always saw Joseph as a younger lad than me, he was not so young as to misunderstand the ways of men and women. But then I could not be sure he would talk the length and breadth of Stanbury's main street. So I spun him a tale.

'Mr. Nicholls is going away...'

'He is?'

'Yes. Most likely very far. About as far as you can go on this earth.'

'Is he to be a sailor?'

'No, no. It's called a missionary. They go all over preaching about the Lord and his good deeds and how you should stay away from Dissenters and recognise the one true way. So they help to make that way. Mr. Nicholls is what you call partial to 'high church' which is why he had a church built here, in Stanbury, where the land is high up. They tell other Anglicans as how the divil himself, dressed as Dissenters, will coax you onto his path, lead you by his clawed hands and with his speared tail wagging round your legs –'

'Get off...' said Joseph who quickly stood up, having none of my tease.

'No, it's not true – at least not most of it. He is going away and he is going to be a missionary. It's what people like curates do, when they've tired of the place they're in. They go off you see, to places like India and Africa and there's even loads of Methodists do the same. You ask your folk. As Christians first and missionaries second, they can agree about many things. They want people who traipse around tigers and elephants and the like to think more about building churches and praying. So that's why he's going.'

'Do you think he'll see tigers?'

Maybe Joseph was not as grown as I'd thought. I told him Mr. Nicholls would let us know if he saw any kind of savage beast and he'd draw us a picture of them. It helped Joseph to think well of him and steered him far from thoughts that Miss Charlotte had anything to do with his plans. Joseph's folk I knew might spread any news they heard, so the less people knew about the truth, the better. With these ideas in mind I devised my own mission. To keep Mr. Nicholls' name in tact.

'Anyway, our Joseph. I do have other news – and it is to do with a teacher at the school. He really is someone you'd like though he won't be teaching you. He's much better than Mr. Sunderland, you know. He'll be there for the younger ones.'

'Who is he?'

'He is me. None other than your old friend John Robinson.'

Exile

*

THE thick mists that blew and spun about the road enveloped us as we made towards the school. With only a yard of visibility ahead we went headlong into a white, vapourous mass that stayed with us down the street and past the houses that rose as shadows on either side. No sign there was of the valleys or moors that our village proudly looked out upon. Only dense, damp fog. We reached the low school wall and I drew breath on thinking what a step it was to be, to take the path that led up to its solid front porch – as pupil-teacher.

We stood there, the two of us. We had seen it being built, on a bare patch of land – muddy, unkempt, where a narrow thoroughfare led down to Stanbury's back lane. We had watched the stranger Mr. Nicholls and his dog come over in all weathers to see it as the stones were raised and the cross and the bell put in place at either end. Now it was my turn to make of it the school he had built in his dreams.

Joseph coughed. I patted his back, but still he went on spluttering.

'Not long now and you'll see me arrive here of a morning,' I said.

'Have to be off,' said Joseph whose coughing had brought tears to his eyes. 'Shouldn't have come out. Cold –'

As I pulled up his scarf about his neck we both suddenly stood still. A voice came through the pale blanket of dank mist.

'John! Is that you?'

I should like to say she was running, but I couldn't be sure. She almost flew or else she danced and being clothed in a cape, she was like an unearth-bound sprite whose airborne feet did not touch the invisible road. When she was close I saw her face all moistened and pink. The only colour in the dull, chill world was the yellow of her hair.

'I thought it must be you, John. I have so hoped to see you,' she said.

'What are you doing out here, Hannah? It's a bad day to be about.'

'Oh but I have to walk, as much as possible. That's what I've been told you see, by a new doctor I have who is really so much better than all the others I've seen in all the different towns. And would you believe it, John, he is not too far away at all. Leeds! When you think that I have even been to the Pyrenees to seek out doctors!'

Joseph, crouched and all-a-shiver, soon went off into the mist without a further word.

'Is he ill?' she asked. 'The poor boy. He's your friend isn't he? Is he unwell?'

'Don't mind Joseph. He's that daft he doesn't wear enough clothes. He keeps them for the animals he finds, making nests for them beneath his bed at home. So, Hannah. Tell us more...'

It was as if the cold did not touch her. She threw up her head and her wild gold hair, though dank, was still bright. She shook it away from her face and laughed.

'You know, John, I'm not sure there is anything at all wrong with me or my legs and I do believe that these doctors with their serious proclamations and the beastly potions they prescribe are not doing a scrap of good. I don't feel anything wrong. I feel no pain nor dizziness. If I lose my balance at times, what does it matter?'

'Nothing at all.'

'However, I ask myself, should I tell Mama these visits to medical men must stop? She does so love to travel. She likes the hotels and the sites of each spa. But you see, I too have been able to discover some marvellous sights in our journeys. Leeds is fairly grim in comparison to Amélie-les-Bains.'

'To where?'

'Amélie-les-Bains. It's named after the French queen and she has been to this country and over there she has inspected all the hot springs – and how lovely they are! And you bathe in them and they are filled with sulphur so the water is supposed to cure things like – oh I don't know. There were far too many rather aged people there and they were wheeled about in chairs like baskets by grim looking guardians and matrons and I had to laugh at times because it was like another world! Like a huge hotel for the infirm with everyone sipping from large pitchers of water and dainty cups and I watched them so. Oh John, I shall never be like them! Still it was something of a wonderful place too. There were wide windows looking out at huge peaked mountains, not like over here...'

She turned to look south but the wide stretch of Smith Bank and the moors round Haworth were hidden beneath heavy shrouds of cloud that hardly moved but hovered, streaked with grey, as if they were poised to stay there for ever.

'Well, nowhere is like here, is it John? Tell me, what have you been doing?'

We had not moved from the school wall. I turned and looked at the small building again and having followed her ramble with delight, was that pleased I could now give her my good news.

'As a matter of fact, Hannah. I am to come here,' I said, nodding towards the path that led from the gate.

'To the school? Why? Have you not done well in Haworth?'

I walked round her, so she did not see the wide smile upon my face – not at once. I put my hands in my pockets though they were not so cold. I lifted my chin and made my announcement.

'I am to be a teacher here,' I said.

She put her head on one side. I felt she looked at me as she might towards a welcome stranger, one who had come from far beyond all those foreign lands she knew.

Or was it that I saw her in a different way? Was it a different light? That grey mist was everywhere. Was she still enchanted?

'Well, John Robinson,' she said. 'I might have guessed it. There is no-one in Stanbury quite like you!'

*

IT was on a Saturday, later, in the spring when the weather was better. Hannah and myself were to go on a railway expedition and I needed to let Mr. Nicholls know. But since he'd been given the order to leave, I thought he might be less concerned about our lessons, so few of them remained. And the state he was in, he was not really fit to teach the way he used to.

'Can I come another time?' I asked him. 'My friend Hannah has asked me to go with her to Morecambe. It will be a day of railway journeys and she thought I'd like it. There's a new jetty being built and she feels sure I shall like that too. She's got that lady with her, Mrs. Parker. There'd not be just the two of us. I shouldn't mind coming to you in the evening.'

'No, John, you would be tired after such a trip.'

'Well, maybe there's not so much to do,' I suggested.

'Oh there is a great deal, John. Above all we need to give some thought to the future months at the Stanbury school – how you will begin them, what subjects you think would be best for their age.'

'Like you did with me?'

'Perhaps not. Those were my ways and may not be yours. We must consider where are your strengths. And how you will compensate for your weaker points.'

'I fear I'm to have sessions with him, for my instruction,' I said, not liking to mention Mr. Brontë's name.

'Good. You will find you need them.'

'But Mr. Nicholls – about Saturday?'

'You would like to be with Hannah wouldn't you?' he said warmly. 'A simple outing...'

'Yes, I would indeed.'

'And so you shall,' he said as he handed me a letter. 'Of course you can miss the lesson. Before you go, I had wanted to show you this. I've received a reply.'

I read the bold print at the letterhead: THE UNITED SOCIETY FOR THE PROPAGATION OF THE GOSPEL.

'What is it?'

'It's an invitation to a meeting in London to discuss my suitability for a particular post they have in mind in Australia.'

'Shall you go?' I said.

'To the meeting? Yes. To Australia? If they deem me fit.'

'But –'

'Go on now, John. I shall not be conducting the service this Sunday. Mr. Grant is again to take it over. We can talk more at a later date.'

'I'll not go to the service, not if it's not you.'

'Don't, John. You must get used to my absence.'

'Well I –'

'Yes, John?'

'I'll tell you what I thought of the sea. Whenever I see you next.'

*

I WATCHED Keighley, a townscape of chimney pots. How many there were I could not guess. Field and moor reached down to the town edges – or rather, the regular lines of building stone appeared to creep up the hillsides over the land's rounded curves, as if to claim all nature for industry.

'Look, John. What do you make of that?' asked Hannah as the train gathered speed and shunted on its way. 'We shall see all sorts before we arrive in Skipton, which is not so far. Then we must change and go on the new line.'

Long, parallel rows of solid blocks, each made up of small, individual houses, were joined at the back and sides. Streets were decked with washing lines hung across the cobbles from window to window where bright white shirts and skirts (and all else that covered a body) blew like festive decorations. I wondered if, when taken indoors, they smelled of smoke. People leaned from window-sills and groups of children played in the streets, the girls' pinafores startling white like the washing. These white spots stood out because of the black patterns made by upright figures, fencing rails and all the sharp lines of an urban architecture.

Now and then I caught sight of a silvery bar of water where the town's canal meandered past buildings at ground level. Slow moving barges carried piles of black coal. The railway crept ahead and I knew I'd follow the snake-like track as I caught sight of the head of the train turn gradually into a long curve. Steam and smoke spat from the black engine.

The window through which I stared was like a lantern exhibition frame. The world went by, slow at first then it gathered more speed as the land went flat. When, slowly, the train scaled a certain height, I was able to look down across that world, so unlike anything I'd seen before.

'I am unsure what I think,' I said at last. 'I can say I'm pleased to see a little more of where we live – but I shall be glad to see fields, the villages. Here, I feel as if I am an insect crawling over a very detailed map.'

Hannah placed her hand upon mine. At last we sped round and away from Keighley's stark outlines.

'I hope you're not disappointed. Another day we'll go somewhere wonderful. You don't mind, do you? If you find it unpleasant, I've failed. Don't worry, I shan't be upset. We'll soon arrive into more country and then we must get off this train, musn't we Mrs. Parker? Then we'll head for the sea!'

Mrs. Parker was sat opposite us in the carriage. She nodded and when she pulled on her gloves – a gesture to show we were soon to arrive in Skipton – she gave us both an amusing wink. I had once thought she was their cook or housekeeper or someone in a role that belonged mostly out of sight of the parlour where people like the Pollards spent their hours. She was not. I wasn't sure what she was except that she was very big and she smiled a great deal and she loved Hannah. Mrs. Parker held her hands between her large breasts and the upper fold of her belly and here her palms were warmed. She sweated a deal as if it were the height of summer, yet it was early spring. The heat from the confined space must have done it. There were other folk in there with us – a bespectacled man who, despite the spectacles, held his newspaper up to his nostrils. Another man wore a moustache that was not shaped with God's hands but with the balm from a pot of wax. I had seen these creations before, sometimes in church, and wondered how much time it took to shape them so. Hannah had noticed this gentleman too. He avoided our glances. His nose did not suit the moustache but fell in a hook over its centre. Mrs. Parker tried to edge away from him as he was sitting next to her. For some reason, during the whole journey he persistently moved along beside her. Luckily we arrived at the station before she had been unwillingly cramped into an uncomfortable corner of the compartment.

'John, you shall see such things!' said Hannah taking my arm as we left the train.

Once on the flat platform, Hannah moved from one foot to the next and tip-toed herself tall to look about her. All the while she held on to my arm.

The way she did that – the way her fingers gripped my flesh – it was not done with any guile. I was a physical support for her and did not object to being so. I even liked it. It gave me a sense of being nicely close to her laughter.

'Shall you want to sit down?' I asked. 'Have we time?'

'Oh John, you are thoughtful. I'm so pleased you came with us,' she said.

Her smile went deep into my heart.

*

I WOULD not have thought the land could change so, considering it was none too far from home. The hills were steep and green, bare and rugged, with low walls that were familiar to me, the way their stones knitted together. These were dales, not the moorland to the south of Stanbury, so changeable and wild, nor the fertile meadows to our north that reached down to the river. Here was a combination of both – stark, pale, solid rock, deep valleys and green turf cropped by straying sheep.

Hannah chattered on and I felt her next to me as the noisy train gathered speed. Her closeness warmed me. She did not check for my attention, which never strayed from her words, but happily talked to Mrs. Parker who firmly spread herself across her own and another seat so as to repulse intruding travellers. She needn't have worried. We were alone, the three of us. And I was deeply happy.

When the land spread flatter, and the sky seemed far wider than I'd ever seen it, Hannah stood at the window.

'We're nearly there!' she called. 'We shall soon see the sea!'

'Shall we?' I said, out of my seat. 'Miss Anne did love it so.'

'Who?'

'Miss Anne. The youngest of Mr. Brontë's girls.'

No sign of recognition appeared in Hannah's face. For a moment I was puzzled. There were not many who did not know the name of our vicar and his family.

'There! There it is!' Hannah cried and instantly she took my arm to drag me to the other side of the compartment. 'We shall be there soon! Mrs. Parker how long?'

'I don't know, child. We've not done this journey before...'

When the train finally stopped and we left it, we were surrounded on all sides by a wide grey and silver watery waste. The cold was very cold. The sea was at a distance, but we smelled it at once, long before we saw it. Gulls wheeled in the air and the chafing salty wind blew in my face so I nearly faltered with the unfamiliar impact of the whole spectacle. The sea.

'There it is! There is where the jetty will go...'

Hannah would have raced about but I held her back. I had to. I knew what it would mean if she began to run, then fall onto the shining wet sands.

'Oh John!' she said and turned at once, unable to move forward with her arm gripped tight. It was not a look of disapproval she gave me. Her maze of yellow hair was blown up in the wind and she laughed and bounded back to me and placed both hands on my chest and laughed again.

*

NO, not ever. Never did I think to hear Mr. Brontë the way he was that day. Martha might have reported it to me, even Mr. Nicholls himself, but I did not expect to witness him rage so with my own eyes.

I had made my plans for teaching, though I was not to start yet. I needed to present my suggestions to Mr. Brontë – simple arithmetic done not with written numbers but with objects placed on a bench, to be counted as they were added or taken away. Writing with quills we'd made from feathers. Reading was the difficult one. I could make pictures on a large slate, together with their letters, and have a try at drawing. What I wanted to do most was story-tell about the ancient world. I needed to know if to start history this way rather than give the children dates to learn was advisable. How could they tell one century from another if they didn't start from earliest times? And when was the earliest? All this was to be discussed.

When Martha led me towards Mr.Brontë's study she pulled a face.

'There's been a terrible commotion,' she whispered as she closed the front door behind her. 'It's since the Bishop, Dr. Longley, left. He's only just gone. We did so much, we tried so hard to make things work right. Miss Charlotte and I, we so wanted everything to go nice and smooth. He's an important guest who's not been here before, you see. She wanted to help clean the church and I let her, seeing as there're reminders there – the burials.'

'What happened?'

'He was a nice man. Miss Charlotte said so too. She called him 'a charming little gentleman' and so he was, to us all. Mr. Brontë was pleased at first. But – sshhh, I dare not speak too loud, John.'

As she quietened her own speech, we heard shouts upstairs. Mr. Brontë's voice was immediately above us. I could not make out the precise words, thanks to the floorboards between us. Martha shook her head.

'Have you ever heard the like? He's up there in his bedroom, all on his own now. He was blowing like a gale to Miss Charlotte and so she's gone out. She was crying. Well you know what it's about.'

'No, Martha. But you're going to tell me.'

'Mr. Nicholls. It's because he was so sullen. Ever so touchy too. They were all in the dining room next door, having their tea. Dr. Longley remarked on the portrait of Miss Charlotte, you know the one. She had it done in London that time. Well Mr. Nicholls spat out some remark and Mr. Brontë had to contain himself. Only he did it again, let out a sharp word about something or other, I don't know. Everyone's in a stew. Mr. Nicholls went off in a dudgeon. Miss Charlotte said to me she felt terrible. You see, Mr. Nicholls tried to speak to her again, just after the evening service and Dr. Longley, well he guessed what was up. He must have tried to talk to him only – sshhh. Mr. Brontë's coming down. I'll leave you to him, John. He's got all his wits wound up...'

If, earlier, he'd blown like a gale, he was now a thunderstorm. His face was red, streaked with the raised blood of anger. He walked into the study, stood still and stared at me then threw down his stick onto the floor.

'John, what is it?' he said abruptly.

'It is me come for the meeting we had planned.'

'Not tonight. I should have told you. We had a visitor, the Bishop.'

'And he's gone.'

'Yes he's gone but I'm out of sorts, can't you see?'

'I can that, Mr. Brontë. I shall leave and come another day.'

'Do. And if you see that blessed master of yours, remind him that the Inspector of Schools is due, soon. It's March in case he's forgotten. I was going to tell him myself only he has run off. If he doesn't behave properly then it shall be reflected in the reference I give him. He risks losing any good words I might have said about him and he'll never find work again!'

He did not stay to sit but stooped to pick up his stick with some difficulty. I might have helped him only I felt my hands would burn if I touched him. He was soon out of the room. I heard him bang the front door as he too went out into the cold evening air.

*

NANCY's failing spirits worried us all. The approach of spring that she usually looked forward to held little charm for her. She talked less and at times I wondered if there was any truth in celestial predictions, when the positions of the moon, the planets and the stars were supposed to have an effect on the likes of us who wandered the earth beneath them.

Things got worse in every direction I turned. Nancy's reluctance to get up in the morning gradually led to her staying put there. Hidden close beneath her bedclothes, she spoke to none of us, not even Betty who was surely her dearest friend. Nor did she eat. When she got up, to go to the privy outside, she was so thin and trembly we did not like to mention her sorry state. As if she was a stranger in our house who had come and taken over Nancy's bed.

'We shall have to think of something, John,' said Betty when we were off on our regular walks. 'To do nothing is irresponsible. I cannot think there is anything in her body makes her ache. She is not in pain, I don't think. Not physically.'

'How is she when she's at the mill? Does she not work as she should and if so, does she not get scolded for it?' I asked.

'I cannot be sure as I'm not in the same line as her.'

'Does she not have friends? She's a likeable enough girl.'

'If you ask me, John, she's just wrong with work. She longs to - to be free of all that she does there. Not just the machines' noise and the regular movements of our arms and how we stand. She's tall and strong as me. There's times when you'd think she was lively and well. I've heard her talk, despite the noise of the looms. I've seen her speak out loud to folks she meets...'

'Do you think she's ailing for some lad?' I said.

Betty did not answer at once but shook her head which I took to mean 'no'. She said she knew of no way to find out without seeming to pry.

'I believe she wants some fulfilment, that's all. And whether that be a lad or a family I don't know. I suspect it's to do with – well, being ever so bored. It's this makes her angry.'

We agreed not to tell our suspicions to Father. He too was no better for seeing the green appear on the trees. His condition was visibly obvious. His bent back was bending further and his groans of a night were almost enough to keep me sleepless. Luckily, I had begun to get used to them, knowing I needed to rest. But silence was no way to help him neither. So Betty and I, being relatively healthy, formed a secret union of watchfulness.

Luckily, Willie Forton kept our spirits cheery. He was now very taken with activites in the newly formed band, down the hill in the hamlet not far from us. Willie fiddled with them on many church occasions. He begged Father to join up with him, even if it was only to thud on a drum now and then. Father declared he would never traipse around the hills after noisy Wesleyans. Their playful banter brought many-a-smile to our evenings.

Mr. Brontë had begun his search for a new curate. Though I was glad to be at the school in Stanbury, acquainting myself with the prospect of teaching there, it meant I saw less of Mr. Nicholls in the week. Still on a Saturday there were our lessons, or what was left of them. Fears grew for me when I knew that his departure might mean I got my instruction from Mr. Brontë. The seven hours a week I was supposed to have were being overlooked considering the unusual circumstances of my teacher.

He became very ill.

The worst of it was at Whitsuntide when all of Haworth witnessed his woeful state. Over the winter months the congregation, when they saw him (which was not often) they knew he was out of sorts and they also knew why. By now every household had heard that he'd asked for the hand of Miss Charlotte and not only been refused by Mr. Brontë, but compelled to leave. No opinion of him was half-hearted. They either sympathised with him or misjudged him.

That Sunday after Easter Miss Charlotte had been away yet again, but she'd come home early, before her return was due. He had taken a few services, glad of the relief her absence gave him. So when she came unexpected back to church he – well, he turned the minds of everyone.

He was shaking. This was not new. His voice trembled. This also was not unknown. When it came for him to stand before the altar, his back to us all as he prepared the bread and wine, all eyes were upon him. Quietly, her head bent low, Miss Charlotte stepped out from her family's box pew. A leaden silence fell throughout the church. In line in the aisle, her bonnet shading her face, she went step by step towards the rail. She knelt down and held her small, cupped hands to her chin.

As he approached her we saw how he quaked. Before each supplicant, he spoke a few words – 'body of Christ...eat...memory...' but little more as his voice quivered. She kept her head bowed as he stood before her and she raised her hands. He stopped.

He stood not still, but on the spot before her, and continued to shake furiously. He would have fallen were it not for Mr. Redman, the parish clerk, who ran through the aisle and held him beneath both arms. A terrible silence rang through the church – you could almost hear a needle drop. Mr. Redman whispered a word or two and Mr. Nicholls nodded, stood upright and moved on. He still had the wine to administer.

The shaking went on and his voice was thin and staggered, barely heard. Somehow he managed to rest the chalice near her lips. Miss Charlotte quickly drank and lowered her face. She walked away, back to her box pew where she knelt so low as to be hid from view entirely.

That's when the echoing noises began. They came from pews in all corners of the church. Tears. Sobs. Noses blown with weeping.

Pity had won everyone's hearts.

Mr. Nicholls

*

OXENHOPE is a little way from Haworth, much the same distance as Stanbury is, making the three places three points on a triangle. When I set off there I went direct on our side of the triangle, down the wide slopes of Smith Bank and up Waterhead Lane. I missed out Haworth entirely and gave myself a fine view of the breadth of our land all the way.

Biding my time, I paused now and then and leaned on a wall to watch the new lambs. Their nimble, long legs sent them dancing across the cropped green turf of the lower hills. When a gleam left the clouded sky, lighting odd patches of ground with rays of warmth, I thought how young and hopeful the lambs were – or at least, young. It was myself that was hopeful. Just a small ray of sunlit hope I was given, but enough to pursue.

It was not hard to find where Mr. Grant lived. His house was opposite the church that could be seen from well away, at the upper end of the village. I knocked at his door expecting to be received by his maid or his wife, but he came himself.

'Yes?' was all he said.

'I should very much like to speak to you Mr. Grant, if you don't mind,' I said. It looked to me as if he did mind.

'On what account?' he said as he held the door close to him.

He had something of an upturned nose which suited his manner.

'It's about Mr. Nicholls.'

'What about him?'

'Well sir, I am that worried about him. I was wondering if you could help.'

'Robinson isn't it?'

'Yes, Mr. Grant. I'm pupil-teacher now, in Stanbury.'

'Ah, very well. You'd better come in,' he said and only then held the door open for me to enter.

He left me stood in the hallway of his house while he went down

156

a short corridor to a room from where I heard a lady's voice tinkle with surprise. Soon the lady appeared.

'How d'you do,' she said tunefully. 'You'll stay for tea?'

'My wife, Sarah-Ann,' said Mr. Grant before I could reply. 'Now, come this way.'

I was led into their neat, darkly furnished drawing-room where a helpless bird stood on a small bar suspended inside a cage. A tall, glossy plant rose from a blue and white pot by a window that looked out onto their well-tended garden and the green hillside beyond. The bird, like Mrs. Grant, chirped. She brushed the surface of a sofa and suggested I sat down. Did I take sugar in my tea?

Mr. Grant did not sit down but stood in front of the cold, unlit fireplace, his legs apart, his arms behind his back. Like this he was able to look down on me.

'Arthur – Mr. Nicholls you say...'

He had a slight lisp, so his '*th*' of Arthur sounded the same as the '*s*' in Mister and the '*s*' in Nicholls. It was not an entirely refined voice, despite the lisp, though I suspected he intended it to be. I was unable to locate the lilt of his accent that did not come from round here. In all the lessons I'd had with him at school in Haworth and the services he'd ministered in church, I had not noticed these quirks of speech – or else they had not signified before. Now I saw how they were attuned to his elegantly upholstered drawing room.

'He's leaving us, I know,' he said.

'Yes but, he is in a terrible state. I am wondering if anything can be done for him.'

'He has it in mind to go to Australia,' said Mr. Grant.

'He should not. He must not.'

'I really don't see how this can be prevented if it is his wish, nor why it should concern you. I believe you are the one who had lessons with him. He's talked of you.'

'I am, yes. I still am, until he goes. But I cannot see why he should leave at all – not really, not when he has much to do here.'

'Mmm,' he murmured slowly as he considered my complaint.

'His departure is the decision of Mr. Brontë and it's not up to me nor you nor anyone in the parish to persuade him otherwise. Our vicar is a determined and rather wilful man, I must admit, and I think we are all surprised at the outcome of this – this sorry occasion.'

'All he did was ask to marry her.'

'He is not the first to have done so,' he said. 'He won't be the last.'

'Someone else? From round here? Or is it her publisher?'

'There have been one or two gentlemen, so I believe. No, not from here.'

'Is that so? I wasn't sure...'

'It really has to be admitted, we are very, very fortunate to know her as well as we do..' Mr. Grant went on and did not continue the subject I urgently wished to pursue. I couldn't stop his flow.

'When I first came to these parts I thought it the most desolate place on earth. I can't say I have altered my opinion on the unfortunate isolation of the parish, but I am prepared to believe that God has placed me here for a purpose. All curates need to accept such a concept as part of their vocation. It struck me as a terribly primitive sort of place. Filled with the uncouth.'

My back began to go up. I felt sweat coming on. Mr. Grant turned, partially, on his heels. His shining shoes I saw were shaped square at the toes, an oddity to my eyes. Perhaps I was mistaken in coming to Oxenhope. All I wanted was to find a way for things to change. He was a strange, fashionable sort of man. Not like a curate at all.

'Ah, but there. You're from the neighbourhood of course,' he said unconvincingly apologetic. 'But you must understand that for me, after Cambridge, it is a little uncivilised. Even desperate.'

Fortunately Mrs. Grant appeared with a tray. Immediately she went out and returned with a second tray. On the first there were dainty patterned cups, saucers, matching plates and a dish of perfectly round biscuits. They were not like our usual rough flatbreads. On the second tray was a gleaming silver teapot, another large silver jug with a smaller spout and an even smaller one which I saw contained milk. In a silver dish was placed a tiny pair of silver tongs and a knife with a bone handle, both balanced on top of a small heap of irregular shaped sugar.

'There!' she sang. 'All achieved. Now – what was your name?'

'John.'

'John, I see...' she murmured as she busied herself with the porcelain, the silver and their contents.

'Mr. Brontë also went to Cambridge,' I said. 'Is it there they teach you to pick and choose who's worthy or not – or who's civilised?'

Mr. Grant coughed, brushed the surface of his trousers and sat himself in a deep armchair to one side of the fireplace.

'I'll have my tea strong, dear,' he said to his wife.

The silence between us did not last long. I had to get my thoughts turned into deeds.

'Mr. Grant. I shall put things plainly. Yes, I have spent many, many hours with Mr. Nicholls over the years he's been here. He's been my teacher and myself his pupil. But when you've been teaching and learning like that, just the two of you, it gets very close. I have seen and heard Mr. Nicholls and come to know the way he's thought about her. He is a – a contained sort of man. You must know this. You've worked with him. His feelings are not light nor easily expressed. I can't say if he's ever talked to you the way he has to me. But what is happening is unfair. You're right, it is up to Mr. Brontë to refuse or accept a man's hand for his daughter –'

'She's tremendously clever!' said Mrs. Grant. 'Is the tea hot enough?'

'Go on with what you were saying,' said Mr. Grant, who I believe flinched at the interruption At last I saw he listened to me.

'Can I think, sir, you might think the same as me?' I went on. 'I mean, if there's any way of holding him back, could we not do it? Even more difficult, can you speak to Mr. Brontë? I'm sure I can't though I have to see him at times, to discuss what I'll do at the school. I want to talk to him about her – only how could I? Could you?'

Mr. Grant moved in his chair and sipped his tea and told Mrs Grant how sweetly she had prepared it. She shook her head and her tubular curls bounced with pleasure as she, in turn, thanked him for thanking her.

'I do know what you mean,' he then said thoughtfully. 'I am sorry for him too. Miss Brontë, you understand, is one of the first people I knew when I came here. I had thought her and her sisters as – rather unfortunate. They were not particularly sociable nor commendably pleasing in their looks. As daughters of a clergyman and as possible wives they promised little. When I tried to converse with them they were – how shall I say – disdainful to say the least. Offhand is more to the point. Miss Emily at times was quite rude. I found them unapproachable. Eventually I was so very fortunate to meet Sarah-Ann, wasn't I my love?'

He held out one arm towards his wife and his demonstration sent her into a flurry of curls, hot water and an alarming shortness of breath. I saw she had spluttered on her biscuit crumbs.

'Were you thinking of asking the hand of one of the Misses Brontë yourself, Mr Grant?' I asked, this being suggested to me by the drift of his words. I knew unmarried curates were always on the lookout for wives. These, like the will of God, was part of the job.

'Tell our guest where we met,' he said as he avoided a reply. Nor did he wait for her to answer him. 'We met in Essex – the south, don't you know.'

'I don't know it, Mr. Grant. I have never been further than Morecambe and that's not south, it's west.'

'Ah well...'

'Essex is where I used to live,' said Mrs. Grant with enthusiasm. 'And I do miss it at times and yet, I am so pleased to be helping my husband here in little Oxenhope. Have you seen our church? Yes of course you must have done. How could anyone miss it, coming up the hill. This has been my husband's great achievement as well as

160

the school and indeed, our house itself. It is a remarkable thing that permission should be allowed for any growing parish to build like that. The same happened in Haworth and in Stanbury. Here also. Not that it was easy to find all the funds. But it happens everywhere now, and so especially good for these more savage parts. It may be inclement in Yorkshire, but the money is still rained down upon us! The churches go up! And ours has such a distinctive style. You have seen it haven't you?'

'I noticed its tower, yes.'

'Well, Mr. Grant has given Oxenhope a real identity. Haven't you my dear? And if you ask me – if I may venture an opinion – I think Mr. Nicholls has done the same. Where do we suppose Mr. Brontë would be without the two of them? Struggling, a poor old man.'

'My dear...' said Mr. Grant as he attempted unsuccessfully to stall her flow.

'I think it very sad that Miss Charlotte cannot be married,' she went on. 'Poor woman. She is quite a dear and I like her well. Poor, poor thing. However, even if she is a poor thing, we are very glad to be her friends. We tell everyone at home that she, such a famous name, is truly ours. Really, we are very glad. You see, we like books.'

'Have you read them all, as well as her sisters' books?' I asked.

'Well, yes – almost,' she said, putting her curls to one side. 'They are certainly distinctive. Most unusual. Mr. Grant went into quite a stir, didn't you my love, when you read – which one was it?'

'Yes, dear. But, back to Mr. Nicholls,' said Mr. Grant. 'I understand your concern, which we both share. I can see no way of changing the situation, however.'

'It would be commendable if Miss Charlotte changed it!' exclaimed Mrs. Grant.

'Her father has spoken!' replied Mr. Grant, alarmed at her outburst.

The subject was evidently one they felt strongly about without being able to agree over its possible conclusion. I hoped they were comfortable enough with my presence to see my own position - genuine concern for Mr. Nicholls. Once the business of tea-time was over, would they talk more openly and reveal their true thoughts?

'If only she, Miss Charlotte – if only she would go against his wishes,' said Mrs. Grant, as her face became quite rose-coloured.

'She could never do that. Never go against her father,' he replied. 'I think we all know he is a determined man. She could not.'

'She would not,' I said and hoped they might consider my own knowledge of the parsonage and the people who lived there. 'She loves her father. They are all each one has. Which is why it's so daft for them not to include Mr. Nicholls. And because of it, he has become so wretched.'

Cups and hot water and tea and biscuits changed places across the table. Mr. Grant, I was relieved to see, had by now become less formal, more thoughtful. Mrs. Grant tinkled teaspoons.

'Well you know what I think,?' she chimed in as she cleared the two trays before leaving the room with the first. 'I think she'll be far more wretched than him.'

Mr. Grant shook his head.

'Please, Sarah-Ann. Leave this to us. I shall try and think of something, but doubt there is much use. You see, Mr. Brontë has held such sway, such power in this wild place. He has made it his own. He is not a cruel man, I've seen that. He deeply loved his family and he has seen them all go, his wife first then his sister-in-law who replaced her, then all his children but for this one. We must try to understand his point of view. He is a fine man, despite his present fury, and I am glad to serve him. It may be an inhospitable land, but I must give its pastor his due. I should also not want to jeopardise my own position here.'

When he stood, a signal for me to go, I walked through into the dark, panelled corridor from where I heard not only the sound of china being sluiced with pouring water. Mrs. Grant was humming.

'Thank you, Mrs. Grant!' I called. 'Thank you for the tea!'

She came forward and tore off the apron she'd put on. She wiped her face and explained they had servants only on weekdays.

'I like to do some household tasks,' she announced. 'Back in Essex, at my parents' house, I was not allowed to. Mr. Grant thinks it is a fine thing for a woman to know her home in this way and – well, I rather enjoy it, though I draw the line at cleaning the grate. Thank you for your visit. I should like to talk a little more to you one day.'

'Can you walk with me now? Even a short way?'

'Yes! I can. I have finished the clearing. I will!'

She brushed back her ringlets and pointed to a door at the side of the house.

'I shan't be long, dear!' she called to Mr. Grant. 'Just a little fresh air with our guest.'

Once we had passed their church, about which she still had much to say, she slowed her pace and we walked downhill, back into the centre of the village.

'John, I'd like to have a few words of my own. Mr. Grant doesn't really listen when I begin on Miss Brontë, but you might. He says I do not know her. But I do and I meet many ladies in the neighbour-hood – well, let's say women rather than real ladies. I daresay you do not know what we – what they all say. Why should you. Some people think we gossip and that's all there is for us to do - tittle-tattle about this and that. Where I come from, Woodford you know, there's much more socialising of a different kind admittedly. But I have found that up here, the ladies are a little more mmm ... sharp, shall we say. Unafraid to speak their minds. Miss Charlotte has naturally become the subject of many conversations. It is interesting to see how they think of her. She could have been one of them you know. She could have gone to all the concerts in Keighley and the balls. Despite her frail looks, she could have been admired if only –'

'If only she'd had a mind to?'

'Not exactly. If only she'd had a little more – artfulness. I'm sure all the sisters – and even that desperate brother of theirs – I'm sure they were all very clever. But they did not know how to – how to – cajole.'

'To what?'

'Well – to flirt. You know there's nothing wrong in a little flirtation, not if it helps you find your heart's delight.'

'Is that why Mr. Branwell got his heart broke?'

'In my opinion, yes. It's known he was in love with a married woman who was always quite beyond his reach. He suffered for it and they say she was the picture of duplicity. He should have found someone more light-hearted, a young thing like himself. The girls were the same. They had aching, breaking hearts. Writing those books was a way to make them feel better. You see, the only lovers they knew were quite unreal, but – but – yearned for. They were not like living flesh and blood. Not like you John, nor like me. They were all dreamed up.'

'D'you think so, Mrs. Grant?' I asked.

'I'm sure of it. I have read those books – well almost. I rather skipped to the end of them. I find them too hard. They are full of so much passion, John, all rather terrifying and not at all real. It's this extravagant display of feeling that's caused a stir. I've never come across anyone like the people in those books. And believe me, John, I've mixed in all sorts of societies. Here I've heard much talk of them, the sisters, and I think our Mr. Nicholls has this other dilemma, besides Mr. Brontë. It's what lies in her head.'

'In Miss Charlotte's head?'

'Yes. She does not see him in the light of a suitor. He does not come up to her idea of perfection. For all I know, the same may be true of all the men who have approached her, whoever they are. Her education – perhaps her cleverness too – these prevent her from seeing their ordinary worth. It's what I think, John, quietly to myself. I have not ever spoken like this to Mr. Grant. But it is how I see the matter. Mr. Nicholls is a fine man but she cannot see him through the - the obstacle of her own ideal.'

'I – I've never thought of that.'

Mrs. Grant now paused and looked back at her house, as if it called for her return.

'You know, love does not need to be so complicated. I swear it! Mine was never so and look at me – look at us! Happy as any married people. When I think of Miss Charlotte I believe there is another man she dreams of, who probably does not exist. But because of this she is headed for the most terrible, frightful kind of fate.'

'Mrs. Grant, what are you saying? You don't think she'll end up like her brother?'

'No, no. Not that.'

'I've noticed she's not very well at present...'

'No. It's the worst thing a living grown woman should have to bear.'

'What's that?'

'Spinsterhood.'

When it came to women, I had never given much consideration to their destiny. Why should I? My only thoughts on the subject were Betty's brave acceptance of Frank's absence and Nancy's strange sadness – how it might work on her health in the months ahead. So Mrs. Grant's announcement alerted me to my state of ignorance.

'You see, John. Education is all very nice, but not if it spoils the chances of a woman being married.'

*

TIME was moving on, yet everything felt stood still. People had their thoughts, their opinions whether voiced or not. Even Martha complained the parsonage was a sorry place to be living in. Mr. Nicholls, still prisoner in his room at Sexton House, was set to leave it in May.

Come face to face with him, his weary resignation was impossible to shatter. So I wrote to him.

> *Dear Mr. Nicholls,*
> *I'm not one for writing letters, so this will likely as not be*
> *short. I've thought I shall keep this paper and the*

envelopes for writing to Australia, if you'd like. I want to
say my own kind of good wishes for your travels and your
work only they don't sound right. It's because I don't
believe you are doing the right thing. It is as much a defeat
as ever Caesar or Napoleon had before them in their
mind's eyes the night before the battle, when they were
war-worn and done for. I think it a great pity you are off
like this.

With all respect and thanks, your pupil and friend,
John Robinson

I did not expect a reply. No-one believed there could be a reverse in the sorry situation that had descended upon the parsonage. Another curate was found and Mr. Brontë, certain of the rightness of all he decided, told Martha of his pleasure at the new appointment. He must have known she'd tell all the world.

She told a few and the word did indeed get round so that folk began to anticipate their new curate, before ever Mr. Nicholls had left. But some, those more loyal, would not let him go without due thanks.

One morning when I came down for my breakfast I found Betty stood still at the table. She was watching out for me. Tipped up against my bowl was an envelope.

'I found it under the door. He must have come over ever so early,' she said.

I took it outside. Already there were carts and clogs about as people made their way on the roads each way out of Stanbury. I went in the opposite direction, to the track that led off to the moors. Some way down I opened the envelope.

Sexton House,
Haworth.

Dear John,
How considerate of you to write to me. I am not one for
letters myself.

Exile

*You know what I have been through in these last months.
I am sorry if, lately, my circumstances have not allowed
me to teach you as was fit – and as you deserve – but I
shall not leave Haworth with too heavy a heart when I
know there are at least some who will have a fond memory
of my many years here. You are one of these.*

*I understand there is to be a farewell gathering for me
at the school here, kindly organised by the parish, this
coming Saturday evening. I very much hope you will be
there.*

Yours affectionately,
A. B. Nicholls

*

EVER so many people were in that room well big enough to take
them. The tall pointed windows on one side were decked with
garlands. I'd only ever known the space filled with children. This
very fact shocked me as I walked in, because I was no longer one of
them. Nor entirely adult. So it was not easy to know where to put
myself among the guests. I looked from face to face and how unset-
tling it was to recognise some, and others I'd seen elsewhere, not in
the schoolroom at all – Mr. Greenwood the stationer who'd provided
us with all those papers and quills – Miss Sugden our occasional
teacher (soon compelled to leave since she'd become engaged) – the
man who signed out books at the Mechanics whose name escaped
me – the curates and yes, Mrs. Grant surrounded by ladies I did not
know. I looked out for Mr. Nicholls but could not see him at once. I
then made something of an effort to see where Miss Charlotte and
her father were placed in all the hubbub of chatter and noise and folk
standing with punch-filled glasses held in gloved hands. Bare shoulders of the ladies. Buttoned up collars and ties. Everyone talking at
once. Sipping the glass edges. Too much laughter.

I walked about between people, to look as if I had some purpose
though it was daft to think that way since I too had been invited –

just as much as all of them. My sisters had seen to me being smart. They'd washed my head and scrubbed my fingernails out in the yard. Nancy had managed to raise a fit of giggles when I had my hair smarmed down. Despite their efforts, I was not exactly comfortable. I went over to the table where drinks were served and before even asking for it was handed a glass of lemonade. If only I'd find Martha, I might talk a bit, I thought. I searched for her. Her father I saw with another man the same height as him so they looked like twins though their faces were as different as a bull's to a rabbit's. I began to tire then luckily saw Mrs. Grant who waved for me to join her.

'John, dear – how nice that you've come. Of course it's awfully sad, but such a lovely gathering! Absolutely everyone is here!'

I had no time to speak before she drew my elbow and me with it to her side and I rather wondered if she was truly glad to see me. The lady she'd been talking to wore an air of great disdain and she looked at me down a nose that seemed to lengthen.

'This is Mrs. Merrall. You know who I mean by that, don't you John?'

'I do. The big mills. My sisters work at Bridgehouse. They start at six in the morning.'

'Now John, don't –' said Mrs. Grant, suddenly flurried.

'Well I'm pleased to meet you,' said the lady and she held out her hand to me which I thought very good of her.

Mrs. Merrall seemed nice enough, considering. Her being stood next to Mrs. Grant showed up the difference between them. The sound of their voices it was – one's chirruping and the other's ponderous. It was also the way they looked as they spoke. When she was amused Mrs. Grant shook her head a great deal and this set off the hanging curls until they bounced. She nodded and they bobbed. Whereas Mrs. Merrall had her hair scraped flat about her ears. More serious, respectable.

It was Mrs. Merrall's husband people did not care for so much – at least that's what I'd heard from Nancy. The mill, owned by Mr. Edwin Merrall and his brothers, was where so many like Betty and

Nancy and countless others worked all hours. And hated it. So they hated him. Without so much as knowing what he was like. At home Betty did not speak out so much as Nancy who would sometimes stamp her feet and cry out at all mill-owners' names. I asked her once, I said: 'How do you think Mr. Merrall would feel at that?' to which she said he was rich and didn't have to sweat each day like her. I said it was not through sitting on their backsides that the Merralls had got to build new weaving sheds.

'And when they're in the counting house, they're not just counting money but thinking how the money can best be used. All for the sake of industry and employment,' I said, which was what I'd heard by those who liked the Merralls.

Nancy said I knew nothing about hard work.

Since I had come to know Mr. Nicholls, though some had been against him (who'd probably never spoken to him either), I was able to have a fairer view of him. So I learned to keep my tongue to myself when Merralls were talked of.

Mrs. Merrall nudged Mrs. Grant and pointed to the far end of the room. There Mr. Michael Merrall stood up at the school desk and the room went a bit quiet and people turned to watch him. That's when my eyes began to search about the place.

Mr. Brontë was not there. Miss Charlotte I might have missed but when the guests all turned one way I saw she'd been at the far end of the room, surrounded by a circle of people. They briefly broke away from her, and I saw how she shrank from the sudden exposure. She was wearing her spectacles though no books were about for her to read or write. She shuffled along by the wall until I could see her no more. As if she hid. So I turned like everyone else. I saw Mr. Nicholls stood at the front of the gathering, his head down, his hands held tight in front of him.

'Ladies and gentlemen...' said Mr. Merrall, calling for quiet. He cleared his throat. 'We have had living amongst us these past eight years, Mr. Nicholls here...'

A man hurried to the front of the crowd, nearer the speaker. He rustled the pages of his notebook on which he wrote with furious speed.

'You know why we have come together this evening...' went on Mr. Merrall and I saw how all eyes were not so much upon him as on Mr. Nicholls himself who still kept his head down.

'...during which time his zeal and energy on behalf of the church and schools, as well as his kind and judicious conduct to all who have known him, have won him the respect and esteem of the parishioners. So it is with extreme regret that we must now part company with him...'

After he'd talked a while he turned to face Mr. Nicholls and took from his waistcoat a small but long, dark box which he handed to him then shook his hand. By this time Mr. Nicholls had looked up and managed to raise a smile. I thought to myself, thank goodness for that, for I felt sure he'd be inclined to shed tears.

I had little chance to talk to him. Everyone else did the talking as they shook his hands and he shook theirs and many words of thanks were exchanged. The room got stifling hot and I searched to see where Miss Charlotte had got herself to, but she had gone. Just as I too thought to leave, what with the heat and the social chatter-ising not suited to me, he was up at my side.

'John –'

'Mr. Nicholls. Have you to show me what you've got there?' I said, not knowing what else to say.

Despite all the years of our talking.

It was a fine gold watch with an inscription: '*Presented to the Rev. A.B. Nicholls, B.A. by the teachers, scholars and congregation of St. Michael's, Haworth. May 25th 1853.*'

'Very nice,' I said.

'John, I – I have so much to say to you...'

A great cuffed hand was placed on his shoulder and he was taken away to say things to those gentlemen who stood by Mr. Merrall, most of whom I did not recognise from these parts. I watched to see the introductions as Mr. Nicholls was herded into their fold. Soon more people stood round him and as I made my way towards the door, about to step into Church Lane, I was comforted with a thought. I would find the time to come over alone, the next evening. I might even go back up in the tower and farewell him in my own unspoken way, one last time, from there.

*

'HE's not in. He's gone to deliver the school deeds to Mr. Brontë and to say goodbye. He'll be off away early in the morning, before we're all awake.'

'But – how long will he be?' I said, my head nodded towards the parsonage.

'As long as it takes,' said Martha. 'If you ask me, John Robinson, that shall not be long. Mr. Brontë has come over ill. Miss Charlotte has set us up to clean the whole house which is why you've found me here, come back to fetch more soap as has run out up there.'

'Cleaning? At this hour of a Sunday?'

'Yes. Cleaning. Now let me get on with it.'

They were cleaning him out of their life.

I returned to my old haunt.

The door to the tower still opened. The gallery steps had not changed. I even fancied the cobwebs might have hung there for years and had witnessed all my comings and goings, blowing in cold draughts as I scrambled past. My heart began to pound behind my buttoned breast and I felt the old excitement, as though a nest of new-lain eggs awaited me. That, or the lamplight on a table where three girls walked slowly, arm in arm.

In his study, Mr. Brontë was not wearing his usual dark clothes though his neck was still swathed white. He had on him a long dressing gown and he stood by his chair and seemed ready to go upstairs to bed. Mr. Nicholls was stood next to him. It looked as though the time between them was bound to pass quickly. Mr. Brontë nodded as he received the papers from Mr. Nicholls' hands. These he put on his table, almost dismissively. Wanting him to go.

Mr. Brontë remained stood up and held on to the chair. Mr. Nicholls left his study slowly, hesitant as he stepped into the hallway. He then disappeared from my sight. I saw no more of him and knew he must have hovered there, unable to leave that house.

It was a while later the front door opened and he came down the few steps into the parsonage garden. He hardly walked at all. His tall figure was solid and straight in the dusk, but his head hung low. My heart lunged. He looked back – at the single lamplit window upstairs. He slowly walked towards the gateway that led to Church Lane. That's where he stopped and fell against the post, head buried against the raised arms that held him fixed to the stone. Hidden behind the old, damp stones of the church tower, I was able to hear him sob aloud.

I might have gone to him, but the door of the parsonage opened. Miss Charlotte stood on the top step. Quickly she followed where Mr. Nicholls had gone until she reached him at the wall. She touched his shoulder.

I don't believe they had many words, but there were some, talked while she held both his hands. She then ran away from him, back inside the parsonage.

*

AFTER he was gone my heart fell into a deep vale. There it was flung about.

I woke in the mornings and I heard the chatterings of my sisters and the groans of my father, but when once I might have been keen to join them and hop noisily down the stairs, glad to smell the hot brew we were about to share – my heart banged.

I studied hard for Stanbury school, working on my own with no instruction which was not how things should have been, officially. Because of the lack of teachers, I was told to go ahead and help with the little ones. I managed, though every new subject I gave them was an old one born of him. I would see him deep in thought, staring at our books yet lost away there, somewhere in the Aegean. The memory tugged at my heart.

At times I met Joseph, now so grown yet still the lad of our wanderings. He asked whatever had happened to Mr. Nicholls. Where was he now? I couldn't say. Because whenever I thought of him, my heart got filled with sorrow.

Night was not an easy time for me. I was kept awake by my thoughts and imagined – such fantasies – what country he might have reached.

My mind's eye saw him on the boat that Miss Charlotte and Miss Emily had taken over to the coast of the continent. Was the sea rough? Did its creatures leap out above the waves? Once on dry land, what language did the people speak in places beyond Brussels? In Italy, would he get by with Latin? Might he not visit ancient Rome on the way, or Sparta and where exactly was Troy? And how far into the east would he go? Did he follow not the footsteps but the galloping dust of Genghis Khan and his armies? No, China didn't really come into it. Such hazardous adventures were surely not part of a missionary's vocation. And yet ... perhaps such was the nature of the test, the trials of an Irish curate who had already endured personal misfortune. Maybe God had decided he was the perfect man for the job and should stomach with it the trials of the holy journey. I tossed about in my bed and eventually fell clumsily into sleep once I realised he was likely to go not by land, but by sea. All the seas of half the world. Far, far away...

Haworth was to be avoided. Mercifully our small school was only a short walk from our front door. I was determined to make fine work of it since it was his idea in the first place, his building, his great contribution to our village. As his teacher there, though only a young one and still a pupil not properly qualified, I determined I would make it my life to teach well. Stanbury was to be mine and the mile that separated Stanbury from Sexton House, the parsonage and the tower, I tried to think of as an arduous, obstacle-laid track. I left Father and my sisters to attend church in Haworth while I remained behind. The school as a Sunday chapel-of-ease would keep me a safe distance away.

No Brontë came here. No-one to bother the likes of me. I was glad of everything Mr. Nicholls had brought to Stanbury and became more attached to my own home ground.

Here I might find some kind of healing in his absence.

I never guessed that already, it was near.

Return

✳

AS you get older your thoughts stretch, they become complicated. More 'convoluted' I should say they are. Your brain takes its time to work things out, but you get there in the end. It is perhaps to do with learning. The things that you learned give rise to more thought. As a boy, I saw things simple. Before my lessons.

After Mr. Nicholls left, when all went strange at the parsonage, I wanted to separate myself from reminders of recent months. Unexpectedly Martha took the trouble to come over to Stanbury to visit me. She said it was to walk on a fine day, though I don't believe she had done much walking before. Mostly talking. Betty greeted her warmly and declared she was welcome whenever she chose, which was good of her. I was glad to see my sisters pay her some attention though I always feared Nancy might be rather offhand to her, what with Martha having such a rarified job, compared to her own work.

After she'd been with us for about half an hour she said she'd wanted to see me since I was such a part of 'those old days' and no longer a frequent visitor to Haworth. That's when I knew she had news to deliver.

Within days of Mr. Nicholls' departure Miss Charlotte took to her bed.

'Nearly two weeks she was there with the influenza. Terrible it was. She was all hot and damp and her poor eyes so red,' said Martha. 'When I went in to her she was just lying there, staring out the window, terribly weak. Once she was up, she started talking about going away. Only Mr. Brontë was then taken terribly bad.'

'We saw he was not at church. We were told he was unwell,' said Betty.

'Well there's some as is not surprised,' said Martha. 'Some call it apoplexy. When I think of all that happened and the state he got himself into, it's as much as I can do not to speak out against him. But he has suffered, mostly from fear. It's his eyes again. They were always bad, but this was worse. Mr. Brontë went blind.'

'Blind?' asked Nancy. 'Do you go blind with the influenza?'

'No because he didn't have that, did he? She did. I just said, with him it was the apoplexy. Folks have all said so. Anyway, I'm that glad he has some sight come back,' Martha added, not wanting to deliver too distorted a picture of Mr. Brontë's stroke. 'Miss Charlotte is still weak and yet I know, once she's recovered, she'll not be as she used to be. Just like everything else. Changed.'

'How odd that this should happen to him now...,' said Betty thoughtfully.

'Well, that is what I say to myself,' said Martha with some eager-ness and she sat bolt upright, prompted by the remark to make a full outpouring of her thoughts. 'Look what happened when the bog on Crow Hill burst. My mam told me, she said Mr. Brontë let fire in the pulpit and read the most awful parts of the Bible and said it was – what was it now – yes, a warning. That we should pay attention to our sins. All the peat flying on the moor and the mud sliding in the valleys so the mills stopped and the thunder in the sky – it was all God's judgement.'

'I should not agree with that,' said Betty calmly, 'but if Mr. Brontë heated himself up over Mr. Nicholls, there's no knowing if his upset mind caused this attack. Bodies are like that. Fits of temper make souls ill.'

'Oh they do, they do,' Martha nodded in agreement. 'I've seen plenty of it. And it's just as well Miss Charlotte goes away when she can. She doesn't write any more. Restless she is and not herself at all.'

That morning Betty had been over at Willie Forton's end of the house to make bread, oatcakes and much more that was now on the table. Willie walked in and delivered from his hands the largest loaf you could imagine and when Martha set her eyes on it – and him – I was certain she'd prolong her visit into several hours, a meal with the warm bread included. His recent courtship of the widow, Mrs. Toase, was on several people's tongues in Stanbury, but not yet in Haworth. If Martha did not know who he was, this fact alone would be reason enough for her to stay.

'Shall you like to see our school?' I asked Martha, thinking it best to take her away from the sure-as-sure gossip our house might unexpectedly provide for her. 'If you've not been over these parts, you'll not know it. It's only very small, but greatly thought of by Mr. Nicholls. He saw to its being built.'

'Thank you, John,' said Martha only rising from her chair once Willie had left. 'It's very kind. I should indeed like to see what Mr. Nicholls did over here.'

Martha, by this time, had become much more lenient on the subject of Mr. Nicholls. Whatever she witnessed in the parsonage had brought her round to almost appreciate him. That I had taken so many lessons from him, over the years, now put me in a special place in her judgement. As a much younger lad, she'd given me such cheek. Was she now trying to make amends? Or did she really care to see his achievement in the schools, since Mr. Nicholls was now gone for ever?

We walked up the short, straight path to the porch doorway where she paused.

'John, I've said some bad things about folk,' she said.

I didn't like to ask what things nor which folk.

'If you'd try and understand, when he first came we were not at all likened towards him. It was the same with so many curates,' she went on. 'How were we to know the way they'd turn out? There was that nice Mr. Weightman who never lodged with us though we always wished he had. He died of the cholera which he caught off visiting the sick and all those who had it. You should have seen Mr. Brontë with him – he loved Mr. Weightman like a son. There was always laughter in the house when he was near and Mr. Branwell and he, they were such good friends. You see, Mr. Nicholls was so difficult – so –'

'Solid,' I said, catching the drift of her conversation. 'I'm sure you'll find other curates will meet with your approval, Martha.'

'That's just what I'm fearful of – finding no more as good as Mr. Nicholls. When we went about clearing his room, there was something about its emptiness that was – well, sad. Even the holes he'd bored in the door. They seem quite harmless now, especially as it's warm and having the air come through them is sensible. Don't you think?'

'Yes, Martha,' I said. 'I'm afraid the school is locked. Shall you come another time when the children are here?'

I had never seen Martha like this, with words that were neither chatter nor disdain but honest and her own, thought out for herself. Still I hoped to curb the way she talked. I did not want to hear how Mr. Nicholls' room now looked. When she told me his replacement, with the peculiar name of Mr. de Renzy, was a plain-speaking but haughty kind of man, I had to insist she was quiet.

'I'm sorry, Martha. You must know that seeing Mr. Nicholls leave the way he did has touched a lot of people, me in particular. My only concern now is to try to work as he'd have wanted of me.'

She nodded and to find Martha in a state of understanding and agreement with me was a welcome change. Before she left to go back to Haworth I walked with her round our little building, and pointed out to her its stones, its tall windows, the bell and the cross. As we came into Stanbury's back lane, I saw ahead of me Mrs. Parker.

I waved to her and beckoned and Martha, suddenly reluctant to leave, asked: 'So who's she?'.

*

OUR paths were the same paths. Stanbury, from the Taylors' farmstead, past the Wesleyan chapel, the inns, the Quaker burial ground and all the homes that faced each other across the street out to the old turnpike, was some 600 yards in length. All features of the village were tight and close, perched up on that ridge. Behind the street, on the back lane, stood Mr. Sunderland's school and the Pollards' house and barn. Every person living here knew of the others. Yet I had not seen Mrs. Parker nor Hannah for months.

'Hello, John. I hear you're with us over here now.'

'I am that, Mrs. Parker. And may I say it is good to meet up again.'

'Hannah would love to see you. We've been away with her mother and I've come back on my own, but she will be returning soon.'

'May I ask where she's been?'

'Oh, to more and more of those places' she said half-heartedly as if they were of no interest to her. 'All over. If it's not for her legs it's for her education.'

'So she is at school.'

'No no, John. Not what you would call school. What her mother likes to call education is more like a waste of time as far as I can see.'

'Then, what is she to do once she's back?'

'I must decide. I can teach her needlework well enough though what she's supposed to do with it apart from hem sheets and darn stockings I hardly know. I should like to teach her some real dress-making, but Mrs. Pollard likes to choose her clothes herself. As it is, she's become very anxious about Hannah.'

'We don't see much of Hannah's mother.'

'No. And you're unlikely to.'

'If she's away, will she not miss her when Hannah returns?'

'I suppose all the travelling gives them each other's company well enough, for a while. Hannah is not a child. She does not need the kind of attention children need. Nor is she yet an adult. This time is crucial for her. That's why Mrs. Pollard is making enquiries.'

'Enquiries.'

'Yes, John. Schools if you like, but for learning the social graces.'

'And what are them, Mrs. Parker, that you can't learn at home amongst your own?'

'What indeed, John. In fact I dread to think. But have no fear, I shall let you know when Hannah's back and you can maybe cheer her.'

That's when the seed of an idea fell into some corner of my brain as if it had been up on the wind, flying around, waiting for the right time to take root.

'Mrs. Parker. What would you think if I were to give Hannah some lessons?'

'You?'

'Yes, me. You know I'm a pupil-teacher at the school, mostly for the younger ones, but I have it in mind to give them more than just arithmetic and written words. I thought, as time goes on, I could teach them about all the countries of the world. Where they are, who lives there and what is done in those places. Do you think Hannah would like that?'

We were still stood in the back lane. Not seconds passed as she gave my thoughts her own.

'Hannah would be overjoyed, John. I know she would.'

The land across the Worth was given a sudden sweep of colour as overhead clouds dispersed. I saw it as I had not seen it before and instantly I felt I was in a new place, not the old home. The trees up over towards Oldfield, the other side of the valley, appeared deep blue and the fields between them and myself were striped with furrows of shade followed by creeping gleams of brilliant sunshine.

'But when and how could I reward you?' Mrs. Parker asked.

'I could not do it until the summer unless it were a Saturday afternoon. As for reward – it would be enough reward for me to teach her.'

The following days, until Hannah's return, I could not separate my plans for her from those I gave the schoolchildren. Hers came first. She moved into my mind through all hours of the day and even unconsciously I thought of her. When I woke, before I heard familiar morning sounds, I realised, with a start, that I felt happy. The promise of her imminent return sustained me at all times.

My sisters saw me in good sorts though I was not inattentive to their own moods. Nancy was still a bother, as discontent at work as ever, so Betty and I, on our walks, tried to think how we could please her. She brought us great unease. Worse than ever before. Food disgusted her and no cajoling with delicacies would make Nancy eat.

Father seemed to bang nails more loud than ever – or maybe that's how it seemed when we sat silent in the kitchen, trying to pass the time with brotherly and sisterly talk. We feared for Nancy's health and if we suggested a visit from the doctor, she scoffed at us, and told us to leave her alone. Father agreed with her that doctors were all charlatans.

It was Willie Forton who came up with some fine amusement that brought smiles to Nancy's face so's we knew she was not in danger. His courtship of Mrs. Toase had been called off since she felt she'd rather keep her dead husband in her dreams than a live body in her bed.

'Told me straight, she did,' said Willie who was also keen on tobacco and whose speech was often interspersed with noisy coughs. He'd bang his chest and we'd hear his phlegm rise before he spat it into his handkerchief. He gasped for breath and laughed. 'So talking of bodies, and not minding my own business since you're talking of the subject, don't forget that time of the cholera when up Smith Bank walked a man no-one had ever set eyes on before...'

'Ah yes, that doctor,' said Father.

'The doctor that stayed with us for months and cured us all that were ill and then went away and no-one had even asked him his name.'

'So they're not all charlatans?' asked Betty.

'No. Any more than widows are all nuns. And with that I shall leave you and wish you all goodnight.'

*

EARLY days of the month of June must be the finest of the year, when nights don't come down until late and you hear birds make their final songs while clouds darken ever so slowly. I sometimes sat out, to watch the sky change. On clear nights, if I looked over towards the west, the wide space above me slowly filled with the colours of sunset fire. As these drifted, before the night was black, a pale speck appeared in the wide blue expanse. It grew bold, bright, like a beacon hanging in heaven – the first evening star. Nervous bats flew about, as if in a panic to make the most of the dying day. When the moon was big and round I liked to consider it. I knew poets made verses about its pale light.

I am not a poet, but I know a thing of beauty when I see it. I did then. If I walked out in daytime, I'd linger to find the wide fields to the north of us were home to a fresh burgeoning of life. Hawthorn hedges were laden with white boughs, as if clouds had stopped here overnight, instead of moving on. Buttercups sprang up across the meadows accompanied by tall, waving daisies. The sweet smell of honeysuckle drifted over walls where I passed, while near my feet tiny white flowers of strawberry plants announced the presence of deep red drops of hidden fruit. That butterfly, the hairstreak, it paused, shimmered together its green wings, then flew off as if it were one of the faerie folk who had stayed behind in the becks and not been banished by mill smoke. Billowing above patches of dried, scrub earth the wild rose briar bloomed.

I could not sleep easily. My head was too warm with the season, too busy with thoughts. Father went up before me and was already flat out like a dead weight once I joined him in our room. I did not draw the thin curtain we had hanging there. The window looked out southwards, on to the bank and the moors, and if I watched that way when the moon shone bright, I'd see a white glow spread about the hills that made the world more of a mystery than a homeland.

I lay in my bed, sheets adrift, wondering what I would do.

＊

I KNOCKED on their door.

'John, how good of you to come. Do you not have school?'

'Yes, soon, but you see Mrs. Parker, I've been thinking things. You know I said I'd be glad to teach Hannah when she returns and you talked of how to repay me. Well, there is a way – indirect it is, but of great value to me.'

'Come in – don't stand there. Have you not time to discuss it?'

'No. Would you and Hannah think it over – I mean – ask her mam if you need and then let me know.'

'What is it you suggest?'

'I was thinking perhaps if I gave Hannah an hour or so, maybe of history or nature studies – or something different – I could manage that well enough. Well if I did and she did, would it be in order for you to share the needlework you do – with my sister Nancy? She's in ever such need of doing things she likes and I know she already sews well.'

Mrs. Parker did not appear to disapprove as I'd feared. Rather, she beamed a broad smile.

'I certainly would not mind. And Mrs. Pollard, who is now somewhere in Italy – well, she'd hardly mind either, would she? But first I'll talk to Hannah. You shall have a reply once she's back, John.'

＊

SCHOOL was over for the summer and many of the children left the schoolroom for the fields, to help with more physical work on the farms. Their shorter limbs than men were fit enough and their energy you'd think was fuelled by sunlight. In ways I was glad they'd gone since I needed more time to make plans. My serious school instruction was to happen in the autumn with a new term and new school year and most likely the new curate.

During the summer I would write. I liked to write on subjects that interested me. I liked the feel of the pen as it scratched on paper. All this I thought as I was collecting up my belongings, my writing book and my pens, about to see the schoolroom clear and closed. That's when I knew I was not alone. She stood in the porch, both arms out against the door frame, the sun behind her.

'John! You are to teach me! This is such lovely news!'

At the time I should never have guessed that Hannah would stay like that for ever, rooted in my memory, stood in the doorway of Stanbury school.

*

SHE came over to where I stood helpless, almost speechless. She hunched up her shoulders and laughed and I feel sure would have reached her arms round me had I not got a pile of books at my chest.

'What shall we do first? Will you tell me about the kings and queens of England? I do so want to know about them and yes – about far far away places like Japan where I've never been. Mrs. Parker said you'd thought of that – history and all sorts and that your sister could join us when we sew and stitch and we shall get to know each other. How old is she?'

'Our Nancy?' I croaked. 'She's older than us. Nineteen.'

'Well I'm sure that won't matter a jot. It will be nice for me to have a friend. Oh John, you can't imagine how tiresome it is to travel, to be quite restless, going here and going there. I know you liked it when we went to Morecambe that time, but I have had enough of smoke and steam for a while. It is so wonderful to be here, in one place. What books are those?'

I put them down on the nearest desk.

She skimmed through the books' pages.

'Hannah,' I said, watching her. 'It is really very good to see you.'

*

FIRST thing of a summer's morning you might find mists as grey as winter's own. Damp and thick and leaving moisted drops on gates and window sills, the air has a strange, hovering feel to it. As if it hopes to tease. For it is not winter. Knowing this, all you can do is wait for the slow disappearance of the vapour. It will pass. It will rise above the earth. Brilliant sunlight and warmth will come in its place.

I headed off to Haworth while the mist still hung about me. Good spirits accompanied my brisk pace, as if I resisted the moving air. I whistled. When I felt a damp heat rise round my neck, I flung off my cap that Betty had insisted I should wear. Above the beck, over the rise of the moor, I watched low-hanging clouds spread flatways as they began to disperse. Glimmering light appeared on the horizon about to send the greyness away. All very slowly.

But my thoughts, like my steps, were quick and happy.

I had it in mind to ask Mr. Brontë if I could borrow the globe. Without mentioning Mr. Nicholls' name, I could say that I knew it was now in our school in Stanbury and I had a particular need for it over the summer months. There was no point in making a pretence of anything and I could even say that Hannah was to be my pupil. After all, the Pollard name was well respected. He could not refuse. He'd even be impressed.

By the time I was in Church Lane, broad patches of blue had appeared in the sky. These made me still more hopeful.

Martha, I could tell, was keen to know why I was there, so as I stood on the parsonage doorstep I steered the prospect of possible chatter by asking after Miss Charlotte.

'She is not yet recovered. She was to have a friend – a writer – to stay, a Mrs. Gaskell, but that's all been put off. I should have liked to see another lady like her. I was going to put her up in their Aunt's old room. But it seems I'll have to wait.'

'How different might you have treated this lady writer?'

'Oh with the best of care and attention of course. She has published much, Miss Charlotte told me, and is even planning to write a book about the north country so she'd be bound to want to visit. Not that this is the reason. It's because Miss Charlotte is now so famous and they have lots to talk about. But it wasn't Miss Charlotte you wanted, was it?'

'No. I have work to discuss with her father,' I said with a deliberate air of importance.

Once Mr. Brontë had agreed to see me, Martha lingered, then took me slowly to his study door. I daresay when the door was shut, she remained there to hear how I was greeted.

'Ah, John. The very person I was wanting to see,' he said not rising. 'Sit down, sit down here,' he went on and pointed to the chair. I now took this to be his audience seat. Curate, bishop, daughter, parishioner, schoolboy – we all sat there as his honoured visitors.

'Well, I was wanting to see you, Mr. Brontë,' I said.

'You know I've not been too well and it is my eyes that have greatly suffered. They were always troublesome, but I have been particularly burdened of late. Still, the sight is back and I can only be grateful and yes, I do see you well enough. Now, John, about the instruction you are to have when you teach next year. We have a new curate...'

The movement in my stomach was not uncomfortable, more like a sudden spell of indigestion. I kept my hands beneath his table desk so he did not see how they shook.

'...although he is a fortunate replacement, I do not feel Mr. de Renzy will meet our needs. So I have it in mind that Mr. Grant should give you the required hours of tuition. He has the perfect educational background, which is demanded by the examiners in the system. It does mean, of course, that you would have to go to Oxenhope for your lessons rather than come to Haworth. I must say, your turning up like this is a fine stroke of luck. I am not easily able to visit Stanbury, unless it were by one of the carriers. I don't have your nimble young legs. So tell me, John, how you feel on the matter. Shall you like Mr. Grant to teach you?'

The picture above the mantelpiece still hung where I'd seen it before. This time I saw it in a changed light. With colour. No longer a black and white print. Swirls of cloud in that terrible sky were now blue-black as night. Lightning flashed bright yellow and the fiery red and orange rays of a hidden sun were harsh and frightening. No wonder the seething mass of fleeing folk were running here and there in fear.

'Come now, this is a fine solution,' said Mr. Brontë, his voice all eager. 'Do you not have a voice, John?'

'I do, that, Mr. Brontë,' I said. 'But my voice has to speak words and I do not know which ones to use for the present.'

'What's this?' he said.

His eyes went small.

How I should have liked to say that I required only one teacher and that he had been cruelly misjudged which made him up and go off to Australia. And all of it was the fault of him, a frail, old man who still had some sight in his eyes to see, but who possessed no vision.

'I should like to consider things awhile,' I stated.

'Consider? Young lad, this is a gift being offered you. There's no-one else in the whole of this neighbourhood deemed fit for such an opportunity. You are. So what do you mean, John Robinson, by 'considering' it?' came Mr. Brontë's angry reply.

I would not let him fright me.

'Well, if you like, for want of a different word or two, I should be glad to think about it all,' I said, as if at ease.

In truth, I had begun to wring my hands beneath the table and pierced their palms with my nails.

How was I to ask for a loan of the globe now? If he were not so aged I believe he may have stood and wrapped me with his stick. Instead I saw his little mouth move about his gums. The eyes, behind his round glasses, sparked. Then he coughed and patted his chest with his trembling, gnarled fingers.

'Well now,' he sighed. 'You're a bright lad it must be said. Don't suppose I do not understand your position and those thoughts that cannot easily be voiced between us. I do know a thing or two. By the time you reach my age and have witnessed ... but there. I expect you have some reservations about Mr. Grant,' he said before he turned his round, white head towards me. 'We all do.'

The eyes shot amused, sparking arrows. He was smiling.

'You do?'

'Yes, John. My daughter, she has even written about him. She gave him a different name of course. She saw him and many of our curates as ridiculous. As the incumbent here, I cannot pass any comment, but as the father of a fine writer I can only congratulate her, for turning those she has known in real life into a life of fiction. Such is her perception of character. If you should care to see what she wrote, you need only look at her book, the second one she wrote –'

'*Shirley.*'

'Ah, you have already read it?'

'No. But I know about it. I know what she said about curates.'

He leaned back in his chair and stared out of the window, towards the tower. I could have asked for the globe then, but was not sure of myself or of him. I just watched him, hoping the right moment would present itself. He went very quiet and seemed to shed something of his age as his face softened, the lines melting into thin flesh. He was lost in thought and seemed not to notice that I was still there, watching him.

A shaft of summer sunlight fell across the polished surface of the table desk in front of him, as if to waken him.

'Now, John - what was it you wanted to see me about?'

'Well, Mr. Brontë, it is about something in our school room. I know it is there – or rather – I know it was left behind, to go there. You see, although I am not instructed yet for proper teaching, I have it in mind to take on a pupil in the summer and to teach a bit of all I know. As I was thinking of tracing the journey of Mr. – the travels of – of Christopher Columbus – I thought it an idea to use the globe. You must know it. The globe that – that –'

'I know the one, John. Tell me, who is your pupil?'

I hardly dared say.

'She's from along our way, in Stanbury's back lane.'

'A girl?'

'Yes, Mr. Brontë. She's Hannah Pollard.'

'Ah the Pollards...' he said as if the name sent him back into a new reverie.

'You know them?'

'It is my duty to try to know everyone, though of course true knowledge of people varies upon circumstance. The Pollards were greatly thought of well over a century ago. Richard Pollard had land in Bradford that was left to his nephew on the understanding that its annual income should be distributed to the less fortunate of both Haworth and Stanbury. It was a fine gesture and still the monies continue to be shared between the two villages.'

'Then – do you know the present family?' I asked.

'I am unsure how they are related. I know that Mrs. Pollard travels widely and has business abroad.'

'I know her too,' I said.

'And there is a woman there...'

'Mrs. Parker!'

'Yes, Parker. I believe her husband was related to the tenor we had, who sang here in Haworth, at the Black Bull. My son did a portrait of him once, holding an instrument. I think it was a viola of sorts. Viola... or maybe something else...'

He went off into a place where his thoughts stretched about him, to lead him, I suspected, into memories of the past and of Mr.

Branwell. Despite all I had thought of Mr. Brontë in recent months, I did not like to see an old man drift like that, only to be saddened by his memories.

'If you please, is it possible for me to borrow the globe? Only when I need...' I asked quickly.

'The globe? Ah yes, the globe. Now then, let me think. You would have to consult it on the premises. I could not let you take it away from the school, much as I would like to. I imagine you have little room at home to do your lessons. Is that so?'

'I could do them at her house, but I should like to stay put. There's our kitchen table. That's all really. And Betty's always using it and Willie Forton slumps over it at times and we eat there though Nancy's lately not joined us so often.'

'Your sisters... how many of you are there?'

'Just father, the two girls and myself now. All the others died.'

'Mmm. They do...'

I had to stop him going off again. All I had recently learned from Martha about his treatment of Mr. Nicholls had formed in me an opinion that Mr. Brontë was a right brute. If this were true, I saw his brutish ways were now less harsh. But why had they happened at all? Was this the outcome of a passionate temperament? Was it to do with his Irish birth? Did this explain his loathing of another Irishman? Would he treat the new curate the same? The passion... was this why his daughters wrote books considered to be dangerous? If so, was being passionate that much of a sin after all? Was it but one way of living a life? It had brought Miss Charlotte and her sisters fine recognition.

I stared at him and I knew his weak eyes did not see how I stared. Of a sudden I felt overwhelmed by him and them and their separateness from me. All I'd wanted had come in the form of my master, who they had sent away.

'Mr. Brontë, please – if you don't mind,' I said, as I stirred myself from my wandered thoughts. 'What are we to do about the globe?'

'The globe... You shall have your own key to Stanbury school.

Return

I'll have a duplicate made at our ironmongers at once. That way you can go in and out as you please. You'll find there not only the globe, but you can use the books. And there will be space, plenty of space in which to teach the young girl. I shall trust you, John. And I'm glad you want to do this. Yes, have a key. That would be for the best. Education is a subject close to my heart, you know...'

*

MR. Nicholls' school was mine.

I went in there late one evening, when the warmth of the day began to die and you could breathe fresh air again. The schoolroom smelled of flies and paper. The tall window panes, smirched by rainfall stains, were hung with fine, dusty webs. Desks stood like soldiers, waiting for action. I stared at the great space.

Mine for teaching. Mine for Hannah.

I walked round and touched the table-tops with my fingers. I peered into the cabinet of books and saw some already known to me. Over the months I'd not thought to consult them. Like the globe, they'd been left behind by Mr. Nicholls. Together we had read them in his room, over at Haworth. Would they be read again? Would Hannah enjoy them?

At nights I lay awake, not tired. How busy my brain was as I thought of all we should do. I felt Father might hear my thoughts, so loud they clanged in my head but he slept soundly, his breathing like short gurgling gusts that marked the passing of the hours as regular as a clock.

Daytime found me outside where I walked with a light step, looked out over familiar land, found it brilliant, rich, strong. Mine. The dark moors seemed warm, without menace. Where the green vales turned into blue distant hills, I felt sure these led to promise and hope.

The day of our first lesson arrived. I washed all over and hoped the soap's smell still lingered on my skin. Betty brewed us all coffee for a change and gave me an extra inch in my bowl.

'So what will you teach her to start with?' she asked.

'Geography. I'm going to set the globe between us and show her where Australia is and where Great Britain is and ask her to find two ways there – one by land and one by sea. Each time we touch a country, we'll write down its name.'

'What a lad you are!' said Father suddenly as he supped from his bowl. 'What's made you think of that?'

'I thought of it while travelling round your snores!'

'Get on! I don't snore.'

'You do and all,' said Nancy. 'I hear you through the wall.'

'I do not. And if I did, it's no hardship to any of you. Is it John? You're nearest.'

'Well, the noise is terrible...' I teased.

'Now then. Just because you teach doesn't mean you need preach on folk's habits.'

'He'll not do that, Father,' said Betty. 'Come on now John, tell us more what you'll tell Hannah.'

'The list of countries will be enough for today. Later on we'll go through each one. She does a bit of travelling, as does her mother. So I thought it would suit her.'

'Shall you tell her I've bought my own needles?' asked Nancy whose first hours with Hannah and Mrs. Parker had already given her some measure of interest.

'You could tell her yourself,' I replied. 'I believe she'd like to see more of you.'

'Then shall I come with you now?'

'No.'

'And why not, Mr. Specially Important?'

'Hush now,' said Betty. 'John's lessons are his own. You can go along to her house another time.'

I stepped out into the road, walked the short distance to the school and soon arrived at its front path where I paused. I thought how Mr. Nicholls had done the same when he watched the building's sturdy walls go up. I walked forward, paper under my arm, the key in my hand. Once inside with the globe upon the table, I waited for her.

*

BELOW her left eye were seventeen freckles. They were not of the same size. Nor were they evenly placed. Their shape was of tiny floating islands on the sea of her skin. Their shade of pale brown varied in intensity. They lay at random, going down to the slight curve of her cheekbone where they dispersed. A few had escaped to follow the rise of her nose. The right side of her face had fewer, in a similar alignment, which resembled the others. In all, during the lesson's hour, I counted about twenty-eight freckles.

*

OUR postman's name was William. His pony and trap I watched as it came across the valley, up wide Smith Bank. I fixed my eyes on it. Even before it reached our ridge, I knew there'd be something in it for me. So few people received letters up there, they had to be important.

Mr. Brontë had said he'd find out more about the future term, what Mr. Grant felt about his tuition and what I was to be paid, once I had passed inspection. Since he was unsteady travelling any distance, even the mile to Stanbury, it was possible he had sent his news by Royal Mail. I remained stood outside to watch the trap reach the top of the hill and turn into our main street. It passed me by, but I followed it. At the Taylors' gate it turned into the farmyard and stopped at our house.

Only Father was at home and he did not hear the knock at the door. I went up to the driver.

'For Robinsons?' I asked.

'Aye. For you, John.'

'I thank you for it.'

Once I saw Mr. Nicholls' familiar hand-writing upon its surface, the broad, pale envelope became as precious as ancient papyrus. The stamp was a regular Penny Red with a portrait of our Queen in profile upon it. I knew there was a British colony called Victoria out there, created only in recent years. Among the kangaroos and Aboriginal Australians, at least he'd been able to find paper and pens. Luckily for me.

> *5th July, 1853*
> *The Vicarage*
> *Oxenhope*
> *Near Keighley*
> *Yorkshire*

Dear John,

You will undoubtedly be surprised to see the above address heading this letter. I have not sent it to Mr. Grant for posting. The address is written because I am staying at it, briefly.

I found it quite impossible to leave Yorkshire. I therefore rendered my withdrawal from the Missionary Society application, and explained it was due to some concern over the rheumatism I suffer. This is only fractionally true. I suffered far more in considering the great distance such work would create between Miss Charlotte and myself. I feel you will understand this.

I have found a new curacy in a village called Kirk Smeaton which is near Pontefract, some thirty-five miles from Halifax as the crow flies. So this is none too far from my old home which can be reached within a day, on sound, main roads. I have done it! I returned so close to Haworth, only to end the journey at this vicarage and be welcomed by Mr. and Mrs. Grant.

I have written to Miss Charlotte to tell her of my changed situation, and although she has not replied, I intend to continue to write to her. I am hopeful that at some stage she will turn her thoughts towards one who

has been steadfast in his affection for her, and whose
feelings remains unchanged.

Mr. Grant has told me much of your news, but I should
like to hear it from yourself. If you are able to walk over
here, I know he and his wife would welcome you. I should
be more than delighted to see you.

I remain, your friend and teacher,

A.B. Nicholls

*

NO runner at ancient Olympia was as swift as I was that day. Apollo himself might have competed with me, still I'd have won. Out of Stanbury, down Smith Bank to the long road leading to Oxenhope I flew and anyone seeing me stopped in their tracks to watch my race. I like to think even the sheep bleated some astonishment.

My heart pounded till I felt it was fit to burst. My forehead dripped with water, my hair was soaked wet. The road narrowed as I entered the village. My pace lessened once up near the church, just in case he was there, but such was my gathered speed I was carried on without a real pause. I arrived at the vicarage door and hammered on it with my fists, and bent myself double to find my breath.

'Goodness, John, what's all this?' said Mrs. Grant.

'Huh – sorry – huh. Heard he was huh – here.'

'You mean Mr. Nicholls? Yes, he and Mr. Grant have gone visiting. I doubt they'll be too long. We are expecting Mr. Sowden to join us, for luncheon. Fellow curates have much to discuss and fortunately are quite close friends. You look terrible.'

'Huh – yes I'm sure. Might I have a little water?'

'Come in, John, do. Go through to the parlour.'

Though I did not meet Mr. Nicholls at once, the joy I felt on seeing his dog was no disappointment. She wagged and bounced, she whimpered and jumped up on my thighs. I knelt to stroke her ragged ears and soon got my normal breath back.

'Yes, it's quite a nice dog,' said Mrs. Grant. 'I am glad it is not here all the time as its tail threatens my porcelain. I have to keep a constant eye upon it.'

'They did not take her with them when they went out?'

'No. They have gone to see an elderly lady who has rather an alarming number of cats that as far as Mr. Grant can tell are the cause of her illness. She coughs and she spits all the time which makes things very uncomfortable. My husband was glad of Mr. Nicholls' company for the ordeal. Not pleasant.'

She had forgotten about my water. I stared down the corridor that led to the kitchen and hoped she'd take the hint.

'About Mr. Nicholls. It's all very intriguing,' said Mrs. Grant as she settled herself into the chair by the empty fireplace. 'We had this letter from him asking if he could come and stay and although I don't mind since it's nice for my husband to have a man to talk to, it does mean I have quite a bit of extra work.'

'Do you not like guests staying?'

'It's not a question of my liking them or not. I don't like the work entailed by all the laundry. We have servants during the weekdays, but I'd sooner they cleaned and cooked and prepared food so I'm not troubled with too many meals, especially in anticipation of Sundays when people tend to come in after church. The changing of linen seems such a nonsense when one has to wash everything after only a few nights. That's how long he's here.'

'I should ask Mr. Nicholls about laundering. It's one of his favorite subjects.'

'Really?' said Mrs. Grant, her eyebrows raised. 'How fascinating. You'd never think so.'

'Oh he's a man of many secrets,' I said.

'Yes, I suppose he is. Since he left, there's been nothing but talk. My lady friends are divided about him, which puts me in a bit of a spot. Some say he is an obtuse and obstinate man who should have known better. Others say he was only being human and really rather touching.'

'And what do you think, Mrs. Grant?'

'I don't know what I think.'

'I remember when we had a chat about him ourselves, you felt Miss Charlotte rather at fault.'

'Fault? I don't know whose fault is what. I don't really know anything. I'm quite confused about it all. I mean, there he was, banished, replaced by Mr. de Renzy – who incidentally I find quite frightful – about to go off to a new life in Australia where he could have done so much good amongst the heathen. As for Miss Brontë, he might have forgotten her. Now he's back.'

'He couldn't forget her.'

'So it seems. What he'll do about her I don't know. His new curacy will keep him busy enough. But you see John...'

She leaned forward, her elbows on her knees, and began to whisper though as far as I could tell, no-one but ourselves was in the house.

'...I think all this feeling is a bad thing.'

'You do.'

'I do. I think one should not question things quite so much, or get oneself upset. For all we know, in staying here, so near her, he may come out worse than before.'

'He couldn't do that. Not worse than being rejected and sent away.'

'He may be rejected again, if he starts to try his luck again.'

'How can he help but try. He's in love.'

'In love?'

'Yes, Mrs. Grant. I believe love spurs you on to do great things.'

'Do you think so?'

'And isn't it what God wants us to do? Love everyone, our neighbours as ourselves?'

'Well, yes... God asks us to love one another, yes, but to be 'in love'- I don't think it's quite the same thing. It's all so troublesome.'

I was sorely tempted to ask if she had ever been in love, but thought it better to request a glass of water once more. As she stood to leave the room, she looked round briskly towards the window.

'Here they are! He'll be pleased to see you, John. He has asked so much about you and you'll see, he does need cheering up. Stay here – I'll fetch lemonade. I made it myself and I can assure you it is sweet as sweet can be!'

Though rested, I felt my heart pick up a racing pace again. I heard his voice, muffled by the walls, but unmistakably his very own Irish. I hoped Mrs. Grant would say nothing about my presence, to surprise him. Fortunately Mr. Grant went through to the kitchen to see what she was up to. So Mr. Nicholls entered the parlour alone.

He bent down to ruffle his dog's fur and did not see me straight away. But once he was stood tall, he lurched forward, his arms outstretched.

'John! John!'

'Mr. Nicholls, sir.'

'John, this is wonderful!'

*

WITH some reservations (more pieces of crockery to wash), Mrs. Grant had suggested I too should stay to eat since I was going to be a pupil in their house, but Mr. Grant soon explained that he and Mr. Sowden would be talking church matters with Mr. Nicholls – from which I was excluded.

I left to go back to Stanbury with the intention of a visit to Joseph Craven before the afternoon began. But as I took to the road I met Mr. Sowden who I knew was a good friend of Mr. Nicholls. During those unhappy months he had been of great assistance, being of the same age and profession as him. They both loved walking. They would meet and talk on the open roads and moors, where no-one would see or hear them, which was of some comfort for my teacher - in ways that I as his much younger pupil could not achieve. Mr. Sowden was a cheerful sort and had the distinction of never having made an appearance in *Shirley*, under Miss Charlotte's critical eye and pen. I nodded to him.

'Oh hallo there!' he said warmly. 'I believe I saw you come from the vicarage?'

'Yes, Mr. Sowden, you did.'

'I know your face – I'm sorry not to know your name – I've seen you and your family in church.'

'Robinson. My name is John.'

He stopped and clapped his hands together.

'Ah how good it is to meet you. I have heard so much about you and about your lessons together. I'm speaking of Mr. Nicholls of course. He is there is he not? And what a turn around! How brave he is, do you not think? To return – to turn the other cheek!'

'Is that what you think he's done?'

'Possibly. There's no knowing if he will be hit once more! Though surely she will have seen the light. Surely she will follow her own judgement this time. Excuse me,' he said, looking at his watch. 'I should love to speak more to you – you were a blessing to him, I can assure you. I understand you were not only his pupil, but Miss Charlotte's also. I really cannot say I know her at all, but I myself can hardly wait to hear his plan, if indeed there is one. Do you know what he intends? He cannot play hide-and-seek. But he is to be commended! I am thrilled. How very pleasant to meet you John Robinson!'

He held out one hand for me to shake. With the other he tossed back his fair brown hair. This sudden appearance of Mr. Sowden, who almost leaped with joyful enthusiasm in the sun-filled lane, to me was like the sighting of a nimble moorland hare. So unlike Mr. Grant...

*

TROUT are a very handsome type of fish. It's no wonder that they hide away in streams and rivers, under rocks or among pebbles. They don't want the likes of us to catch them.

When we were young at school, when Mr. Nicholls first came

to teach us, he would take us children off to tickle trout and it was a wonderful thing, to know that beneath the sometime cruel landscape of our home, the water that ran in our valleys contained such vigorous life. He had a favourite spot, down on the river not far from Griffe Mill, a short but steep descent from the school. With breath held we'd watch the water and not speak unless it were to cry out that we'd seen them, the trout. The shallow pools were of a crystal clearness where we also saw, mirrored, our own shadowy forms like dark intruders upon their watery world.

'We could always go back there, John,' Mr. Nicholls had said and it was agreed we should spend the whole afternoon together once the Grants' lunch with Mr. Sowden had finished. 'Let's meet in Stanbury.'

I waited for him. I knew at first I would see him as a small speck on the distant road. How hard it would be for him to continue forward up the wide expanse of Smith Bank rather than take the road that led to Haworth. Was he making a terrible mistake in returning to the place from where he had been so cruelly exiled? What was the nature of the hope in his heart? I had to find out.

Despite the warmth of the season, he walked fast, his arms almost flailing as he strode ahead, his dog at his side – I recognised them at once. When at last he was at the edge of the village the arms waved. I was about to lead him from the gate towards the school porch, but he refused.

'No, John. I do not belong here.'

'It's your school, your church. You saw to its building. What's more, I have a key – it's my very own,' I said, smiling triumphantly.

Only minutes earlier I'd thought to fetch the key from home. I brandished it before his eyes.

'See! We can go in.'

'It was built for others, not me, John. It is not my school. Thank you for the thought which I appreciate, but please understand I would rather not enter unless it was with a purpose relevant to its use,' he said in a tone so serious, I felt we should not venture into the village at all, but take to the fields at once. 'You can tell me how you managed to obtain this key – on our way to the stream. Come, let's go down there...'

I wanted to tell him. Everything.

That Miss Charlotte was ill and Martha had been run off her feet.

As far as I could tell, Mr. de Renzy was not well liked.

Had he heard of the Pollard family?

Mr. Brontë had gone blind for a while.

I'd sat in the chair in his study, the very same one where he'd always sat.

Our Nancy had taken up embroidering.

The book called *Villette* was now placed in Haworth Mechanics Library.

Willie Forton was resigned to be single.

What exactly was 'apoplexy'?

Joseph Craven's voice was gone funny.

As ever, Merralls and mills were talked about all over.

Father had thought of playing an instrument.

Mr. Grant was to be my teacher.

I had the key so I could teach Hannah.

Hannah...

I said nothing.

We made our way down to the river.

Trout will stay still as they hover against the flow of the water, faced upstream, yet moving. The great joy of tickling them is after you've found them, the ones that hide under boulders or the overhanging verges of the riverbank. You have to not mind getting wet, half way up your shins or more, depending on the water's depth. You crouch, but you don't kneel. You have to keep your balance. You can lie flat on the ground, your head over the bank, close to the surface of the water. Either way, you put both hands under the rock and carefully feel about there. Keep arms about a foot wide. Fingers going, moving. The idea is to wriggle your fingers about, underneath the fish, until you feel it's belly which you tickle, ever so gently.

'Have you found one, John?' asked Mr. Nicholls.

'I have that. It must have gone into a kind of swoon. It's letting me tickle away and I do believe it likes it...'

'Good. I'll try for another after you.'

We didn't say much, not while we watched out for the trout. I felt he was generally loosened, even though his mouth said nothing. He sat on the bank and eventually lay down, his face in full sunlight, one arm on his brow. I'd not seen him like that, but as my fingers busied themselves in the cool water, I thought how peaceful he looked. Untroubled.

I could not tell if thoughts played about in his mind or if he had given himself up to the peace of the moment. Where else could he be so entirely calm? No-one was near to disturb us. The sun was not harshly bright, though from minute to minute was shielded by white, foaming clouds that passed at a steady pace and changed the patterns of the sky. It was very warm, almost hot. The only sounds were the hushed lapping of water, the drone of bees, a wood-pigeon cooing its steady refrain accompanied by incessant whirrings of the nearby mill.

I stood up and held the trout in my hands. I saw its moving gills and its round startled eyes as it gasped for breath. The fine marks of its sleek, wet body gleamed in sunshine. In order to stop its tortuous wriggling I had to hold it with some pressure. I threw it back in the water.

Mr. Nicholls was asleep. I watched him. In case he ever went away again, I tried to remember how he looked.

*

'SO another key was made for me, which was a good idea when you think of it. What I do is move the table out from the wall and we work there. There's room on it for the globe and my books and hers and I can see how she writes. The desks would not have served my purpose, them being too small and each one quite hefty and stood facing where the teacher – that'll be me after the summer – where the teacher stands. So best not to disturb them and besides, my teaching Hannah is not the same as the regular class. We manage well in our own way. She did say she would like to go to Siam as it's such a funny shape...'

'That would be difficult.'

'No more than going to Australia. I've not found it easy to describe those countries and since we've finished making our lists, it might be time to move onto architecture.'

Hannah's lessons were not going as well as I'd hoped. What I dreamed I'd achieve, as I lay in the dark at night-time to look blindly up at the beams, was less possible to realise once she and I were in the school room. I explained to Mr. Nicholls that because of this I even doubted I'd do better in the autumn with a full class, following Mr. Grant's tuition.

'The two situations are not comparable, John,' he said. 'In a class room you have a sea of faces and yet you know that mass is made up of individuals. The teaching you offer is in the hope that most of them will listen and understand. With a single pupil you are bound to pay attention to that person's individual ways and adapt accordingly. I know this. I did so with you.'

'You did? How do you mean?'

'I detected what interested you most. I gave you more of the aqueducts, the roads, the amphitheatres and less of the wars. I needed to keep up your interest so that you did not become bored. Sometimes I changed my preparation entirely – all the work I had done the night before!'

'You never did!'

'Oh I did, John. But I was pleased with your interest and it meant that I was also encouraged not to become complacent. Find out what Hannah likes best and work with this.'

Much as I knew him and was glad to hear his welcome returned voice, I could not find the way to describe to him what Hannah's lessons had become to me. The worst of it was my growing lack of confidence. This had come about through Hannah herself. Not that she did anything amiss. She was the same as she had ever been. I believe it was myself who was not the same.

All the preparation I did for her was well done, but was almost made useless once I was sat close next to her. She brushed back her mop of hair and stared at the books as if hungry for their nourishment. When we travelled to South America you'd think she'd been part of the Beagle's crew. She took hold of my hand that was lain on the table and wrung it with her excitement. A sudden rush of warmth, like if you stand near the stove when you're cold, ran through my body and I felt I should faint.

Should I describe and explain all this to Mr. Nicholls?

'Architecture might take her fancy,' I said.

'Perhaps.'

'I thought of going through the whole history – from the Egyptians to the Wesleyans…'

I walked part of the way back with him, intending to go down only to the beck. We were nearly there and still I found the more we talked, the more there was I wanted to say to him. He slowed his pace, perhaps to accompany his tired dog who sat in the shade of a tree with legs sprawled. Her pink tongue fell over the teeth on one side of her open mouth.

Mr. Nicholls paused. 'Shall you show her the buildings we have nearby? The nearest pyramid I fear is in Rome, but in Keighley we have the work of Mr. Pugin…'

The brilliance of my idea dimmed.

I stroked the dog who continued to pant noisily and was not about to move.

'Hannah does not do so well if it's far,' I said. 'She could never walk to Keighley. There's something wrong.'

'Ah…I'm sorry.'

I saw the coolness of the grass verge, so sat down next to the dog and stroked the fur on her heaving body. Mr. Nicholls sat next to me. The shade of the trees created a welcome shelter.

'For all I know it might be nothing, just some kind of limp that thousands of folk have,' I said. 'But she's been taken all over, abroad and here and there and looked at by doctors and pulled and shoved and touched. It makes no sense to me. I don't see that it matters much. Not when you see her. Not when you know her...'

In this way I must have gabbled on to Mr. Nicholls, not really telling him of my innermost feelings but nearly. He listened, or rather he did not lie down and sleep. Leaned forward, his arms on his knees, he heard all I had to say about Hannah's absent mother ('how could she leave her daughter for so long?') and about the motherly Mrs. Parker whose cousin or so in-law was the popular singer known in Haworth, that Mr. Brontë had told me about.

I then realised I had mentioned that name. One I'd meant to avoid.

'It's all right, John. You can talk about him. I bear him no ill-will at all. I only hope the day will come when I may see him as a friend. Funnily enough, there were always subjects we agreed upon, where there was no hint of conflict. One was that very Tom Parker, your friend's relative. We did not believe he should perform his songs in the church.'

'No more does our Nancy.'

'There are plenty of souls of the same opinion. Strange... Mr. Brontë and I were once so much in agreement.'

'Well – have you been over there? Have you see him again? Have you seen her?'

His face crumpled into creases.

'No...no I have not.'

'Is it that you dare not, sir?'

'I do dare. But am fearful that this daring is inopportune. Miss Charlotte has not replied to my letters at all. I am glad of friends like you, and indeed Mr. Grant and especially Mr Sowden...'

'He's a good one. What did he say?'

'He – he feels I should hold fire. He said if I advance too much, she may retreat. I have to give her the chance. Let her be the one to move forward a little...'

The talk of retreat and advance made me think of them as toy soldiers on a battlefield. Was this how love was played out? As a calculated campaign? For a while we said little as I contemplated the idea that here we were brought together again, only the lesson's subject was changed.

His forehead was drizzled with warm beads and he frowned and I thought how there was little I could do to help him now, especially if he took the advice of men his own age. Speechless we sat on that bank and the valley stretched out calm and sunlit before us, with no answers to offer from its quiet beauty.

'But about Hannah,' he said as he picked himself up. 'Why don't you suggest something in the musical line since through Mrs. Parker's cousin there is a connection?'

'Music?'

'Yes. Concerts are held in Haworth, in some of the different meeting halls. Tom Parker was encouraged not to sing in our church, but such performances have their place in Haworth's small social sphere. Mrs. Parker will know of them. In fact, I would think Hannah already has attended some of these.'

'Do you think so? I don't believe they go about the place.'

'Music is a fine entertainment,' he went on, encouraged by his idea. 'You should hear Mrs. Grant on the subject! I have heard her say that the little concerts are 'the light of civilisation'. Ah dear – Mrs. Grant. How glad I am of their civility. How kind they have been to me...'

Music.

Here was something I knew nothing of. Not a note. If I took to whistling at times, it was my own sort of invented tune. I had seen manuscript books of music in the library and wondered at the railway lines upon them and the dots and hooks like tiny tadpoles that were understood by some, but mystified me.

Music.

'You must ask Hannah what interests her.'

'Yes, but music?'

'Ask, John. Don't be fearful.'

'If it's music she likes, I shall be more than fearful. I shall be vanquished.'

We remained seated for a while on the bank beneath the tree. When the dog was recovered from the heat, she rose and barked to continue the walk.

'You're very fond of Hannah, aren't you John?'

'Oh I am, Mr. Nicholls. I really, really am.'

'Well, if ever you should like to discuss how you feel, you know I would listen. If a time comes when I return to the Grants more frequently, we can meet again there and talk. Otherwise write to me. If you need. If I can unburden you.'

*

AT times I could not remember her face. I closed my eyes to try and conjure up its features. These I recalled, each one individually. Her nose with the small channel beneath it above her petal mouth. The dark brows that almost met. Her full cheeks and round chin. But I could not put them together. I saw her haze of wiry, fair hair but the face that it framed moved about so much as I tried to make it still, to bring it back into view. It almost became smudged. Then I'd have a flash and see her laughing, hear her laugh – and the face would return. But I was driven into the very pother of a state whenever I forced myself to think of her. Not apoplexy, but certainly a state of agitation. Yet I was not too anxious, because I knew that a day would come, soon, when I'd see her again in the flesh. Still I was restless and my fingers and my stomach I found to be full of nerves.

*

SINCE it was summer, I had more time on my hands and would dust around Father when he let me and I'd sharpen and polish his tools in our back yard. Betty left me instructions for peeling and pie-shaping though on some mornings I'd accompany my sisters out of the village to their work. The mills over Haworth way – Ebor, Lees, Mytholme and Bridgehouse – each had a group of buildings round them that employed families and provided them not only with the work, for money, but also many struggles. At least that's how many saw it. With no canal, no railway nearer than Keighley and roads none too substantial and more like tracks, we had not been early leaders in the field of wool weaving. The Merrall brothers changed all that. Now, it was thought, the manufacture of cloth had taken the life out of the workers only to put money into the millowners' pockets. For many, there was no choice in work but to contribute to the success of the worsted industry in our area, despite personal hardship. Engine houses, warehouses, combing mills and weaving sheds had marked the landscape for years. Great chimneys rose like pinnacles into the sky. Over at Ebor's a line of workers' cottages followed the lower slopes of a hill down to the great pond that powered the mill's looms. It was here I paused, on a morning wander, about to retrace my steps again when, instead of turning home I thought to explore a little. I would first circle the pond then take the steep route back to Haworth.

That's when I saw our Nancy again. I was surprised as I'd said my goodbyes to both girls some distance away once they entered the gateway to Bridgehouse.

She was hurrying. She ran along the bridge and over to its corner arch that led to the wheel pit. From one of the cottages came a figure. He walked towards her. They greeted each other close and stood to talk a while before she raced back to the door where countless more people approached. I knew it was her. I'd not mistake my sisters. The other figure I did not know. He returned to the cottage. But she stayed to talk to the growing numbers of workers as they arrived at the start of their day.

Was I to mention it? Did she have a young man who she did not want us to know about? If I did, if she did, there'd be more than her sullen looks and sharp words at home. Should I tell Betty, the way we often talked about Nancy – out of concern for her? Or did Betty know what was up? Father would be best kept in ignorance. Ignorant of what, I repeatedly asked myself. She had met someone to talk to before beginning her work. Nothing wrong with that. But I felt it rather amiss.

I decided it was best to put what I'd seen out of sight and mind. When it was time for them to leave the mill, of an evening, I went back again, to wait and greet my sisters cheerfully and return together to Stanbury. Nancy came out of the door at Bridgehouse first and stood with me on the bridge and seemed to have no intention of doing anything but wait with me for Betty. So we walked back.

At the meal I began what I considered to be a wise plot – to ask Nancy about her sewing and with one throw, kill two birds. Find out more about Hannah.

'Well are you for making some real clothes yet, our Nancy?' I said.

'One day perhaps. For the moment Mrs. Parker is teaching me embroidery as well as how to cut cloth and hem lengths and do different stitches. There are all sorts of ways to sew. I'd never have known it,' she replied, surprisingly talkative.

'I'm glad of it,' I said.

'Why should you be?' came the more familiar harsh ring to her voice. 'It's not you doing it. You're all set to teach, to earn a fine wage.'

'Salary.'

'Get off with your teacher's airs, John.'

'Well, it's good enough if you're learning what you want and Hannah is learning what she wants and I'm teaching what I want. We should all be happy and not pulling faces about things. It's a good thing to like your work, I say. And you know it. The idea was to keep you from the mill one day, when you can make clothes and never go back. Shall you not like that?'

Nancy was silenced.

'Tell us, Nancy, what you're doing next with Mrs. Parker and Hannah,' said Betty, to stall the imminent quarrel.

I returned to eat my meal.

'Hannah is for making a bonnet which is far too difficult for both of us,' she said at last, quietly. 'Mrs. Parker said it will be possible only if she can find the right support and the right bits to go round. I'm none too interested in bonnets, not having much use for them.'

'Well if you go courting a young man one day, you will,' I said boldly.

'Will I heckers like!' she hissed.

'Now then, now then,' Father chimed in. 'We'll have no squabbles at table.'

'John's got his brain inside out,' Nancy went on. 'It's all that geography has done it. Doesn't know which side of the planet he's on.'

'I do that. I know more than you, Nancy Robinson,' I retaliated. 'What's more, I'm giving geography to Hannah because she loves it, which is just as well. It's all so's you can sew.'

'It's not all so's I can sew. It's so's you can see her!'

'It never is!'

'It is! It is! I just know. She almost says so!'

Deep red went my face. My heart began to beat loud in my ears.

'She does not,' I said meekly.

'Well she does and all,' Nancy went on. 'We're sat there being instructed, her and Mrs. Parker and me, and we talk about things. She asks about the looms, as does Mrs. Parker and though I don't like to talk on them, I tell them, I do. But it's when she asks about you – oh then I've things to say.'

'What things?'

'Never you mind your clever head.'

'What does she ask then?'

'There you are – you want to know!'

'What does she say? Tell us.'

'Well she says she likes the lessons with you, and that you're – what is it now – 'such a sweet thing, such a dear' – that's what she says. You'd almost think she was fond, you would.'

My heart's blood must have surged about in great quantities as I felt my neck warm up and I'd have hid beneath the table so no-one would see me, had it not been for Betty.

'Leave off him, Nancy. And do as he says – remember the lessons he teaches Hannah are in exchange for your sewing with Mrs. Parker. It's very generous of him and if he stopped, then where would you be? Stuck at Bridgehouse for ever more like.'

'That's what you think,' said Nancy.

'It is. Having work at all is a blessing round here. Only I don't moan over it.'

'Moaning is not a bad thing. Specially if it makes things change.'

'Well it's John is changing things for you, so stop now, Nancy.'

As ever, Betty's clout seemed to work. She had a way of settling things and she ladled more supper onto Nancy's plate as if to show she was not as annoyed as she sounded. Just wise. The heat went from my veins though my heart still bumped. It fired a thought into my head that was not kind.

'At least I don't see Hannah in secret,' I announced as I stood to leave the table.

I walked out into the cool evening.

*

WHEN the fields were harvested, I liked to watch. Many of the children I knew from school helped out with the work. I wondered which ones should have liked to stay there once the corn had been reaped, gathered and stored. Which ones looked forward to a return to the classroom. The fields were bright yellow. When I walked by the walls that enclosed them, I'd pick up stray stalks and think to make something of them. I chewed some as I went. Some I looked at closely. The small wheat grains were tightly knitted together – woven into strong, plaited ears. A fine structure. A thoughtful invention of God's.

Perhaps I should use a stalk of wheat to introduce Hannah to the idea of how vaults and spires were built. Would she like that? Or, before the cold weather set in, we could draw the body of a wall, the courses of its stones, the capping. But I had to be sure these thoughts would meet with her agreement.

That's how my thoughts were going. Spires and beams and all over the place.

There'd not be many lessons left. I was to bring them to a halt once the new school term began and I had my tuition with Mr. Grant. With only hours remaining for me to be with her, I had to be sure she would wish to see me again, even if it weren't to do with teaching. If it were just to be together. Somehow.

She was waiting in the school porch and waved as I walked down the path. So full of fears was my head, I hardly noticed that I had left the key at home.

'John! I have good news. We are to make another trip, Mrs. Parker and myself. I thought you might like to come. We are going to Manchester, on the train from Hebden Bridge. I'm not sure how long it will take but imagine if Mrs. Parker again had an amusing passenger sitting next to her! John, will you come?'

'Why are you going?' I asked.

'For the amusement of it. There are several tunnels on the journey and when we arrive, there's a library, John, that anyone can visit. It's only recently been opened. You'd like that wouldn't you?'

'You're going for the amusement? Not to see a doctor.'

'Goodness, no. I've had enough of them. There's nothing wrong with me! There's everything right! What shall we do today? Shall we think about Manchester? You like buildings and things, shall we look at our books and the encyclopaedia in the cupboard? Shall we find out all about it?'

'…find out all about it?'

'When are you planning to go to Manchester?' I asked.

'In September – or October – I'm not sure, but Mrs. Parker said it will be during the week when the library is open and we could look at the books together. That's why I thought of you, John!'

'Excuse me for a moment, Hannah. I have to go back home for a second.'

'I'll come with you. Is Nancy there?'

'No, she's gone out.'

'And your other sister, Betty. Is she there? Your father?'

'I have to fetch the key, that's all. Then we can work.'

'Of course. I only wanted to talk. I'd like to get to know them, that's why. Here I am in Stanbury again and I hardly know anyone who lives here at all!'

'We're supposed to have our lesson...'

'I know, John. I was only asking. I shall stay here and not move.'

On my way home thoughts surged through my mind. Weekdays in the autumn, with the new term, I would be more than usually busy. What excuses could I make? I'd possibly have a whole class to myself. What would Mr. Grant think if I requested a day away? Not much of me. And then Mr. Nicholls might get to hear, that I'd shaken my responsibility, that I'd preferred to be with Hannah and go to Manchester. But he would understand. Because if I didn't, she might find someone else to go with her. Who? Who round these parts? A young fellow like me? She might meet one on the train. She might refuse to have lessons at Christmas, being so taken with her admirer. And he – he might be older than her, and educated, wealthy, with a fine income. Marriageable.

I was almost ill with thoughts. I had to smile and cheer myself up. To not let her see. Get back to her, with the key. Teach her well. Keep her near.

'You know what I think we should do today, Hannah,' I said as I turned the key inside the door. 'I thought you could tell me what you'd like to study best. Where your interests lie most. Apart from railway journeying...'

We settled into our places at the table. Her hair was like a golden orb, not far from my left ear. My hands shook so I put them under the table where she could not see them. She was looking at me, wasn't she. I could tell she was smiling. I should talk. Sound strong.

'I thought you said you found trains and travelling tiresome. You'd done so much abroad,' I said and hoped to get Manchester out of her thoughts.

'Oh yes I did. I did once I came home. But that was after doing months of it, from guest-house to hotel and boarding place and all the stations were so noisy and filled with people. A single day with you and Mrs. Parker is a completely different prospect! You would teach me things. My mother thinks that visiting museums, which tire me, and seeing monuments and statues that are made of stone and don't even speak, I learn that way. But I learn far more with you!'

She did it again. She got hold of my hand, the way she always did, only this time she held on to it, as if it were a treasure, never to be lost. It made me feel quite unsteady and my eyes glazed a second.

'Hannah,' I said, recovered and all serious. 'Hannah, I have to start at school – here. I have to be here more than ever I was before. I have to teach the others...'

She let go of my hand and I almost drew hers back.

'I see,' she said.

'It's a terrible responsibility. It means I have to stop – with you.'

'What about Nancy? Shall she stop her needlework if you no longer teach me?'

'Nancy...'

'Yes. Mrs. Parker and I like having her. Her fingers are a bit clumsy which I suppose is to do with the looms, but we like to hear her tales. She says so much. I should not be pleased if she no longer came to us.'

'What tales?'

'About the mill. The unrest. About the people there.'

'What people?'

'John – are we going to do some work today? I should really like to.'

I was making a right fool of myself, the last thing I had intended. It was time to pull myself into the kind of person I hoped she thought me to be.

214

'Right now, let's have a think about things Hannah. What have we done over the summer? We've travelled to Australia, looked at the route, thought about those countries on the way. We've drawn pictures. Made lists. You've told me a little French and I've told you some Latin which I don't think you'll need so much...'

The golden mass of her hair now bounced as she laughed. I hadn't wanted to be humorous. I wanted to keep her close to me, that's all. The only way I knew was to keep on talking. The only thing I ever did when I was nervous.

'We've not gone into that much history, and there's centuries of it still to do. The kings are one thing. There's wars, but I don't care for them. You see, Hannah, it's best for me to do what I prefer, but only if you prefer it too. I wanted to teach you about architecture - windows and gables and if we were to go down to the mills to look what's about here, there's all sorts. There's the launders that carry the water up on mill wheels, there's the span of the bridges over becks - we've no need to go into Manchester, nor Keighley, not really Hannah. So what do you say? I'll teach you still on Saturdays, after my time with Mr. Grant. I'll come straight up here. But I need to know what you should like to do best. I do, Hannah. There's no point in anything unless you really, really want to learn – so what do you want to do most?'

She sat quite still. Her face didn't move much and I thought I had probably hurled myself into a perilous pond of talk. I thought she might have taken up my hand again, the way she did, which would have sunk me. Instead she sat upright, both hands cupped together on her lap.

'I shall tell you what I want to do, John,' she said.

'Do, Hannah. Do.'

'More than anything I want to learn how to waltz.'

*

BEESWAX was high on Mrs. Grant's shopping list. Once you were in their parlour, you were almost overcome by the sweet smell of the

Grants' gleaming furniture. It tickled the throat. The straight doors of the corner cupboard, the thin framework of triangular glass pieces on the front of the china cabinet, the bowed drawers of a solid chest, the exposed planks round the floor's edges – even those square ends of Mr. Grant's shoes – all these surfaces shone and flickered with white light that passed by the windows' heavy drapes. The darkened room was enlivened by polish.

'So you see John, to study buildings is all very well, but the parts must be named appropriately.'

Mr. Grant did not sit still. He walked round the room, his nose upturned as if he searched for cobwebs on the ceiling.

'Frankly, I doubt your young children will retain the difference between the abacus and the impost of a capital…'

'What is the difference, Mr. Grant?'

'Well – it's hard to define.'

'I wish you'd try, sir.'

He moved towards the window that looked out onto high fields. He moved the curtain, slightly, as if he had spied something there worth inspecting.

'We can talk about that another day, John. I appreciate your desire to explore your own interests, but as I say, we must confine ourselves to what will be suitable for your class.'

He didn't write much himself, but he liked me to write what he spoke. Dictation, he felt, was a solid way of learning. He would sometimes dictate for my own benefit, he said, not for the children at all. I was about to be in a privileged position as a teacher, an informer, and so should learn not only facts for them but principles for myself. I soon grew to know that the words I wrote, when he walked about the room, were indeed his own dictates.

'The responsiblity of the public figure is a serious one' he said with authority. 'His or indeed her writings may reach beyond the marketplace into the homes of those who read and from there into the wider world. As the great philosopher declared "To avoid criticism say nothing, do nothing, be nothing"…'

He was telling me about Aristotle, whose ideas he claimed were exemplary, but I think he was really on about Miss Charlotte, whose portrayal of him in *Shirley* he probably still resented though he and his wife claimed she was their friend. Severe hints like that often came into his vocal perambulations round the room. Often I wanted to interrupt the dictation.

'But Mr. Grant, if people did nothing, nothing would get done.'

'Yes, John, I'm sure that's how you feel. Indeed we need men of action in our lives and especially in our times. I'm talking about fame, so often misplaced, and the weight it brings with it, no matter what its source whether of admiration or of contempt. Fame is not always merited.'

Sometimes he wiped his brow with the handkerchief he kept carefully folded in an inner pocket. I did not care to catch him out, but I came to believe that he'd probably not planned the time he spent with me and that our lessons were the result of spontaneous thought, once he had overseen Mrs. Grant's activities in the kitchen.

At times she left her weekend domestic duties and would first knock at the door then coil her head round it, hesitant, hoping not to disturb her husband in his flow. She always treated me with gentle civility and was concerned for the feeding of the five thousand or so cells I had in my brain. Her appearances were a relief to me though a source of irritation for Mr. Grant. This she must have detected for she usually at once returned behind the door, rather like a mouse that has dared to come out of its home only to discover the presence of unforeseen danger.

How different was my trek back to Stanbury from Oxenhope after my Saturday lessons there. Before, when I came from Haworth and Mr. Nicholls, I'd stared at the wide sky on my way and my feet would take flight as I thought of all he'd said. Now I looked at the ground and counted my steps as if each one had been weighted with fresh, clinging mud.

*

'HAVE you heard from Mr. Nicholls?' I asked several times over the weeks once our lessons began. I usually waited until Mrs. Grant had been released from the kitchen. She joined us in the parlour with all her dainties and tasty cakes. As she offered these, kindly, she was more free with local news than Mr. Grant, even if it weren't entirely true.

'Well he intends to come back – I daresay to force his way into the parsonage once and for all...'

'Please, Sarah-Ann, he is hardly likely to do that,' her husband checked her.

'He's coming to stay here, with us. We said we'd always welcome him and we shall, indeed. It's only a jot more work for me, but will be worth it if he can go and demand to see Miss Charlotte. Forcibly.'

'My dear, you must not make a fantasy of plain facts,' Mr Grant continued. 'He has simply asked to stay. For all we know it might be to see some of the many people whom he left behind when he went. There are plenty who will be glad to have him visit them. Then there's Mr. Sowden, another friend. They often walked together. He might like to do so again.'

'But he is not staying with Mr. Sowden!' Mrs. Grant remarked with a raised voice. 'And the reason for that is that Mr Sowden lives in Hebden Bridge a good six miles away – which would make it from there about a seven mile trip to the parsonage and seven back again – and it's getting chill now the autumn is approaching. No, Mr. Nicholls is staying here in order to woo Miss Charlotte from the close range our home provides. Properly this time.'

'Have more tea, John,' said Mr. Grant as he took up the pot with the hint of a scowl across his face. 'I wonder, Sarah-Ann, could we have more hot water?'

*

Return

10th September, 1853
Kirk Smeaton
Near Pontefract
Yorkshire

Dear John

I think you will know that I am to return to Oxenhope. This time it will be for over a week. My living here in this pleasant village is unlike the work I did in Haworth, it being much smaller and without the threat of illness that the mills there provide. I can therefore avail myself of several days when I am not greatly required.

You would be interested in the church here which has a fine gallery but the whole is in need of repair. We have no organ, but two willing violinists provide the accompaniment to our hymns.

I should like you to know that I continued to write to Miss Charlotte five times. On receipt of the sixth letter she replied to me. I am hoping I shall be able to meet her this time.

I know I will see you. I shall ask Mr. Grant if I may take one of your lessons during the time I am there, which will give me the greatest of pleasure.

Yours very truly,
A. B. Nicholls

*

I DO not know what Mr. Grant was given in the way of a salary for teaching me. For myself, the small fee placed in my hands I did not consider was thanks to a distant council committee, nor as a personal reward. I preferred to think of it as a celestial gift.

Before the evenings became too dark Nancy was able to see well enough to work inside. She made great pieces of linen that she'd cut into shape on the kitchen table. Hour after hour there she sat, her back bent over her sewing. By the time she had stitched together a quantity of working aprons, she was all set to sell them at the draper's in Haworth.

In Father's eyes, though I was still at school, I was earning which meant all three of us had now well and truly grown. Sometimes he'd talk about our two brothers and one sister who had not lived beyond childhood. I did have some recollection of William who was of the same age as Joseph Craven. Already I had begun to play with Joseph at the time William died. He'd been a sickly child.

'He was a darling,' said Betty. 'I used to take him to fetch water at the well where he loved to let down the bucket and hear it splash. It was always too heavy for him to draw up, but he did love going there. He'd throw stones down and I told him not to. He'd want to play in the road and I had to watch him when the sheep came past. He was a lovely boy...'

When Father's eyes went damp, we changed the subject quick before he started on Mam.

'Well our John, now that you're earning some pennies, what shall you buy with them?' said Nancy who was all for telling us her own spending plans.

'I shan't buy anything yet,' I said. 'I shall keep my pennies safe and I shall see they mount up and I shall think on what to do with them later.'

'You miser!' said Nancy. 'I shall be after something in Leeds one day. We'll go together shall we Bet? Go and pretend we're real ladies like Hannah Pollard.'

'She's not a lady!' I said at once.

'She is that,' Nancy replied. 'Anyone knows it who talks to her. She doesn't talk like us. She's never worked and doesn't have to. Most girls her age have been in the mills for years.'

'Talking money is not a good thing,' said Father, when he tried to keep things peaceful before our voices rose.

'I'm not talking money now,' Nancy went on. 'I'm talking about how Hannah is different. There's no-one here like her either, except for Miss Taylor at the farm only Hannah's shy of her, she says. Anyway, I think she prefers you, John, to anyone else.'

'Get off, Nancy.'

'She does, too. She says you've set her thinking and you've been ever so kind that way. She and Mrs. Parker are going to make a dress for her – a lovely one, silk and all.'

'What the use of that round here?' I asked.

'It's not for round here. They're planning to go away and join Hannah's mother somewhere.'

*

AS she was close to Hannah during her needlework hours, Nancy learned a lot. When they sewed, the three women talked together about women's things. How was I to be a part of their world, unless it were to take up sewing myself – or dancing – which I was unlikely to do.

I needed to know more.

The extraordinary thing was, when the subject of Hannah did crop up, I was sent into a spin in my head. There was Nancy, full of knowledge. But I hated to seem forward in asking, despite her being my own family. At table I was liable to redden in the face. This happened often enough as to make me think I need not eat after all. Anything to avoid eyes on me.

At length eating did not have its usual appeal. What with that and not sleeping so well I was turning into a right scarecrow and I could not keep from having a stomach that shook. Fortunately, I found this state gave me a rare source of energy, created by nerves, and in the classroom it was turned to a lively form of instruction.

The new term got well underway. I kept the children on their toes, mentally, and dotted my questions about (not so loud as to disturb that half of the class that was writing). I had them learn a poem by playful repetition – in whispers. The little ones giggled. Those that forgot the lines had to turn round on their benches until there were only a few who faced forward. Then it was a game for them, competing, memorising, paying strict attention to what I said. I too was on my toes...

Out of school I stayed in the road, where I hoped to catch sight of Hannah. I walked up and down but did not quite dare to venture into the back lane as that would look like I sought her out. I began to bite my nails and Betty disapproved. She said she'd put dandelion milk on them while I was asleep.

What state had I come to? When I thought everything over, I knew that Hannah was my friend from years gone. But the years had seen us grown and changed. Why could I not now go and call for her, as I had done once? Mrs. Parker was not her mother, but a pleasant enough woman who always made me welcome. She would not bark me away. So why not go – up to the door – knock?

*

HE would know what to do. His advice would be worth seeking.

As I reached Oxenhope I was more than surprised to see Miss Charlotte walking towards me on the road. Within seconds I guessed she must have been there to see Mr. Nicholls who had arrived the day before. She almost strode as she walked, at a fast pace, deep in thought.

'Miss Charlotte...' I ventured to say.

She looked straight at me. Since she was not wearing her spectacles I cannot say what she did or did not see.

'It's me, John Robinson from Stanbury.'

'Ah John, how are you,' she asked in such a dull manner I almost fled.

'Me, very well thank you. But how are you? I see you have come from the village.'

'That's right, John. And you are going into it.'

'Oh I am that. I am to have my instruction there, as your father may have told you. Only –'

'Yes he did tell me.'

'My lessons are with Mr. Grant now.'

'They are. And do you feel you have made progress?'

Her face was like a bird, her nose the beak, her eyes round and lifeless but for moments when she blinked. Yet here she was, the very person who held the happiness of another in her power. There was I, reduced to polite chatter that went round in merry circles of confusion. Nearby was he. Not in Australia, but just down the road. Had she seen him?

'Well, is your tuition going well?' she asked, still with a drear voice.

'It used to. I mean with him. Not him.'

'Which him are you referring to exactly John?'

'Oh, Miss Charlotte –'

She looked so fierce I wanted to blurt out the terrible mistake she had made in refusing Mr. Nicholls and that most folk had understood it was probably not her choice but on account of her father being furious. Much much more, I wanted to tell her, about the hours I'd spent confronted by his anguish, for never had there been anyone so struck with love. It was surely a fine thing for a woman to be so loved. Did she not know?

Of course she knew. She'd written about it.

Still I had not read her books and so I could not tell exactly what she made of love. Though I had the idea she thought a lot of it, from what people said, that day she looked a stranger to affection – as if she had been into battle.

'And how do you find your teacher, John?' she asked.

'My teacher.'

'Yes, Mr. Grant. He has done well in Oxenhope.'

Oh but so did Mr. Nicholls in Haworth, I wanted to say. And he will be ever so faithful to you if you'd only let him...

'He has?' I asked feebly.

'Yes. I should say Mr. Grant quite wore out at least fourteen pairs of shoes as he went about the neighbourhood, begging for money for his church. More than that. He wrote letters with no thought of hesitation. I believe he even wrote to the Queen herself.'

She was a little more talkative. She almost smiled, but not quite. I wanted to ask her, have you seen him then, Mr. Nicholls?

'Have you seen him?'

'Yes. He was there. As was his wife.'

His wife?

'Ah – you mean Mrs. Grant?'

'Yes, John. Mr. Grant's wife is Mrs. Grant. Are you quite well?' No. No I am not. Tell me if you saw him.

'I'm ever so sorry, Miss Charlotte. I think the changed season has got to my bones. That and all the learning and teaching. I wonder that I'm not fit for it.'

'Don't say so, John. Not someone as young as you. We depend on you. Where would we be without you?' she said as she paused in the road and her voice changed, as if she were about to plead with me.

She did not seek answers, nor even a conversation. Her mood was raised from sullen and about to become angry again.

'I shall tell you where we'd be...' she said and she turned away from me and faced back down the road to Oxenhope. 'We would have the likes of only Mr. Grant. And may heaven deliver us from him and all curates.'

'Miss Charlotte – don't say that. Not all of them – surely?'

Her wide eyes fixed upon mine. I did not know where to put myself.

'No, you are right John. Perhaps not all of them.'

*

IT was an autumn marked by an unusual event nearby – the strike at Lees Mill. It had brewed for months, with the mill-workers' anger aimed at the two-loom system imposed on them who were not rewarded for the greater effort this required. A fear grew that the Lees strikers would influence the workers at all the mills of the neighbourhood. But early in the morning women, Betty and Nancy included, they rattled through the village in their clogs while in the distance and from the mills either side of Stanbury's ridge, the sounds of the water-wheels in motion and the banging of the looms and the sight of grey coils of smoke from the stark chimneys went on as ever.

Nancy, disappointed, explained much. She had wanted to fight the mill-workers' cause. She'd spoken to them at other mills, not just Bridgehouse. She'd met them on her way to work. To incite the fight. A fight that had been stalled, hardly won. How glad I was that I had never asked her who was the young man I'd seen her with. For all her grieving ways, these had led her to consider the plight of people like herself.

At home we listened to her. Even Willie Forton liked to hear of the disruption over at Haworth. Fortunately he had the wisdom not to linger over sorry words and news. He stood up and took a turn on his fiddle, to bring the smile back to Nancy's face.

'Now here's an air I learned some fifty years ago. Your age I was and a better thing we thought it, to dance, not to strike. What do you make of this...' he said as he played his music and banished the evening's words with notes so lengthy and drawn out, you'd think wild mewling cats had joined us round the hearth.

My fight was not hers – or theirs. The ruddy cheeks of those children who, during the summer, had worked outside for weeks by then had paled once they'd returned to the schoolroom. With a chill in the air first thing and later, as the lowering sun lost its colour, we knew we would soon be spending longer hours in twilight. Of an afternoon we'd look up at our tall windows to see a cloud-strewn sky. Warning of a brutal winter ahead.

*

Mr. Nicholls

16th October, 1853

> *Kirk Smeaton*
> *Near Pontefract*
> *Yorkshire*

Dear John,

I am sorry not to have answered your letter earlier, but many things have been on my mind. You may guess that my last visit to Oxenhope was not a happy one and I must apologise not only for this prolonged silence but especially for my absence when you came to the vicarage there. I should have loved to give you some teaching, as of old times, but I was compelled to walk away from Mr. Grant's house. I did in fact seek out Mr. Sowden whose presence is always a balm.

I had had a difficult meeting with Miss Charlotte. She agreed, by previous communication, to meet me in Oxenhope but things did not go well between us. I believe this is because she came to see me in secret, unknown to her father, and therefore the occasion was strained for her and it became so for me.

You have written to me about your friend, Hannah Pollard. It is difficult for me to comment since I have never met her, but I believe I understand your feelings for her. My only advice, John, is to persevere. This does not mean you need place yourself in her presence every day – or indeed every week – but to put your faith in God who will listen to your prayers.

I hope we may yet meet again. I have every intention of keeping my feet on the path I have set myself to take.

> *Yours sincerely,*
> *A.B. Nicholls*

*

Return

FATHER and my sisters had never stopped going to Haworth's church on a Sunday. Nancy in particular enoyed the services. She had always found the quietness of prayer a solace for her lively, questioning mind. Now that I knew Mr. Nicholls was not the other side of the world but occasionally over the moor, I joined them there. Mr. Brontë conducted the morning service as often as he could. He was attended by Mr. de Renzy of the peculiar, foreign-sounding name. Some said he was from a Latin country, because of the '*z*' in that name. He therefore must have known the Latin of the scriptures and was a suitable choice for curate. He only had to open his mouth for folk to find out that here was another Irish. Unlike his predecessor he was a man of mighty indolence, as far as any of us could tell. His expression, as he stood beneath those tall windows and administered the bread and the wine, was one of boredom. He stared at the congregation as if we had been a field of cabbages. Not one soul, as far as I have heard, was ever visited by Mr. de Renzy. Nancy did not like the shape of his ears.

It was a relief for me to come across Martha on these occasions. I suspected she had little news for me but to describe the hollow rooms of the parsonage and the quietness that existed there. But on one point I had to be certain and I knew that if I asked Martha about visitors to the parsonage, she would be more than willing to inform me.

'Gentleman publisher? No no,' she said at once. 'We've had no-one from London. Miss Charlotte was there in January but since then she has visited only friends. She does not like to leave her father, which I suppose is to be understood. No, there has been no publisher here. Not long ago we were that lucky having her lady writer friend, Mrs. Gaskell, come and stay. She was good company for her. They walked out often and they stayed up late, talking. What was nice was the fuss the lady made of me. She took me outside, for a stroll she did, while Miss Charlotte was busy. I showed her the stone in the church with the family's inscriptions on. She asked me things and as I spoke, she wrote things down. We sat in the pews there. She wanted

to know all about them – Miss Charlotte and her sisters too. She
wanted me to say as much as I could.'

'You'd have had no trouble there, Martha. Must have enjoyed
yourself.'

'Oh I did. I told her lots. She was ever so interested. 'Good
company.'

'She must have found you so – filled with all your chatter.'

'Don't get on so. You asked me how things were and I told you.
Not much happens and it has been very quiet. With the winter on its
way, I daresay it will be quieter. Luckily Miss Charlotte has taken to
writing again.'

From what I gathered, life in the parsonage had resumed the
pattern of earlier days. But in near silence.

*

Stanbury
12th November 1853

Dear Mr. Nicholls,

*I have not forgot what you told me, when we went after
the trout that time. Nor have I forgot what you wrote to
me. You said that perseverence was a fine thing and that
sounds like a good word to me. The trouble is I do not
know how far I am to go, when it comes to Hannah
Pollard, because I don't get to be with her any more, now
that I'm at the school, and I was wondering if a gift at
Christmas time would be an idea? I am earning now and
could afford something nice.*

*I'm sorry you are down-hearted and that Miss Charlotte
has said such words to you. What were they? Would you
tell me or might that be difficult. You see, I should dread
the same of Hannah. Perhaps we might find ourselves in
the same position one day.*

The cold is setting in, but we are used to that up here.

Nancy is asked to make more clothing, which pleases her, and Betty has made a new friend at Bridgehouse. The strike at Lees Mill has caused much confusion and two weavers shot a gun into Butterfield's mill, to get them to stop using the two looms. No-one was hurt, but some damage done. Joseph Craven and the Wesleyans, you will be interested to hear, are singing their usual noise of a Sunday as we go past and Father has set up a new great pile of wood to dry in the yard. These are for his clogs only it takes up most of the space there. Willie Forton's fiddle noise makes us block up our ears. He wants Father to join the Lumb Foot brass band.

I have not told the little ones about all that happens in the Crimea but we have the book about the American slave come to the Mechanics which I hope to read them as a story once I've read it.

I hope perseverence goes well with you. This is the longest letter I have ever written, so it works for me.

Your friend,
John Robinson

*

JOSEPH was all for the Christmas sport we used to do when younger, but I was fearful of being seen by Hannah and taken for a child.

Joseph sulked about my decision and it was not easy to cajole him out of it with words of learned wisdom. Though his voice was almost that of a young man's, he had not yet made it to that privileged state, not entirely. He was grown quite big so I knew he would not fit down folk's chimney stacks, the way he once did. He said he wished he'd come to Mr. Nicholls' small school, not the old one along the road, since they were now having fewer lessons with fewer teachers and they were 'useless as a sheep's horn'.

'So what's it like, being a teacher?'

'It's a fine thing, Joseph. You could do it yourself if you put your mind to it.'

'No I could not.'

'You could and all. Anyone could.'

'Not anyone. I've a mind to go into Keighley and work on the trains.'

'Doing what, exactly?'

'Don't know. Don't know yet. But I'm not staying round Stanbury. There's no-one here.'

The old endowed school was just along the back lane from Hannah's. I rather wished I taught there if only to walk past the windows of her house each day and peer inside. With dark falling so early, I had the idea of being conveniently hidden in it and I sometimes went out of an evening, before supper, and from the lane I looked in to see where lamplight lit the rooms – and her.

Stray cats prowled in that lane. They went along walls and into barns, stealthy and sure of their feet. I wished I could be like them. Once the leaves were shed, trees' branches touched each other, tapped and creaked like the voices of throats that were wanting to speak. They rose black and tall, and waved about when the wind was up. I sometimes saw the moon behind them all, round and clear like a heavenly torch in the night. The chill air found its way inside my jacket and though I shivered, I stood fixed by the stone wall of a yard that backed from our street onto Hannah's lane. No-one was around.

So I was able to see her. She sat on the sofa where I'd once sat when we took her mother green shoes. Mrs. Parker was usually with her, in another chair by the wide fireplace. Hannah would look up from her book or needlework to talk to her companion who'd reply then return her gaze to her own work. I guessed it was very quiet in there but for the noise of their clock and the rippling flames in the hearth.

One night there was much more activity. Hannah's mother was there. I had not seen her for well on a year and at first did not recognise her – or else was not expecting her. She was fatter than I recalled.

She talked a deal, and used her hands when she spoke. Hannah would go over to her and embrace her and be enclosed by her arms, staying like that for a while. I saw that the two of them were fond as could be. Hannah herself talked more and stood at times and walked – yes walked, as if on show, her head held high to make her tall, her arms out, her weight balanced. Mrs. Pollard placed a book on her head and laughed and made her walk round her chair, round the sofa, round the room. She was stable as could be. It occurred to me she had practised this walking, ready for her mother's return.

Night after night I went and watched. I told Betty it was to get some fresh air, though when it rained it seemed an obvious lie. I took up my place again, by that wall and if a dog came and sniffed me in the dark, I sent it off. I settled my feet in the turf, stood firm and watched her. Her yellow hair was a wonder, and if her mother tried to tame it into some shape against her head, I was jealous of her fingers. Mrs. Parker brought a mirror for her to look in which she took eagerly and she tilted her head from one side to another, admiring the sight. Laughing.

I was so near, as I watched this intimate scene. But I could not have been further from it. Other scenes there were. I almost put my face to the window to see what they were up to next. Always Hannah was the centre of the parlour stage. Always she ended what I guessed was a recitation or a song with that walk round the room – upright, straight, confident.

When had it happened? Where? Did she go into the lane and find it secret and close, as I had found it? Had she practised her walking there? Or with the length of her legs grown, had they become more stable? As I watched I felt she would never fall down again. I thought of my first sight of her and how she'd followed me out of that same house, into the road, near the puddles, and she'd called after me. She was still that same girl, wasn't she?

*

14th December, 1853

> *Kirk Smeaton,*
> *Near Pontefract*
> *Yorkshire*

Dear John,

I must thank you for that last letter which was indeed a great pleasure to read. I enjoyed hearing about the people near you.

I am sure your Hannah would love a gift at Christmas and I imagine you could make her a very pleasing trinket. Remember what I said about 'perseverence'. For myself, I find it more difficult. I had told you that Miss Charlotte had written to me. We did indeed meet that time, which was not good. She found she was compelled to speak to her father about our correspondence and our meeting and all I can judge from this fact is that he still does not take kindly to me. She has implied that I should accept the situation as Providence, that my lot is the will of God, that I should cultivate patience and resignation. Her words are hardly encouraging. She has talked of 'great obstacles' that lie in my way. But you see John, it is the way itself, from her own words, that I feel will open up, as long as I persist.

The lady writer, Mrs. Gaskell, has become a most unexpected ally. I believe that whatever took place when she was in Haworth, in the way of conversations between her and Miss Charlotte, has cast me in a favourable light. She has put my name forward, together with good words on my account, that have led to offers for me to take up one of two livings. These posts are in Lancashire or in Scotland. I refused them both. They would be too far from the one place I have set my hopes upon.

This is the nature of perseverance, John. Despite all her refusals and the fact that her father barely tolerates our communcating, I am steadfast. She does communicate.

Return

I tell you these things in the hope you may understand them and learn from them yourself. You see, I am still your teacher.

Yours very sincerely,
A. B. Nicholls

*

THE Taylors, in their big house over the road, had a tree in their parlour which I spied one night when I was outside. I had thought to walk over to their door once I'd heard about the tree. They said that plenty of grand people had them in their homes at Christmas because the Queen did and the idea was to decorate them with sweet things and nuts and apples and the like. Some folk fixed candles to the branches of the trees but these were dangerous. I also heard that a lady got her dress on fire as she tried to light one with a taper.

The Taylors' tree was a tall conifer, felled some way away and brought up into the village roped to a cart. Though theirs was a big front door, they had a job getting the tree through and the Taylor brothers, standing there, only got in the way. Eventually it was one of the men from the farm who held one end while the others got inside, waiting to receive it. Even then, its top branches had to be sawn off to get the tree stood up inside the parlour. Quite an exercise.

By day, indoors, it must have looked rather peculiar, this great dark tree like a strange, giant visitor trapped in one corner. But at night time it was certainly a pretty sight from the road. Lamplight fell on the branches that had been tied with coloured ribbons and lacy trinkets made by the family.

For the rest of us, it was our windows and doors that we hung with evergreen sprays. This got both Betty and Nancy hurrying here and there to make the front of the house look worthy of the season. Christmas was sung aloud not only along at the Wesleyans', but in our little church too. I had asked the children to make decorations for the window sills along the wider walls. These were of paper, washed with colour and cut out into patterns. At the centre of each sill we placed a candle, their holders bound by twig and dried corn and berries saved from earlier months' activities.

I did not venture out to tease the old folk from their hearths.

On Christmas eve the little church was filled – and how glad I was. I'd thought that most of our particular flock would go over to Haworth where Mr. Brontë was to minister. But many preferred to stay at home. Father had said that for once he would do the same and I believe he knew how the absence of Mr. Nicholls over there would touch me, though he didn't say it. So we did not traipse down and over into Haworth but walked only yards to the church, our school-room, where unto us was given Mr. de Renzy.

I hardly listened to him. This was not only because his voice was dull, almost inaudible, but because at the back of the room was Hannah, Mrs. Pollard and Mrs. Parker. I lifted my cap a little, as if to let my hair breathe, and hoped it sat well on my head since that was all Hannah could see of me. I kept my eyes forward, looking at my own work in the garland that hung on the wall above Mr. de Renzy's head. I said the prayers, gently, and though Nancy nudged me to speak up, I took no notice. When it came to the songs I held my chin up, so it looked as if I was in full voice.

Father kept pulling at his crisp white cuffs. He was not used to wearing them and they'd been starched only the day before when Betty was all for ironing our best clothes. His fidgeting made me nervous, unkindly so, especially when he started at his neck, fingering and scratching. I felt sure Hannah would notice.

It was as if the whole of my back was alight, so conscious was I of her stood there behind me. Her torch hair a beacon, aflame with rays. Her mother and Mrs. Parker her attendants, sentinel at her sides. Everyone else in the schoolroom melted. They sunk into a sea of moving mist. The singing rose, noisily. The candles quivered making wispy shapes upon the window frames. I closed my eyes, not in prayer. Feeling faint.

'What's up with you, John?' asked Nancy.

'Nothing. Just a bit warm.'

'We'll be out in fresh air soon.'

As the small congregation left, Mr. de Renzy stood in the porch to shake hands with each worshipper. His palm was damp and his grip no more than a reluctant brush. His smile was fixed and he nodded again and again. You'd not think he was meeting some parishioners for the first time.

People chattered together on the path and past the gate in the road where they held lanterns that shone out in the drizzly air. As I waited for Father and my sisters I stiffened with dread to think of Hannah gone without another sight of her. I looked round anxiously and could not see her nor the women. People wished good tidings on us and I nodded the same. But Hannah had fled round the crowd ahead of me and when she touched my shoulder, I had not guessed who this was.

'John – you and your family must come and have some punch! I have asked Mama and she says yes, certainly, and Mrs. Parker has gone ahead to prepare glasses. You will come, won't you?'

She took hold of my arm and pulled me close to her side.

'Let's find Nancy and your sister. And your father. He hasn't gone home yet has he?'

My head reeled. I wasn't sure where they'd gone. Thoughts and doubts and wishes and all sorts spun through my mind at once. I had not completed the gift I hoped to give her. It was beneath my bed, hidden. I needed a spell of time to finish it. There was no time now. Would there be time tomorrow? What was I to do? Not leave her side. Not while I felt her warmth against me.

'There, John! There you are,' said Betty as she approached me. 'Mrs. Pollard has kindly invited us to her house. Ah – you've told him Hannah.'

'Yes. How lovely this will be. Come on John...'

*

NANCY was quite at home there. She'd continued with her needle-work in that parlour and was almost like one of the household. She was on the point of inviting us to sit, when Mrs. Pollard came in with her solemn look. I tried to see what colour shoes she was wearing. If only Father were to stop his scratching, which he did almost furiously, I'd have been more at ease. We did all sit but Hannah remained stood up.

Was she to walk round the room the way I'd seen her do from the road? She had no book on her head. She fled out after Mrs. Parker and returned with a plate of biscuits and then again she went out to come back with glasses and again, and again. She did not sit at all. Nor did she fall.

'Our very good wishes for Christmas,' said Mrs. Pollard as she raised her glass. 'Let us hope it is a good one for us all.'

I thought she might bless us the way she talked.

Father now moved about in his chair, his feet so firmly on the floor in front of him he resembled the chair itself, the way he had his arms on its arms and his legs alongside its legs. With a glass in his hand he did not scratch so much, but the cuff began to bother him.

Nancy chattered to Mrs. Parker and Betty watched us all.

'Shall we tell them, Mama?' said Hannah who, again stood by the great fireplace in front of us all, had no intention of sitting down.

'Yes, dear. If you must.'

'Well everything is thanks to John, really,' she said and she turned to me and I could have folded up and crumpled on the spot. All eyes were upon me.

Red hot I was.

'You see John helped so much in the summer when we were learning all sorts of things. And you've been a truly good friend...' she said.

The best thing to do was look down and hope no-one saw the heat in my face. If I went over to the fire I could pretend the flames were the cause. She was saying things. I could not grasp their meaning. Not completely. A firebolt. A spear. A gun.

'So I did tell him what I wanted to do most. And I thought it a good idea to tell you, Mama. Oh you seemed so far away in Europe, I didn't think you'd read my letters properly, but you did. I doubted you and I shouldn't have, Mama, but you see it was quite difficult living here,' she went on and looked fixedly now at Mrs. Pollard as if she were saying these things to her for the first time and our being sat there helped her speak. 'Sometimes Mrs. Parker and I felt you had abandoned us to the elements! But luckily there was John and Nancy too. We've loved having you here...'

My uneasiness did not match her enthusiasm. Hannah's position – stood there, talking at us as if we were her audience, her mother to one side – it was all different, as if things had changed forever. She was so firm on her feet. So confident, commanding and beautiful.

'It has been all planned. We are to go to Vienna, very soon after Christmas.'

So lost to me.

*

BELLS get rung, but the sound does not always reach round moorland heights. Over in Haworth those great heavy weights of iron I'd seen inside the tower – they moved and they clanged but I did not hear them. Mr. Grant's eight bells at the Oxenhope church were also silent for me. Christmas morning was hushed and damp.

Earlier in the week I had been over to the Mechanics Institute library where I'd sat and read Miss Emily's poems. I had thought to write one out for Hannah only it was difficult to choose which one. I spent several hours reading, hoping I'd find in them nice descriptions of our countryside since I knew Miss Emily had been fond of walking out on her own. But they were not all gentle words. She'd said much about heaven, but less to do with sky and birds, nor even summer flowers. So I gave up the idea. The little book I'd made I left blank and I found myself with no gift for Hannah. Then I had a better idea.

I went off, courage risen from the knowledge that I'd not see her for a while and would need to act. When she came to their door she was as winning as ever. She even took my hands and kept them clasped in hers. I let go quickly. Hastily I took the little book I'd made out of my pocket and cast an eye on it to see its ribbon was still tied with the feather tucked beneath it.

'This is to wish you a merry Christmas, Hannah. It's for your thoughts. You can write about the things that you like on all the pages. You can write about all that you see.'

*

IN the early days of January, snow fell. Snow fell and fell. Every person in every household watched through windows as the heavy flakes dropped from the sky and settled on the ground. Within minutes the roads and tracks were covered with a thick white layer that, given the greyness of the sky, appeared like a murky stain.

Our animals were cautious and watched the snowfall as we did, not venturing out to test its depth. Out on the farms, horses remained stabled for fear of them slipping on roads or tracks. Amused by the snow's novelty, a few dogs bounded headlong into it, their front legs leaping, their black noses daubed with white patches that melted at once. They soon turned back once their masters called. Cats stayed still, perched at secure heights on ledges and sills that were freshly covered. Stooped, the cats padded softly, paw by paw, nor blinked as their whiskers were spotted. Out in the fields the motionless sheep bleated helplessly as snow drifts formed. Farmers paced across the land to gather each one in their arms and take them to gaping, empty black barns. Rodents hid. No birds sang.

Quiet. An uncanny silence descended as the thick, white blanket wrapped the world with no warmth. No carts rattled, no wheels, no clogs, no footsteps. The hushed land stopped.

More snow hung in the sky above us like a dense grey wall against infinity. Foreboding and dull, shutting away air. Snow.

Return

So we were stranded. The snow rose to three feet, four, over five in the drifts. Not only were all the roads out of Stanbury impassable, but between our rows of houses the only way to reach one another was to send out the men with shovels, to create a maze of pathways and these did not melt as they were dug. They stood like short corridors with upright frozen walls. At night the tracks were left solid and firm. Channels wound their way from one door to another like giant snake tracks. Huddled, bent, fearful, keeping close watch on each step as we went, we made our ways from one house to another with food and hopeful words.

'There will come a thaw,' was a reasonable thought.

No thaw came. Not for weeks.

*

I KNEW I'd not see William the postman since he could never venture further than his own home in Haworth. Still I watched for him, despite knowing he would not come, and I fancied the contents of his bag. I hung from my window to look out over wide Smith Bank for the tiniest stir of a speck upon the road, willing such to become my messenger. My eyes were sore with rubbing as I watched – and hoped.

Mr. Nicholls would keep me informed not only of events in Kirk Smeaton — the people he grew to know, the curing of his rheumatics and how the snow affected his parish – but of the letters that were exchanged between him and Miss Charlotte. For the present they'd be collected together somewhere, maybe in a pile tied with string, delivered all at the same time, once the melt began. I imagined him reading them all, his brow knitted, his eyes fixed as he drank up her writing, page upon page...

In that unfamiliar Austrian city, Hannah would find a quiet spot to tell me of new lessons, new moves to learn, the music and the elegance of her fine new clothes. She'd describe her dancing, how her legs were strong, how she looked forward to demonstrating many wondrous waltzing steps to me.

I waited.

As long as we were cut off, I held hope in my heart. But once the thaw began and the first carts proved safe on the dun coloured roads, I knew the world beyond us had opened up again. My hope was let loose in it. Gradually that hope disappeared.

Weeks passed. The cold was severe, later accompanied by rainfall. Water now gushed between the hills where, during the snow, river and becks had formed gulleys of solid ice. Torrents ran. The land was soaked but still dotted with small mounds of snow that lay in the freezing shade of stone walls and would not melt.

No letters came.

The heaviness of my heart was such that I grew tired and listless with its weight. Unwilling to do much, I had to force myself to my studies and gained a little reward from their distraction. Time could pass. But it would lead me where?

One note was delivered, with no stamp on its envelope but in the hands of a merchant from Haworth.

'Is there a Mr. John Robinson at this house?' he asked Betty at our door.

Betty called out for me in the yard and I came at once.

'From Mr. Brontë,' he said as he passed the letter to me. 'I told him I was coming this way and he wrote it there on the spot.'

My immediate thoughts, that raced at once through my mind, was that something bad had occurred there – to do with Miss Charlotte.

> *The Parsonage,*
> *Haworth*
> *29tth January, 1854*

Dear John,

*   The recent spell of winter weather has affected us all, but you may be interested to know I have a fine pair of ice spikes to attach to my shoes that prove worthy once the*

effort of attaching them has been overcome and I can venture forth without fear. Your young bones won't suffer from falls, I am sure, and you are well balanced to deal with any unsteadiness. My daughter assures me that the shoots that have sprung up in our garden are a good sign that spring is on its way - a warming thought. Whilst it was absent we had fewer pupils in the school here but now they are beginning to return. She would like to continue her teaching hours, but we find we are a little overburdened by the numbers of children, especially since Mr. de Renzy has not proved a suitable leader of a class.

We are therefore hoping you could continue your apprenticeship over here in Haworth. Your tuition, I know, is already with Mr. Grant but I myself might be able to replace him. The small school in Stanbury we believe would survive well on its own from occasional teachers nearby.

Please give this matter your consideration. The reports we have had about your work are most encouraging and we would welcome you back.

Trusting the appalling weather of the new year's season, now gladly past, did not prevent you and your family from thriving well.

Yours, P. Brontë

When the roads were almost clear, I went.

To stay long hours in Stanbury, so near to where Hannah had been, and in the very school where I had taught her in the summer months, was a grievance to my heart. It's not as though the outside world spurred me forward – February and March were as grim as the early weeks of the year had been, but without the dangers that the snow had brought. The hills were still overshadowed by dull, featureless cloud and the damp air left moisture on every exposed stone.

William came and went, and most times strode through the village, past our house. After a while, I no longer hoped for a letter

from his hands. But I did believe that Mr. Nicholls might yet persevere in keeping our friendship afloat. Somehow.

It was while I was over at Haworth, when I walked into the
school one day, that I felt sure I saw him. Many men wore long black
coats and were muffled by worsted scarves in the winter months. But
who else beat his arms about his shoulders as he walked? Had it been
him, he'd have had his dog with him. Was I beginning to become
sick of mind in my disappointment?

I had to ask the Grants. They would know if he'd visited.

But when I asked straight out – 'Have you news of Mr.
Nicholls?' – the subject was abruptly changed.

'Do you know, there have been some homes in Oxenhope that
were completely flooded when the thaw came, ' said Mrs. Grant. 'I
would have gone out and helped but you know, I am a bit unsteady
on my toes...'

'Is that why Mr. Nicholls has not been to stay? Because of the
weather?'

'It's true, the weather has been particularly bad. You're right. I
wonder how you manage up on that ridge. Does the wind catch your
home? Aren't you facing south? I think you said your windows look
out over Smith Bank...'

Mr. Grant was even more unhelpful. He just went silent. He tilted
his nose up and blew it with his handkerchief.

I thought to walk over to see Mr. Sowden who had always
seemed such a welcoming kind of person and certainly more open,
with few airs to blow about. Then I relented, and simply toyed with
my own thoughts and at last came out with the idea that if he wanted
to, Mr. Nicholls would let me know how he was.

He didn't want to.

For all I knew he was set on being a missionary again. Or Miss
Charlotte had written to say she was no longer to write to him – nor
he to her – and there was an end to it. That was it. Or that she had
accepted an offer of marriage from Mr. Smith, her publisher. Mr.
Nicholls' grief had made him bad again, just as I knew him. Only

this time he had no John Robinson to turn to. The small village of Kirk Smeaton offered him nobody and nothing to relieve the repeated refusal that she had given him. That was it. Australia again.

As for Hannah, her silence was of a different nature. My imaginings blew and grew and in my mind's eye I saw her waltzing in the arms of a fine-clothed gentleman through the wide Viennese streets. In the library I looked up what the place was like, and when I saw photographs and engravings of its grand columns and stately facades I nearly wept with my own grief.

I came to believe that Mr. Nicholls and I were in the same boat and out at sea. All adrift. Yet there was a difference. He was a man of God with his duty laid out ahead of him, despite the yearnings of his heart. He would persevere.

Prayer did not help me. I found no God among all those biblical words. Although I could now spell them, their meaning became hazy mystery. Who had written them anyway? Matthew, Mark and John – their names were just like ours. Father was called Luke. And he couldn't write for a halfpenny. Even the simple words became confusing. What exactly was meant by 'grace'? As for 'trespasses', I'd not been in that tower for well over a year and had no more care to go there. The Bible was full of stories, very attractive ones, but none that I could recognise nor feel were related to a lad like me.

Unlike Mr. Nicholls I was young, with no rheumatics and strong limbs. But I came to realise that I, like him, suffered from a complaint that was common to folk of all ages, at all times, and it had no obvious cure.

It was known as a broken heart.

*

MY family never mentioned Hannah's name, nor asked what had happened to her and her mother, not even Mrs. Parker. The three of them, being gone, did not prompt conversation the way they had done, once. I would have borne every flush of my cheeks, every tease from their lips, every rapid beat behind my chest for such talk again, but the name of Pollard gradually became a never-to-be spoken word, such as a forbidden oath.

My sisters watched me. They could tell what was up – that I could not forget her. In their small, kind actions, they tried to mend the blow that had stopped the life in me from flowing freely. Betty left the house early, striding off to Bridgehouse when the world was still dark. Always she left behind a cheerful word to try and encourage me. Only a few hours later I followed her path to Haworth, retraced her steps and recalled how she too had known what it was like – that break in the heart. But she was better now. So it was possible to recover. Somehow.

I thought of those who had hearts that did not break. Weddings in the village were proof enough that hearts bound together should be celebrated. Hearts not fragile, not like Mr. Nicholls' and mine. Hearts that were strong.

At the time I still had not read the books of Miss Charlotte, nor Miss Emily's nor Miss Anne's. They wrote of passion and patience, of love thwarted and rewarded. Such experiences I would not have recognised. When I witnessed the weddings that began to take place in the warmer months, I was almost inclined to agree with Mrs. Grant. She'd said how love and being wed did not have to be complicated.

There was a saying I'd heard told about a man who wanted his wife to do his bidding: "If she will, she will, you may depend on't, but if she won't, she won't – and there's an end on't." This was surely true when it came to the whole question of courtship and betrothal.

Wedding festivities were simple and merry and took place at the nearest public-houses to couples' homes. Outside the groom would stand with a ribbon in his hand that was stretched across the road and held by another. This ribbon was run for. Not a long distance away five or six men would strip off coat and vest, take off hat, shoes and stockings and then run for dear life to touch the ribbon. The first to reach it claimed it. Nothing more. Later in the evening the couple would march off to live in the parents' home. Until they found a house of their own. All straightforward.

Love could be achieved.

*

IT was in June, late June of that year.

I was pupil-teacher in Haworth and my tuition continued with Mr. Brontë. And if one thing got me off thinking badly on Hannah Pollard, it was thinking better of him. He was not really an old, old man. Maybe in years he was, and the whiteness about him made him look it, but the eyes behind his glasses were keen – and so much alive. Into those eyes came his thoughts and I imagined he could actually see with them whatever he talked about. So when he'd done with my formal lesson I asked him things and he liked that.

'What is it you want to hear?' he said and the sharp eyes sent gleaming, playful darts of light at me.

'Tell me about the explosion of Crow Hill...'

'I wrote a poetic account of it that was published in the *Leeds Intelligencer*.'

'Then have you a copy I can have? Or at least look at?'

'I do, but John,' and here he smiled. 'If you're in no hurry to return, I shall tell you about it...'

He told me everything as if it were yesterday, not thirty years earlier. He described the slimy mud that followed the course of the rivulet up there, how it carried with it rocks and timber and uprooted trees – right down the valley – and destroyed fields of corn, and entered houses and how the sky went the colour of copper and a hurricane blew – and the quiet that came after. I was spellbound.

He seemed to enjoy my company. Now and again I caught sight of Mr. de Renzy who paid me scarcely a blink of the eye while Mr. Brontë – he winked with amusement. He helped me on my way. He was pleased, he said, that the school could continue to flourish with my contribution towards it. For this I was more than glad, I was proud. I felt I had taken up Mr. Nicholls' banner and I took to my role as pupil-teacher with a sense of personal accomplishment. This was an antidote to the lingering grief I felt over my bruised heart.

I went on my way. Forward. Trying not to look back. Quieter in mind. A sense of regularity, of routine, was in itself a kind of balm against infectious, invasive thought. Each day. Every day.

So it came as a surprise that on one of those days, as I approached the school I found Martha's father, John Brown, waiting for me in Church Lane. His face was hot and anxious.

'John – you're to get up out onto the moor and watch out for them!'

'Watch out for who?'

'Watch for the three of them – Mr. Nicholls, Mr. Grant and Mr. Sowden. They're headed over here together. There's a wedding. It's Miss Charlotte's. She's to be married to Mr. Nicholls only you've to watch out and when you see them, run back to the parsonage and tell them they're coming. So's Miss Charlotte and her friend can start for the church...'

*

THE moor was bathed in morning's early rays of light, when heat has not yet descended on the earth but the sun makes a promise of a fine day ahead. The heather, widespread purple and green, scratched over my boots on my ankles as I ran, nearly toppling over. Birds flew up, surprised. My heart pumped fast and my face smiled – I could feel it – and now and then the smile turned to laughter. Out there, as I ran.

Stood still, I put my hand up to my brow to shut out the sun and look hard Oxenhope way. The brow of the moor was a wide line across the sky. Soon the line was broken by individual shapes - three of them. I waited for them to come close. I saw Mr. Nicholls on the left, his head high, his arms outstretched. He moved them as fast as he walked. Unmistakable.

When he saw me he waved. That single gesture on that singular day brought with it, for me, a belief in the infinite measure that is hope.

*

I RAN back to the parsonage to find John Brown waiting at the gateway.

'They here?'

'On their way,'

'Good lad. Now go down to fetch the clerk, Mr. Redman, quick as you can.'

When I got to Mr. Redman's I found him in his kitchen about to light the fire so once I'd told him what was up I said to put everything down and that if he didn't hurry, Miss Charlotte would already be at the church door.

'Come on,' I said. 'There's no time to waste!'

The speed at which all this was performed, together with its great surprise, set me on my toes and still my heart raced. Still I smiled wide. I dragged Mr. Redman away and once we were out in the street he called out.

'I must stop John – have to – lace my boots…'

He did stop and I looked here and there as he put his feet up, one by one, against a wall. People were already in the street and I guessed that few, if any, knew what was about to take place in their church. As we approached, I heard the clock up in the tower strike eight. The three men arrived and turned their steps to a very slow pace as they walked into the door at the front of the church, not far from where I stood to watch. Mr. Redman took my arm, to follow him inside.

*

SHE looked like a snowdrop. Her bonnet was white, trimmed with lace and a band of flowers and leaves. Her pale dress was embroidered with green and I knew I should have to memorise these details, to tell my sisters. Never had I seen her in such fancy clothes.

There were not many of us in the pews to see Mr. Nicholls wed to Miss Charlotte. Not many knew, did they? Mr. Sowden did the nuptuals, and he too wore a smile, like all of us. I was surprised to see she was led down the aisle and given away by a lady. This was her headmistress, Martha told me, from the time when she went to school. Mr. Brontë was not there.

The ceremony was passed over quickly and I had every intention of going back into the school to prepare for the children's day. How hard it would be to concentrate! As I settled the little ones and handed out their hymn books, the door was opened and Mr. Redman was stood there, as if already about to leave.

'John – you're to come to the wedding breakfast.'

After some explanation to Miss Sugden (who flushed pink and had to fan herself with the news) I flattened my hair, scraped my boots on the bar outside and left to join the small party.

Into narrow Church Lane came a carriage and a pair of horses, a bay and a grey. The driver turned round up by the edge of the moor and came back to the parsonage wall where he halted. He was to take a bridal couple to Keighley station, he said.

When I entered the parsonage as Mr. Nicholls' wedding guest, I found the smile had not left my face. I wondered if ever it would.

Very Much Later

*

THAT young man from the newspaper does not understand that memories are like trees. There are some that grow and spread naturally with the thinking of them, though you cannot be sure how they seeded themselves. You just find they are there. Others not unlike them have deep roots that will never be upturned. The branches'll be buffeted about by storm and wind, but the roots will stay fixed and not be displaced by any intemperate weather. Then some blow away, as if they are leaves on the wind. You have to make an effort to capture them. Trees don't grow all at once nor in the same direction. Such is how memories work.

The lad's visit is prompted by my sixtieth wedding anniversary. A nice enough story for him. I shall gladly tell him how I met Sarah and the years we have spent together and the children we've had and those they have had. If he cares to hear it, I'll tell him about my later career, once I stopped being a teacher. He's found me because I've a fine reputation in these parts and they've named me the 'King of Wombwell'. That's to do with all the public offices I have also held.

He'll write all sorts down. All very interesting for them that don't have much to read about in a day.

What he really wants to know about is the Brontë family. First hand facts from an old man who once knew them. That's what. He'll ask me to tell him as much as I remember. He'll sit there like a clown he will, with all kinds of questions – mostly what happened before and after the marriage – their marriage, not mine. That story would take a whole book to write.

I'll not tell him all.

*

EVERYTHING changed.

In our house there was Nancy who, by her own efforts, managed to leave Bridgehouse. The day called for celebration and we went up over the road to the Cross Inn where our neighbours soon understood our cheerfulness and joined in its noise. Nancy was asked to make a dress for the publican's wife. The first whole one she ever made.

She was a changed being. I asked her to help out when there was need over in the Stanbury school. She taught the little ones, as she'd always had a secret mind to do. Only the infants. More than them she could not teach, not having had the opportunities I'd had.

The dressmaking she loved. Her work brought her a grown confidence so she took it upon herself to knock at the Taylors' door and ask to see Mr. George. He agreed to let her have one of the rooms at the far end of our building, where Joseph Craven's grandmother lived. Said he'd be glad to smarten it up for her. Here she kept a wide table on which to spread her cloth that was left untouched all day, not upscuttled for any meal. She spent hours there and from the window she looked down over the wide green fields of Smith Bank and the line of Haworth Moor above it. No weaving sheds rose about her, no noise of banging looms to beat inside her head.

Nancy took to reading more and at times, when she laid down her cloth, she'd go into the room next door where Joseph's grandmother might have sat away her last years in silent solitude. Nancy read her stories, loud so she could hear, which made us know she was not that deaf after all. She moved the old woman's great chair so she too could watch the fine view – which she might not have seen in months. Nancy witnessed the sad misfortune of a dwindling mind that is not sure why it stays alive.

One day when Nancy thought to look in on her, she found her sat upright in her chair, but with no sign of life. Willie Forton insisted on playing at her funeral. The old dear was accompanied to the grave by the strains of Willie's fiddle that her dubious hearing had always found irksome. He never knew this and believed he was doing her a favour, something she'd have liked. The emotion of the thought brought tears to his eyes as he played.

Betty continued at Bridgehouse. She walked off to Haworth defiantly each day, never looking back. She'd arrive before the bell rang out, to be at her place as she had been for years. That the work was deafening, repetitive and lacked all interest did not deter her. She was there, like thousands of others in our valleys, to earn a wage and keep alive. Her good humour kept us going, as did her mothering ways.

When she had time, when she was not at work, she'd also visit Joseph's grandmother but Betty's chores were more to do with feeding Father and Willie. As it happened, the two men liked to seek each other out. For company.

Father, as cordwainer, together with much help from Betty, made shoes that matched some of Nancy's clothes. In all the years he was at the work, I never saw another pair that was green. Stocks of wood remained piled in the yard for his clog soles, even when he was beyond clog-making. His bangs, like his nightly groans, had remained the only rhythmic sounds in our house until, finally, he joined the Lumb Foot Brass Band. It had not been an easy persuasion on Willie Forton's part. Unwilling at first, Father joined Willie in a few of the rehearsal hours that took place in the dining area of the mill down there, thanks to Mr. Butterfield's permission. It was not a long walk from our end of the village. So no excuse about aching limbs. The steps he took with Willie and the music they made together strengthened his body and soul. Naturally he swore he'd shut his ears to any Wesleyan warbling, but he liked to play his pipe in time to songs. He'd listen to the top notes, the ones that held a melody. He blew hard and we all believed it was his throat sang the tune that came out the pipe's other end, rather than the pipe itself. The band welcomed any eager player of any instrument. With Willie, the two of them went off on familiar trails from one village to the next. His pains disappeared entirely. On summer nights the pair of them paced about the yard, blowing and fiddling. Though he was not as young as its other members, the Lumb Foot band was the saving of Father. Banished were his weary declarations of becoming an old man - he thought he might instead become a musician.

Songs rang out across our street whenever the Dissenters took to public demonstrations and even though his sympathies were not in tune with their own, Father made sure his piping was. The band accompanied all sorts of events. He was there when, at a wedding celebration, some scoundrel took his knife to the drummer's drum. Stones were thrown at the band, but Father was unscathed in the scrimmage. One year he was proud to play in the Trawden contest over near Colne. The Lumb Foot band was one of ten competitors from all round those parts. They did not come in the winning first five, but the excursion for Father was memorable. He talked of it often, right until the weeks before he died. We thought to put his pipe in the coffin with him, in case he cared to play it in heaven.

*

MARTHA reported to me the activities that went on at the parsonage – as ever she had done – though after Mr. Nicholls' wedding there was less sense of urgency in her news. The household was calm and she went her round of domestic duties cheerfully. She too had a smile on her face.

Mr. de Renzy was not an easy one to farewell. To everyone's surprise he'd had little difficulty in finding himself a wife. She came from none too far from Haworth, but since Martha had not seen them at their courting, few people got to hear about it.

When it came to Mr. Nicholls' wedding Mr. de Renzy had been all noise. He complained to John Brown and several others and insisted on upsetting the marriage plans with all his talk of this and that and how he wanted things to be. Mr. Brontë, who was the one to take him into account, agreed to pay him three weeks' leave but this was not enough for him. He lingered about the place and said he needed a holiday on top of the leave. So the wedding date only took place once he was finally gone. He'd not made his mark on Haworth and I still believe there was something suspicious in his peculiar foreign name that makes it no wonder.

Mr. Nicholls was reinstated in his role as curate.

And as my teacher.

Can I say that the cares of his difficult courting days were gone? They did not disappear at once. His rheumatism was a constant worry to him, and though it made him groan at times, he'd not let this impose itself upon our lessons. These were now taught in his newly papered study, a small but light room transformed from the peat shed to the rear of the parsonage. Did I ever imagine it should be so! No longer was he a lodger at Sexton House where he went to his window to listen for a step or a voice in Church Lane. No longer the cautious stare over to where Miss Charlotte lived. He now lived with her in that house.

I said to him one day, I asked him what it was that had changed for him, that had made Miss Charlotte accept him as a husband when things had seemed so stacked against him.

'Perhaps my stubborn refusal to be dashed...' he said.

'No, but – there was a time when she was more than just unsure. She was against you.'

'Yes, that changed...' he said thoughtfully. 'It changed when I was accepted back into the parsonage – something she insisted upon, despite her father's opposition. I believe she developed a sense of the injustice that had been done towards me and knew I had been harshly treated. This encouraged her to question her father's actions and to look upon me in a different way. You see, my reason for being there was changed. I was no longer her father's curate. I came as a suitor. At the same time I think I proved myself to be her friend. If you like, there was a shift in the alliance of two opposed to one. Her will became greater than her father's. And he – it was not that he was out-manoevred. He was simply less strong than her.'

Mr Brontë suffered fragile health and Mr. Nicholls' duties at home and for the church became numerous, as Mr. de Renzy took his time to leave. Still he did not fail me as a tutor. As I prepared for college training, we sailed many seas of learning! The small school in Stanbury thrived and the two of us taught there together at times, when the size of the class was too great for one soul. As a lone Anglican island, it continued to become a church on Sundays where Mr. Nicholls spread the Word – his way. According to Martha, his wife often teased him and complained he was a Puseyite, which she thought was some kind of insect.

*

IT was good to see them together – as Mr. and Mrs. Nicholls. I never did think of her as a famous lady, perhaps because he rarely mentioned it. She was the same as ever she had been, though she often went about with him. They walked through the village freely and chatted to all sorts of folk, and if he was not ministering himself he took up his place with her in the family box pew in Haworth church. You'd see above its panels his great, dark head and her little bonnet beside it as they listened to Mr. Grant or Mr. Sowden who walked over to assist when Mr. Brontë ailed. The two of them were always together. He hardly left her side – as if she might disappear. As if his struggle might return. As if their peaceful life might be a dream, so long had he held it as a far-away hope. When I found her on her own I did not hesitate to talk to her as I no longer feared her occasional stern words. They did disappear.

Martha described to me how delighted she was with Miss Charlotte's new position and their shared daily chores. As the seasons turned, the inhabitants of the parsonage settled into a quiet routine. Miss Charlotte (whom I could never call by her married name) was still eager to take her usual walks. These were no longer taken alone. Now Mr. Nicholls accompanied her. In late winter, when the snow had begun its great thaw, she hoped to see the swollen waterfall above Sladen Beck. The ground was sodden and wet, but still they went out to the moors – him at her side, helping her, the two of them arm in arm. They seemed a true pair, as if no obstacle had ever stood in the way of their union. Nor was there reason to believe their life might change again.

'Tell me, Martha,' I asked her once. 'Does Miss Charlotte have time to write?'

'Ah no,' she replied. 'Not with the two of them. She now has father and husband to look after.'

*

IF the steps of the tower grew dank and moss-ridden I was not to know it. For I never did go up there again. I had no need. To look upon the parsonage would have been a truly sorry act.

Not a year went by after Mr. Nicholls' wedding before Miss Charlotte died.

*

A CHILD might have lived there, a little one to inherit the rare gifts of the extraordinary family who'd spent such years at the parsonage. Mr. Brontë had survived them all and from the time of Miss Charlotte's death he was looked after devotedly by his son-in-law. Esteem for Mr. Nicholls rose further amongst most of their parishioners, though there were those who were always set against him, perhaps because being 'solid' he seemed fierce. Or maybe there were some who never forgot the laundry escapade. Haworth is a small place, after all.

Visitors came to find it. Though far out of reach for most, fame had put it on a broad map. Now Mr. Brontë and Mr. Nicholls were known not only because of the sisters and the brilliance of their novels and poems, but from the wide renown of the biography written by Miss Charlotte's friend. It was published not long after she'd died. Others followed it.

Their lives were no longer private. People questioned the shopkeepers nearby, some of whom made tall stories of their acquaintance with the family. Strangers stared into the parsonage garden from the churchyard or went as far as to knock on the door to see what the two men were like. These two men who now found themselves together, alone.

I was up to the age of eighteen when I had to leave, to make that start in a world with which I was unfamiliar. Mr. Brontë received me in his study and the tight grip of his hand I shall not forget. He held me firm as he spoke and thanked me for all I'd done in his schools. He warned that I would find things very different away from there. I think I told him I was not afraid of adventuring. Kind, he was, and he gave me a portrait of himself that he signed in true friendship.

Mr. Nicholls and I went up on the moor.

His face wore the signs of a saddened man. Shades hung beneath his eyes, but his mouth was firm set. He held his chin up and walked fast with purpose. He stared ahead to the heights beyond Stanbury as if the horizon were our destination.

'I will write to you, John. I hope you will write to me.'

'Oh I will, Mr. Nicholls. There'll be that so much to say.'

'I should like to hear it. Tell me everything, all that you learn, all that you enjoy. They'll teach you how to teach. This would interest me greatly.'

'I will. And I shall be glad to hear of your news, all that happens here.'

'Yes, John. You can be sure I shall tell you.'

'I'll see you when I return, won't I? When I come back for holidays?'

'You shall indeed. Meanwhile, keep one idea in mind, whatever lies ahead for you, whether in your work or in – in more personal situations.'

'What's that? Or can I guess...'

He laughed and put his arm round my shoulder as we gained speed and strode ahead.

'Perseverance!'

*

BEFORE I left Stanbury, I needed to give back that key.

It was understood that Hannah and her mother would never return. The house in the lane with the magical letters above its door had been emptied back in that spring. Pollard was a common enough name and word went about they'd had no claim to descendancy from its earlier resident. They'd attached themselves to the reputation of a single benefactor who had lived there years before. They left as mysteriously as they'd come, a time no-one could recall with precision. Not unlike that doctor who arrived, healed and disappeared again.

Ours is a distant land. Remote. I believe that for as long as Hannah suffered the disability of her childhood plight, it was thought best to hide her away there. Until she grew out of it. Until she was more socially presentable. So the old house became the stage for a great performance where names were adopted as if from the cast of a play. When asked, Tom Parker knew nothing of his namesake.

So they departed from Stanbury's heights and when they were no longer talked about, they withered from people's minds entirely, as if they'd never existed.

I did not forgot Hannah entirely. I cannot know her real surname. But when I sometimes try to think of her, she fades off into a fair mist and I wonder if I dreamed her. Then, remembering our small school, the key to which was once mine, I see her stood there at the doorway, the sun behind her wild hair. I often ask myself if she has any thought of me and I am put in mind of a verse by Miss Emily.

> *Day by day some dreary token*
> *Will forsake thy memory*
> *Till at last all old links broken*
> *I shall be a dream to thee*

*

WHEN I met my wife her name was Sarah Webster. I had completed my tutelage in York and come over here eventually to be headmaster of the National School in Wombwell. As we stepped out we found we both cared for many similar things. She was born and bred not far away and she took an interest in all I told her of my childhood in Stanbury. I found her company pleasant and close and a fine addition to the hours when I did not work. We liked to make expeditions out of town and I explained to her I had a particular preference for open countryside.

One day we took the train into Sheffield and from there went a further five miles to Hathersage, a beautiful village in the Derbyshire Dales. The landscape there is not entirely unlike my homeland and on high ground it is scattered with stone outcrops. There is a bold ridge of gritstone like the battlements of a castle that stands above the village as the formidable edge to that higher land. I knew Miss Charlotte had stayed there with her friend, Ellen. In Hathersage church were memorials to a family named 'Eyre'. So I told Sarah all about Miss Charlotte and her books and said how I'd known her well and that if it wasn't for the attention she'd paid me, and the years of lessons I'd had with her husband, I should not be where I was in life.

Sarah listened to me. When she said she'd love to meet some member of the Brontë family, I had to explain they had all gone. Only their writing remained alive. The books and the stories about their life.

I told her about my lessons – much more than I'll tell the newspaper lad. In time she grew to understand my attachment to Mr. Nicholls, and all he had meant to me. As well as to others.

I told her how, when Mr. Brontë died, he was not succeeded by his son-in-law as incumbent of the parish, despite all the devoted care Mr. Nicholls had given to him and to Haworth itself. Many people were alarmed, even ashamed, that the man they had known as curate for so long was obliged to leave them. Some fools said it was because he was Irish. They forget the bold tone of the old man's voice that they'd heard in the pulpit for decades. But Mr. Grant, also shocked, told him it was the perverse decision of the church Trustees. I'd even heard talk that Mr. Nicholls was too 'High Church', betrayed by a Methodist – a notion that grieved me sorely. Another said the reason for the Trustees' decision was to have less fame about the place, less association with the Brontës.

The idea...

Mr. Nicholls did not intend to fight, nor rail against a committee of men with a joint idea in their heads. He was, after all, a man who accepted the blows flung his way. A certain Mr. Wade won the job by the narrowest of margins – a man with no knowledge of the parish, its history, or its land. A stranger who was to make changes that no-one cared for but himself.

I told my wife much more, and I found my thoughts clear, thanks to the way I think round my memories. It was Aristotle who said 'Memory is the scribe of the soul'. My thoughts, and even my written words, have helped me to understand much.

Those sisters and that unfortunate lad, their brother, are now known in the world way beyond Haworth. Their work and their life has made them familiar to many more than me.

Sometimes I hardly recognise them now, given what folk say – those who never set eyes on them. Such is the danger of fame, that none of the family cared to court. I suspect the reporter is after making a fine story – thanks to my memories. But since I've written them, I've come to understand what Aristotle said. My own less godly soul than theirs is glad to have known them. Remembering them has made me feel enriched.

Theirs was not a family of girls and a boy who fought a strict father. They loved him well, as he did them. Few people knew how his pale, furrowed brow could melt like the snow. They never saw the tears he shed when he talked of his dead children. He was a good man.

Much talk and words there's been about the place where they lived, as if it were another continent. That writer friend of Miss Charlotte's at the beginning of her book said the hills round Haworth contained a '*wild rough population*' and that the likes of us who'd been born there were '*lawless*'. It was her way of explaining the way the sisters wrote, that because of where they lived, they were unlike others. But she and others did not know them.

I shall always think of Miss Emily accompanied by that great dog. My own eyes saw her with the dog. From our house, above that wide bank, we saw the way she strode and how the dog bounded ahead of her. It was Martha told me she had beaten and scolded Keeper for sitting on the parsonage beds upstairs and that she'd wept and caressed the penitent brute. This I can believe. I do not think of her as a young girl running over heather to reach Withins farms, nor tapping on their windows. I never even saw her with a young man. She loved being at home, in the parsonage, where she liked to tend the house and to cook. She even had a book propped up on the kitchen table, so she'd learn while she made a loaf of bread.

The book she wrote I could hardly understand. The words were written to resemble the way we speak. Not easy to read. But then the books of her sisters, like hers, were not really them. They were works of art. They were words that spoke language, absorbed from other books, written with the pens I saw them use when I watched them from the tower. To see them, you'd never guess the three of them were brilliant.

Miss Anne, she looked round her bonnet and smiled at people. Shyness was something she overcame, perhaps through the work she'd done as a governess. It was work she did not like, but it made her watch the ways of others and learn how to adapt to them. Some cannot. Our Nancy never did, not when she worked at that mill. She made herself ill with it. Miss Anne was quiet and for all I know she suffered quiet, even when the children in her care made her wretched and unhappy. She did not let on. I'm guessing that being godly, they had a faith that made them strong in times of hardship. Her suffering was never known to us pupils at the school nor the people who talked to her in Haworth. Only in her written work might you detect it.

They say that Mr. Branwell was the model for her tragic hero, whose dissolute life caused terrible grief. If that is so, all three girls would have shared Miss Anne's distress over him. Still they did not always write about experiences they shared. Maybe they each had secrets. I am grateful that I was privy to Mr. Branwell's notes on Horace. The translated words. The written ink. Not many have seen that. The family may have lived together up near those moors in a house set at the edge of them, but it was their educated minds drove their pens. That and their imaginings.

Imagination played the larger part. It made so much more of the plain governess or the drinking man, the heathland farm or the cruel school. Imagination transformed real life into books. They selected from the truth. They made choices, rather like I shall do when that lad the reporter comes back.

*

DOWN on the cobbles of Church Lane went the horses and the carriage that took Mr. Nicholls away. Down the steep main street of the village. People stared from their windows to watch him go, some half hid by curtains to shade their damp eyes. Down into the valley and on to meet the railway.

Over the seas to Ireland.

He was not entirely alone when he left Haworth. As he boarded that carrier he took much with him. There were his own memories that he'd keep throughout the rest of his life. There was much of the family furniture and the portrait of Miss Charlotte that had hung in the parsonage dining room. There were the manuscripts. With him also went more vital accompaniments – two dogs and Martha Brown.

*

IT's when you find yourself old, you make new discoveries. This has to do with looking back and seeing the events of a life in a long line, with landmarks that seem to point to others on that same track. I should never have guessed that Martha would set off with Mr. Nicholls, on a sea I had only been able to imagine from what he'd told me. Yet it was she who went – to sail right over it!

When I saw her again she told me about the place, Ireland - that Island I had once dreamed it to be. She said how the lay of the land was unlike our moors, though the green was as green as the valley of the Worth. She talked – at length. Mr. Nicholls had a large and fine family, she said, many good relations who were that kind towards her. The school where his uncle had taught, and where he'd lived as a child, was one of the biggest most beautiful houses she'd ever set eyes upon.

'If only I had known...' she said. '...what a grand place they had. And John, it was so big, with space enough for at least four houses the size of ours to fit inside. There were tall walls with fancy white trimmings round the top and cellars and stables and buildings outside. If I had known...'

'What if you'd known, Martha?'

'It's just – to think of him upstairs, lodging as he did with us, in that small room. I never guessed what he'd come from...'

Martha returned frequently to Banagher where years later Mr. Nicholls married the cousin he had known all his life, ever since he was a small boy. Mary Anna Bell. They had played together as children and during the intervening years had never lost contact.

'Miss Charlotte met her, when she honeymooned there. They

knew each other well,' Martha explained. 'And she knew how much Miss Charlotte meant to him...'

When he gave up the profession of preacher and ran a farm, he hoped Martha would stay on with them. She did not accept, though she was given a room at his house in Ireland that was kept for only herself. She divided her time between there and here. On one visit, when she was back to see her family, Martha died and was buried in the churchyard, close to the parsonage wall.

If ever I had guessed ... but it seems right to me now, that Martha and Mr. Nicholls should have finally shared a good friendship. It thrived in letters when they were apart, but was born in a place that for both of them, in different ways, was home.

*

SOME years ago I had it in mind to go back to that home. For there was still an old friend of mine I cared to see. I may be eighty-four years old, but I am not averse to a little shaking up in a motor car. To ride out and see how the land has changed was a grand thought, as long as Joseph Craven knew how to steer a wheel. I'd only ever seen him skim stones across the surface of a stream.

He was there at Keighley station. Grey hair, bent back and all the signs of age did not disguise him and we settled in the vehicle with no complaint of creaking bones. We'd written to each other for years, and on occasions had met in Leeds which seemed like a half-way halt from here. He too had been active in a public capacity and was once a member of the Keighley town council. We found we always had much to tell each other.

The motor chugged out of town and at once I saw how Keighley was grown outwards, with buildings added on every side.

'When I was a surveyor, after I'd stopped teaching, I remembered that church,' I told him, as Mr. Pugin's edifice entered my gaze. Since his eyes were on the road, and he was none too sure how to miss the sharp bend ahead, he did not look at it. 'I worked as an architect too,' I said, though I cannot be sure he heard me. 'I was always interested in buildings.'

We agreed to go to straight over to Haworth.

It was a fine day which allowed me to look about and see clear. As we came down towards the Worth, I saw the railway line that ran alongside the river there. It had been built thanks to money from the mills. How much easier it would have been to go those four miles into Keighley by train! Especially in the winter. Because of the line, more houses were spread on the hills, and still more were built in snaking trails of terraces, to herd in the mill-workers and have them all nearby. The chimneys were still there – black, smoking, hard at work.

Once we had passed the crossroads and come in view of Haworth's steep hill I held my breath. I told Joseph to move on slowly, but steady. We decided not to take the motor car up the steep climb to the top and fortunately, after several moves, Joseph managed to park down near Bridgehouse.

I was put in mind of Betty's daily traipse to work and the change it gave her to spend her latter days with me and my family in Wombwell. We were able to look after her and I hope the home we provided was filled with the kind of children's noise, of laughter and of song that she'd missed while she cared for others.

Once at the top of the street I hesitated. Most of the church was changed, built by Mr. Nicholls' successor, the wealthy Mr. Wade. It was a shock to see the wide nave and the larger windows completely gone from the church I had known. But the tower remained. As I walked round this I remembered how I'd gone there secretly, so as not to be seen. I tried the small door and was glad to find it locked. I looked up at the pinnacles on the corners of the four sides. I steered my gaze fast over the sundial and looked through grown trees that grew in the parsonage garden and sheltered that home.

It did not seem so bleak and lone upon the moor. The trees softened its austerity. A great lump of masonry made a clumsy addition on one side, to the right. Gone was the graceful symmetry of the earlier façade I had once liked to watch.

All gone.

When I glanced over at Sexton House I was surprised to see it entirely unchanged. The top window was wide open to greet the morning's fresh air.

'Come on, now Joseph,' I said. 'Let's get over to Stanbury.'

'Do you think the small school is still there?' Joseph asked.

'They won't have pulled it down.'

'You never know. With enough Wesleyans like us, they've maybe no more use for it as a church,' he teased.

*

WATER. The entire valley in front of our old house was filled with water. From the lane that led to Oxenhope, right over to just below the turnpike – the very length of the village – everything was gone. The farmsteads, the walls, the barns, the rough paths of Smith Bank – all were beneath water.

'You know what, John' said Joseph. 'If we were young now, we could make a boat and sail over that lake.'

'It's not a lake.'

'I know that, but we could pretend, couldn't we? If we were young lads.'

'It's a resevoir. Built by Keighley Corporation, as you well know.'

'Well, if we were lads, we'd say it was built by pirates...'

For over a decade the valley had been brutalised, ripped apart. Steam cranes and excavators had driven the earth out of its bed to be taken away in trucks on rails. Long wooden tracks, like earth-bound ladders, were struck into the hillside. Other rails transported clay dug out from the further moors. A deep and wide embankment was built, a huge concrete dam, right above Sladen Beck.

During the Great War work on the resevoir had been halted. Later, in peacetime, many of the navvies who lodged in Stanbury went on strike. The proposed imposition of a 47 hour week (in all weathers) together with their complaint over a pitifully low wage led them to it. In the end, despite their hardship, their work was finished and they went away.

Water, contained and controlled, was left behind.

'You could bring your grandchildren here. They'd love it,' said Joseph.

'They would, would they?'

'Admitted, they could not sail on it. But it's a fine expanse of water. You'd never think we ran about underneath there, would you? Think of it – the beck, the boulders, the games... Never. Still, we can only be proud of it – as a great achievement,' Joseph enthused. 'They say the Marquis is to open it. And a marquis is a grand sort of man, John. Not like the likes of us.'

Joseph could tell I was not in agreement with him.

'Anyway, John, whatever you think, you could say it's our water, from our land. Water that's come from these hills.'

'And flows to the seven seas...'

*

I DID not care to visit our old home. The Taylors' farmyard was still in use and I guessed that others lived in the house and had made it their own. At the other end of the street I did not turn into the back lane though I saw it from where I stood in front of the small school. The school was unchanged. Trees that stood at either end of the building were tall enough to touch the bell and cross. The structure was as modest and welcoming as it had ever been, but I had no key to enter.

I walked to the end of the village, to the turnpike house and thought for a while of the long, straight road leading west, trekked upon not by navvies, not by scholars, nor even by drovers with their cattle. It is said that 'Stanbury' comes from a Viking word that means both 'stone' and 'farm'. Some have even said that the Romans once knew Stanbury.

I prefer that – to think of the Romans there. It puts me in mind of my first lessons with Mr. Nicholls. At times I like to go in for a spot of imagining myself, just like those sisters did. To have the familiar place inhabited by others I care to dream up. In my mind's eye, as I stood there, I saw soldiers in helmets from ancient times. They were traipsing up and down our street. They spoke to each other in Latin.

I looked out, over the wide moors. They never altered. Unlike our valley, no-one would ever touch them. They remained vast and wild, of colours changed by moving clouds. They invited thought – upon their very nature and the source of their creation. Imagination could make of them a dread place or a home.

Over beyond them was Crow Hill, not that I could see it. I knew it was there, a distant heath that had once exploded and startled the likes of everyone who heard it's terrible burst. It had settled down. Nearly a hundred years had passed since it vomited up its mud and caused chaos wherever it flowed. You'd never know it, to look at the moor's sombre, flat brow. As if it had thrown up its very core, shocked and alarmed, then settled to remain the stuff of memory. But it existed, it exists. Memory need not be mistaken, not when it is planted well. At times out of nowhere come images prompted by other recollections.

The same is true of people. Their actions, their works and words are held in the mind's eye and ear – vital, alive, never entirely gone. There are those who flit in and out of memory's store like sparks, like stars – and others that linger there in beams of brilliant light.

They say that once, at the same time, two suns appeared in the sky. But it was not for long.

Acknowledgements

I SHOULD like to express my thanks to:

Carole Angier and Alex Martin of 'The Writer's Project'
Juliet Barker for her outstanding biography on the Brontës
Ann Dinsdale of the Brontë Parsonage Museum
Steven Wood for his several volumes on Haworth history
and many more whose genealogical researches revealed John's
family to me.

Extracts from the following books appear:

Shirley –
Charlotte Brontë, first published by Penguin English Library, 1974

The Complete Poems –
Emily Jane Brontë, edited by Janet Gezari,
published by Penguin Books, 1992

The Brontës –
Juliet Barker, published by Phoenix Giant, 1995

The Life of Charlotte Brontë –
Elizabeth Gaskell, first published by Oxford University Press,
World's Classics,1996

The Author

JULIET HESLEWOOD was born in Leeds and grew up in Yorkshire. She lived in France for thirty years where she worked as an art historian. At Toulouse University, her Masters paper in English Literature was on 'A Sense of Place in the Work of the Brontës'. She now lives in Oxfordshire and continues to write.

Also by Juliet Heslewood:

Tales of Sea and Shore
Earth, Air, Fire and Water
The History of Western Painting
The History of Western Sculpture
Introducing Picasso
Tales of Two Rivers
Hualachi and the Magic Sandals
Mother: Portraits by 40 Great Artists
Lover: Portraits by 40 Great Artists
Child: Portraits by 40 Great Artists
Myself: Portraits by 40 Great Artists
A Travelling Actress (BBC Radio Four Drama)

Investigate our other titles and
stay up to date with all our latest releases at
www.scratchingshedpublishing.co.uk